A Brilliant Defiance

LAURA BEERS

1

England, 1814

Lady Jane Lyttelton counted the eight long, wiry silver hairs protruding out of the Duke of Brackenford's nose. And the ones curling out from his ears were even worse. She resisted the urge to shudder. This was her wedding day, and all she felt was dread.

How had it come to this?

The vicar droned on in a smooth, monotonous cadence, completely at odds with the chaos in her chest. Her hands were trembling in their satin gloves as she struggled to breathe.

As the duke gave her a tight-lipped smile, he revealed two discolored teeth and a faint whiff of tobacco. He was ancient. Nearly eighty. And yet, he stood straight and radiated power, like a general surveying a battlefield. *His battlefield,* she realized.

Her gaze slid to the vicar again, who cleared his throat expectantly.

"My lady?"

She blinked. "Yes?"

"You will need to answer the question," he replied in a coaxing tone.

Jane opened her mouth, but no sound came out. Her heart thundered. "I... uh..." Her words trailed off, wishing the earth would swallow her up whole.

The duke turned to her, his eyes narrowing. "Just answer the question, my dear," he said, the smile gone. His voice was low, impatient.

This was it.

If she agreed to this marriage, her life was over. She would be his and go from one gilded cage to another. She would be a duchess, but a prisoner, too.

She had heard the rumors about the duke. Everyone had. Four wives. All dead. All within a few years of marriage. His last one had fallen down the stairs, but many people suspected the duke had actually beaten her to death.

The duke reached out and gripped her arm. His fingers dug in, firm and bruising. Jane gasped, and she blinked hard to stop the sting behind her eyes. *He's hurting me.* And they weren't even wed yet.

If he did this now, in a chapel full of witnesses, what would he do when they were alone?

She looked out over the pews. Her father's expression was thunderous, and his mouth set in that way she knew too well. Her brother looked just as grim. They had arranged this match. It was a brilliant connection, they'd said. "A gift." *A sentence,* more like.

The duke's fingers tightened. "You are embarrassing me," he hissed, his voice steely and biting. "Do what you are told and answer the question."

Pain shot up her arm.

She couldn't do this.

She *wouldn't* do this.

Something in her snapped like a dry twig. She yanked her

arm free and stepped back, shaking. Her voice came from somewhere deep inside, somewhere that had never been allowed to speak.

"No."

A collective gasp rolled through the chapel like a wave.

The duke's face contorted in disbelief. "I beg your pardon?"

She squared her shoulders, even as her hands trembled. "I said no."

He stared at her as if she'd just grown horns. Then, disturbingly, he smiled. "You think you have a choice in the matter?"

"I do," she replied, the quiver in her voice barely concealed.

"The contract is signed," he said, each word a dagger. "You are as good as mine."

"I have the right to say no, and I signed nothing. Only my father did."

Leaning in slightly, he replied, "That is true. But do you think I care?"

Her throat tightened. "Please," she whispered, desperate now. "I don't want to marry you."

His expression shifted—amusement drained away, and something cruel took its place. "You're playing coy, aren't you?"

"No, I'm not."

"You think you can treat me like this and get away with it?" he demanded.

The slap came out of nowhere.

Her head snapped to the side. The sting was instant, followed by an awful, hot ache. She staggered back a step, stunned. She raised a hand to her cheek and stared at him in disbelief.

He struck me. In public. In front of God and everyone.

She turned towards her father, hoping he would intervene now. But he did not move. Nor did her brother. Their gazes were cold, their silence louder than any rebuke.

They won't help me. She was alone.

The duke took a step towards her, fists clenched.

"Your Grace!" the vicar said sharply, stepping between them. "Need I remind you this is a holy place?"

The duke paused. His lip curled. "You're right. This is a private matter between me and Jane." He unclenched his fists and held out a hand. "Come now. Let us finish this wedding. We can... converse later."

Jane stared at his liver-spotted hand, thick fingers curling like claws. If she took it, she would seal her fate. She would be lost. Forever.

Run.

Her mind screamed the word before her body caught up. She turned on her heel, lifted her skirts, and fled down the aisle. Gasps and shouts followed, her brother's voice rising behind her, but she didn't stop.

Out the chapel doors. Down the steps. Onto the London street.

She didn't know how far she ran. Only that when her legs finally gave out, she collapsed onto an iron bench in a small square, heart pounding, breath heaving.

What had she done?

She had walked away from everything. From security. From the title. From her family's expectations. She had no income. No future. Just a reticule with a few coins tucked inside. She was ruined. None of her family members would take her in now.

Tears burned in her eyes but she blinked them back. This was her first act of defiance and she had sure made a muck of things. She didn't even know where she was and the sun was beating down on her.

Rising, she tried to muster all the courage she could find. She would find a way to survive. She had to.

A short man with greasy-looking black hair bumped into

her, causing her to step back. He tipped his head. "My apologies, Miss."

"No harm done," she replied graciously.

The man ran off and that is when she realized he had taken her reticule from around her wrist. She ran after him but lost him in the crowd of people.

Drat.

Now she had nothing.

A thought occurred to her. *Olivia.* Lady Westmere. If anyone would help her, it would be Olivia. She would understand. She had to.

Jane lifted her chin and began walking. Her feet ached in her thin slippers, each cobblestone a fresh torment. If she'd known she'd be running from a wedding, she would have worn sensible shoes.

But she hadn't. She was alone, aching, humiliated… and free.

And for now, that would have to be enough.

Jane's feet throbbed with every step, but she pressed on, drawing strength from the rhythm of her pace. One step, then another. She would get to Olivia's townhouse in Mayfair if it took her all day. What other choice did she have?

As she passed a narrow alleyway choked with shadows and refuse, a sudden *thump* caught her attention. Then a groan. Voices followed—low, angry, and violent.

She paused, heart stuttering.

Peering into the alley, her eyes adjusted just enough to make out a brutal scene: two large men were holding someone upright by his arms, while a third landed a vicious punch squarely into the man's gut.

"Stop!" she cried without thinking, her voice echoing louder than she intended.

The attackers froze mid-motion, their heads snapping

towards her. Three rough-looking men, all wiry and strong, their eyes hard and unforgiving.

And she was just one woman. *What in heaven's name am I doing?*

One of the men, the one still poised to strike, sneered. "Go away!" he barked—and then drove another fist into the bound man's ribs.

"No." Her voice was quieter this time, but firmer. *No more looking away. No more standing aside.*

She scanned the ground and spotted a broken broomstick handle near a pile of old crates. Without hesitation, she rushed forward, snatched it up, and held it out in front of her like a sword, albeit a rather pathetic one.

"Leave that man alone," she ordered.

The two brutes released their victim, letting him crumple to the ground like a discarded sack. Then all three turned towards her.

The tallest man took a step forward. "And what do you think you're going to do with that, love?" His voice dripped contempt.

Jane's legs trembled, but she kept her spine straight and her chin high. "Whatever I must do," she said, proud of how steady her voice sounded, despite the fear coursing through her.

The man's sneer deepened. "Perhaps we should have some fun with you first," he said, eyes raking over her.

Jane's breath caught. *Oh, no. What have I done?*

But before she could speak, another voice rang out.

"The constable!"

The word came from one of the other men, panic lacing his tone.

All three attackers bolted from the alley without a backward glance. Jane exhaled, shaky and slow, and tightened her grip on the stick. She would be forever grateful for the constable who happened to be walking past.

She stepped cautiously towards the fallen man, who lay in a heap, not moving.

"Sir?" she called out. "Are you all right?"

A low groan answered her.

Still wary, she prodded his shoulder with the tip of the stick. "You need to leave before those men return."

He groaned again, but didn't lift his head.

Concern overtook her fear and Jane crouched beside him, her skirts sweeping the dirt. As her eyes adjusted, she got a clearer look at his battered face—bloodied, bruised... but unmistakable.

She stared at him in disbelief, not sure if she believed her own eyes.

"Alistair?" she whispered, reaching out and pressing her hand to the sleeve of his coat. "Alistair, it's me. Jane."

His swollen eyelid twitched. "Jane?" he rasped, barely above a breath.

Relief swept through her, sharp and overwhelming. "Yes, it's me. We need to get you to a doctor."

She tugged at his arm, but he barely budged. He was dead weight. She wouldn't be able to carry him herself. "Please," she urged. "You must try."

With a pained grunt, Alistair shifted and began to rise. Jane slipped her shoulder beneath his arm, bracing herself under his weight.

He leaned heavily into her. She stumbled slightly but found her footing.

"Why are you here?" he mumbled.

"That's a very long story," she responded, panting with the effort of supporting him. "And we don't have time for it right now."

Step by step, they slowly made their way towards the street. Jane's muscles screamed in protest, and her shoulder was already sore, but she refused to stop.

"Where is your coach?" she asked breathlessly.

"I don't have one," he murmured. "Rent a hackney."

The request seemed simple enough, but it was nearly impossible for someone like her. "I've never... rented one before."

He gave a weak huff of amusement. "It's not so hard."

She spotted a hackney farther up the street, its driver slouched lazily on the box. With determination tightening her spine, Jane shuffled Alistair forward.

"Excuse me!" she shouted, waving with one arm. "Is this a hackney, sir?"

The driver glanced down at her, brows lifting. "It sure ain't a flying carriage, your royal highness," he mocked.

Jane didn't have the energy for his humor. "We need a ride."

At the sight of Alistair's condition, the man sobered. "What happened to him?"

She thought it was best to lie. "My husband was attacked. He needs a doctor. We live in Mayfair. Viscount Alcott's townhouse."

The driver straightened. "Right. Get in."

Jane helped Alistair up into the carriage, her limbs aching with strain. Once they were inside and the door shut behind them, she sank onto the seat across from him, her heart still racing.

What had begun as a walk to Olivia's house had turned into something far more complicated.

And she had a feeling this day was only just beginning.

Alistair Winslow, Viscount Alcott, groaned as the hackney jostled over another rut in the cobblestone road. A sharp bolt of pain lanced through his side, and he shifted on the hard bench, cursing under his breath. What in the devil had just happened?

One moment he'd been walking along the pavement—unarmed, unguarded, and foolishly lost in thought—and the next, fists had rained down on him from all directions. Three of them, at least. Maybe four. His vision had blurred too quickly to tell. He prided himself on being alert—had survived two campaigns with scarcely a scratch—but now, here in London of all places, he'd been taken unawares.

Complacency. That was the real culprit. He had let his guard down, thinking the war behind him.

And now, he paid the price.

Through one swollen eye, he glanced across the narrow compartment at Lady Jane, who was seated as though this were a quiet afternoon ride through Hyde Park and not a rescue mission from a violent ambush. Her gown was pale blue with a delicate net overlay, her blonde hair was pinned atop her head in perfect order, and a diamond-studded bandeau glinted with every flicker of sunlight through the windows. She looked lovely, as she always had.

But it was the look in her eyes that struck him most, concern and something else... something unsettled.

"Do you know the men who did this to you?" she asked, breaking the silence.

"No," he rasped. Even that single syllable scraped at his bruised ribs. He drew a shallow breath, and pain lanced through his side. Cracked, perhaps. Or worse.

Jane leaned slightly forward. "Perhaps we should take you to a hospital?"

He shook his head, immediately regretting it as the world tipped and then righted. "No. I've suffered worse."

"You took quite the beating, my lord."

A huff escaped him, half-amusement, half-indignation. "Since when do you 'my lord' me?"

Her lips twitched—just barely. "We aren't children anymore. You are a viscount, and I..." Her voice trailed off as she looked away. "I am the daughter of an earl."

"Titles be hanged," he muttered. "You saved my life today. I shall call you Jane for the rest of my days, and you may call me Alistair—or 'Fool' if you prefer."

She didn't smile. Her hands remained tightly clasped in her lap. "I'm only glad I was there in time."

"So am I. But why were you in that part of Town? Alone?"

Jane hesitated. "I went for a walk."

"Without a maid? Or a footman? Surely you know better."

Her tone sharpened. "My reasons are my own."

Alistair fell silent. He could hear the defensive edge in her voice, and though every instinct urged him to pry, he refrained. Jane had always been composed, careful, and obedient to every societal rule. The fact that she'd been alone in one of London's rougher neighborhoods was strange indeed.

She suddenly reached for the velvet curtain and slid it aside. "You can let me out here."

"Here? We're nowhere near your townhouse."

"I'm not going home."

That gave him pause. "Where are you going?"

"To Lady Westmere's."

Alistair pressed his fingers to his forehead and winced. "Is she expecting you?"

"No."

Realization dawned on him as he studied her closely. "Today was supposed to be your wedding day... was it not?"

Jane stilled. "It was," she admitted. "But I changed my mind."

He straightened despite the pain. "You changed your mind?"

"I don't know why that sounds so surprising," she said. "The duke and I would not have suited."

"When did you come to this realization?"

"At the altar," she whispered.

His brows shot up. "At the—? Good gads, Jane."

She wouldn't meet his gaze. "The duke struck me when I refused to marry him. And I ran."

"Oh, Jane... I am so sorry," he said, not sure what else he could say in the moment.

Her chin lifted, proud despite the tremor in her voice. "I don't need your pity, Alistair."

He managed a smile. "At least you've stopped calling me 'my lord.'"

That, too, earned no smile. She tucked an errant piece of her hair behind her ear. "I will be just fine."

He wasn't certain if she meant to convince him or herself. "And you're certain Lady Westmere will receive you?" he asked.

"She will. She's one of the few who might still look at me and see a person, not a scandal."

Alistair leaned forward despite the agony in his side. "Then she's wiser than most."

Jane gave a small nod, but her expression betrayed doubt. "My family will disown me entirely once the gossip spreads. I've embarrassed them and myself."

"For what it's worth," he said, "I think you did the right thing."

She looked up, startled. "You don't mean that."

"I do. Marriage without affection is a prison."

"That is a rather bleak view."

"I am merely being realistic," he countered.

She bit her lower lip. "I thought I could surrender my own dreams for the sake of duty... but when the moment came, I couldn't do it. I couldn't marry a man whom I feared."

Alistair nodded slowly. "Then you were braver than most."

For the first time, something flickered in her gaze—relief?

Gratitude? He wasn't sure. But the silence that followed felt less strained than before.

"I was not brave," Jane murmured, her voice laced with quiet regret. "I was a coward. I shouldn't have let it get that far."

"You spoke up when it mattered," he said firmly. "Don't question yourself now."

That drew a faint smile from her, softening the tension in her jaw. "Thank you, Alistair."

For a moment, she seemed to take in her surroundings for the first time. Her gaze wandered around the interior of the hackney, her nose wrinkling in distaste. "I've never been in a hackney before."

He smirked. "It's not for the faint of heart."

She leaned slightly towards the window and sniffed. Her face puckered with theatrical disgust. "Does it always smell like this?"

"Worse, I'm afraid."

A surprised laugh burst from her lips, light and unguarded. It did something to him—eased the tightness in his chest and momentarily made him forget the ache in his ribs.

"I didn't think that was possible. It smells like the inside of a chamber pot," she remarked.

He chuckled, then immediately regretted it as pain stabbed his side. Just in time, the hackney lurched to a halt, and he winced as he pulled back the curtain to peer outside.

"It would appear," he said, bracing a hand against the doorframe, "that we've arrived at my townhouse."

He reached for the door, but Jane's voice caught him short.

"Wait!" she shouted. "I can't be seen exiting a coach alone with a gentleman. Not without a chaperone."

"But you can leave a duke at the altar?" he teased, hoping levity would settle her nerves.

Her frown returned. "Point taken."

"Regardless, I won't let you travel alone in a hackney. It

would be deeply ungentlemanly of me." He pushed open the door and stepped out onto the pavement, wincing as his boots hit the ground.

The street was quiet, the faint clatter of distant hooves echoing down the row. Reaching into his inner coat pocket, he found a few coins and handed them up to the driver.

That was odd. If the men had meant to rob him, they'd done a poor job of it. They hadn't even searched his pockets. What, then, had been their purpose?

Jane alighted beside him, her expression alert, almost wary. She glanced up and down the pavement.

He offered his arm. "It will be all right," he said. He wasn't entirely sure it would be, but he suspected she needed to hear it.

She placed her hand on his arm, and he led her up the stone steps. Just as he reached for the handle, the door was flung open by his butler, Malone, whose formidable frame nearly filled the doorway.

"My lord!" Malone's dark eyes widened at the sight of him. "What happened?"

"I was attacked," Alistair said, brushing past him into the entry hall. "Send for the doctor."

"Yes, my lord." Malone bowed. "At once."

"And have a coach readied."

With another crisp nod, the butler disappeared to fulfill his instructions.

Left in the quiet entryway, Alistair turned to Jane. She stood near the doorway, uncertain, her hands clasped tightly once more. The familiar strength in her posture had returned, but he could see the vulnerability behind it.

He felt a swell of gratitude that startled him. "I owe you my life," he said simply.

"You owe me nothing."

He shook his head, stepping a little closer. "If you hadn't

intervened, I'd still be bleeding in some alley—or worse. I must do something to repay you."

Jane offered him a weak smile. "Can you turn back time?"

"No. That's beyond my abilities, I'm afraid."

Her eyes dimmed. "Then I'm afraid there's nothing you can do. I made my bed. Now I must lie in it."

Her voice was firm, but he could hear the weariness beneath the words. She wasn't just tired—she was bracing for the inevitable.

"Let me help you, Jane," he insisted. "Please."

She met his gaze. "You are kind. But I must go about this on my own," she said. "Besides, you don't want to be associated with me. Not anymore."

He opened his mouth to argue, but no words came.

Because the truth was, she wasn't wrong. She was ruined. And he had to think of his sister's reputation.

"It is all right," Jane said, her voice threaded with compassion. "You need not worry about me."

But he did. He couldn't not worry about her—not after what she had done for him, and certainly not now, when she stood in his entry hall with nowhere to go, her life upended and her future uncertain.

Alistair's fists clenched at his sides. Blast it, he needed to do something. She had dragged him—half-conscious and bleeding—from a filthy alleyway. She had saved his life. And now, she meant to walk out the door and face Society's judgment alone?

He stepped forward, ignoring the fresh flare of pain in his ribs. "At least allow me the honor of escorting you to Lady Westmere's townhouse."

"In your condition?"

He offered her a crooked smile, the best he could manage with one side of his face aching and the other already stiffening with bruises. "It looks worse than it is."

Which was a lie. His left eye was nearly swollen shut, and each breath sent a sharp jab through his side. But the discomfort was a welcome distraction from the sense of helplessness gnawing at him.

She studied him, unconvinced. "Very well," she said at last, though her tone made it clear she thought the gesture excessive. "But I think it is unnecessary."

"It is wholly necessary," he replied, allowing just a touch of formality into his voice. "You deserve to be treated with dignity, Jane. If I can give you even a shred of that, I will."

For a moment, she didn't speak. Her lips parted slightly, as though she meant to protest. But she didn't. She simply gave him a quiet nod, and that look in her eyes—wary, grateful, exhausted—settled something deep in his chest.

It wasn't about what she *needed*, not really.

It was about what *he* needed.

To show her she wasn't alone.

2

Jane sat stiffly in the corner of Alistair's coach. Her back was rigid and her hands were clenched so tightly in her lap that her gloves had wrinkled. The plush interior of the coach seemed too soft, too opulent for the turmoil roiling inside her. She stared unseeingly out the window, watching London blur past.

She was trying to be brave.

For Alistair's sake? For her own? She wasn't entirely certain anymore. The mask of composure she wore had already begun to crack, and the farther they traveled, the more difficult it became to keep her fear at bay.

What am I going to do?

The question haunted her, looping endlessly in her mind. She had no home now—of that she was certain. Her father's glare as she had fled the church would forever be seared into her memory, a promise of his fury. She had no hope of returning to her family, and if Olivia refused to see her—

No. Stop it. She refused to let that thought spiral. Olivia would help her. She had to. She had no one else to turn to.

She turned her head, glancing at Alistair. Even with the bruises marring his face and a swollen eye that had darkened to a sickly shade, there was still something steadying about him. His broad shoulders, the way his long legs were crossed with forced casualness, and the familiar dark, unruly curl that refused to stay in place—it all transported her back to childhood. Back to a time when he was simply Alistair, the boy who had let her ride his horse and rescued her bonnet from a tree.

But now? Now he was a man who had no business escorting her anywhere. He needed rest. A doctor. He shouldn't be worrying about her future when he could scarcely stand upright. Yet here he was, doing his duty. That wretched word.

Jane's throat tightened. She had done her duty, too. Smiled when she was told. Curtsied. Obeyed. She had donned her mother's bridal gown and walked to the altar of her own ruin. And still, it wasn't enough.

Will I ever be enough?

"It will be all right," Alistair said gently, his voice breaking through her musings.

She looked at him, her heart aching. "No. It won't be."

His brow furrowed. "You don't know that."

"I do." Her voice cracked, despite her efforts to keep it steady. "I left a duke at the altar. Not just some obscure gentleman with a country estate, but *the* Duke of Brackenford. One of the most powerful men in England."

He opened his mouth to respond, but she pushed on, her voice rising. "You don't understand. I have no home. I am ruined. Shunned. No one will receive me now."

"I'm sorry," he said.

Her shame returned like a rising tide. She was being rude. "No, I should apologize. You are only trying to help me. And I am grateful." She paused. "I'm just... frightened. Of what comes next. Of the unknown."

"It's normal to feel that way," he offered.

She sighed. "I had everything. A future secured. A title. A life others would envy. And I threw it away. For what? A foolish hope that there might be happiness out there for me?"

He leaned forward, his bruised face sincere. "You deserve to be happy, Jane."

"Happiness is fleeting," she murmured.

The worst part was that Alistair remained silent, as if agreeing with her.

The coach rolled to a halt, and Jane's stomach clenched. Olivia's townhouse loomed outside the window, elegant and imposing.

Alistair opened the door and stepped onto the pavement, then turned to offer her his hand. She hesitated for the briefest of moments before placing her gloved hand in his. His grip was warm, steadying.

"Shall we?" he asked.

They walked towards the front stairs, her steps slowing with each one she took. When they reached the threshold, Jane froze, staring at the heavy brass knocker.

Her hand hovered, then fell.

"I can't do it," she admitted.

Alistair turned towards her, surprise flickering in his eyes. "Sure you can."

"No." She took a small step back. "I can't do this to Olivia. She's only just begun to recover from the gossip. Her marriage to Lord Westmere has given her some measure of acceptance. I won't destroy that with my scandal."

Alistair glanced up and down the street. "I don't mean to rush you, but the longer we remain out here, the more curious the neighbors will become."

"I know, but—"

"Then good, we are in agreement," he said. And with that, he reached for the knocker.

Before his hand landed, the door opened. The butler's expression shifted from practiced neutrality to alarm.

"My lord," he gasped, "are you well?"

"I am," Alistair replied, stepping inside.

"Shall I fetch ice? A physician?"

"That won't be necessary."

Jane stepped over the threshold behind him, her heart hammering. This was it. There was no going back now.

"Will you inform Lady Westmere of Lady Jane's arrival?" Alistair asked.

The butler bowed. "At once, my lord."

As he disappeared, Jane took a trembling breath and tried not to show it. What if she had made the wrong choice to come here?

Alistair turned to face her. "Take a deep breath."

"That won't help."

"It will." His tone was calm, anchoring. "What's done is done. All that matters now is what comes next."

She shook her head. "There is no 'next.' Not for me."

"You are being quite the naysayer."

Lowering her gaze, she replied, "Sorry."

He stepped closer, his hands lightly touching her shoulders. "Will you stop apologizing?"

"Sorry." She grimaced. "I'm afraid it is a force of habit."

He chuckled. "Remarkable. I don't think I've ever seen you so undone. You were always the prim and proper one."

Before she could respond, a sharp voice rang out.

"Alcott!"

Jane turned to see a man emerging from a side corridor. Tall, scarred, and commanding. Lord Warwicke. She recognized him immediately. Everyone did.

He narrowed his eyes at Alistair. "Why do you look like death?"

"I feel like death," Alistair replied wearily. "Why are you here?"

"I was visiting Westmere, and I was on my way out. What happened to you?" Warwicke asked.

"I was attacked," Alistair replied. "If it weren't for Lady Jane, I might not be standing here. She saved me."

Lord Warwicke's eyes sharpened. "Do you know why you were attacked?"

"No. I assume it was a robbery, though they never took my coin purse."

In a low voice, Lord Warwicke asked, "How many attackers?"

"Three, I think," Alistair said. "But it all was a blur."

Jane interjected. "It was three men. I remember."

Lord Warwicke turned to her. "If you were called upon in the future, could you recognize them again?"

"Yes, I could," she said.

Alistair swayed slightly in his stance. "I don't... feel so good."

Warwicke moved quickly and caught his arm. "Let's get you to a chair."

As they moved towards the drawing room, a voice called from above.

"Jane!"

Jane turned and saw Olivia standing on the stairs, smiling down on her.

"You're here!" her friend exclaimed.

Surprised by Olivia's exuberance, she asked, "You're... glad?"

"Of course! It means you didn't marry him." Olivia reached the bottom step, her eyes sparkling. "Dare I ask when you came to this realization?"

She winced. "At the altar."

Olivia giggled. "Dear heavens, I cannot wait to hear this story. You must tell me everything," she said. "How did the duke respond? Was he furious? I bet he was furious."

Jane touched her cheek. "He slapped me. In front of the vicar. That's when I knew I had to leave."

Olivia's face fell. "I'm sorry. Did your father or brother say or do anything?"

"No, they said nothing. They just looked... furious, as if I were the problem."

"I take it they disowned you."

Jane's eyes burned. "I have nowhere else to go."

Olivia reached out, her voice kind. "You're not alone. You're here. With me."

Another voice entered the room. "My wife is right," said Lord Westmere, appearing beside her. "You can stay as long as you like."

"I don't wish to intrude."

Olivia smiled, slipping her arm around Jane. "You would offend me if you left, especially now."

Tears spilled freely down Jane's cheeks. "Thank you."

With a glance at the drawing room, Lord Westmere asked, "Did I hear Alcott was attacked?"

Alistair answered from the doorway. "You heard correctly, but do not worry. I'll live."

"Have you seen a doctor?" Lord Westmere asked, his eyes perusing his friend in concern.

"Not yet, but now that I am assured of Lady Jane's well-being, I can be on my way," Alistair said.

Jane turned to him, her heart full. "Thank you... for everything."

He inclined his head. "Take care of yourself, Jane."

After he departed, Lord Warwicke joined Lord Westmere by the window.

"I can't believe Alcott was attacked," Westmere said.

"I can," Lord Warwicke replied. "The streets of London can be dangerous, even during broad daylight."

"That's why I carry a muff pistol," Olivia shared.

Jane's eyes went wide. "You do?"

"Oh, yes. It's been quite useful." Olivia gave her a warm smile. "Now, how about a bath and some chocolate?"

Jane managed a laugh. "You know me too well. And now that I won't be a duchess, I can eat and drink as much as I like."

With Olivia's arm linked through hers, Jane allowed herself to be led upstairs. Her chest ached, her future was uncertain... but for the first time in days, she didn't feel entirely alone.

Alistair's entire body ached with each jolt of the coach. His ribs throbbed, his jaw felt as though it had been struck by a brick, and every muscle protested the very idea of movement. He had kept up a brave front for Jane's sake since he hadn't wanted her to see how close he'd come to collapsing. But now that she was safe, he could no longer ignore the pain that radiated through him like a dull, merciless drumbeat.

The coach lurched to a stop in front of his townhouse. Before the footman could come around, Alistair forced the door open and climbed down, gritting his teeth against the fire in his side. He ascended the stairs slowly, one hand gripping the railing for balance, and pushed through the front door.

Malone appeared instantly and moved forward with concern etched into every line of his face. "Doctor Wentworth is waiting in the drawing room, my lord."

Of course he was. Alistair gave a terse nod, barely able to summon the strength for civility. "Thank you."

He had no desire to be poked and prodded by a physician,

but the pain in his ribs had not dulled—it had only intensified. And he was tired of pretending it hadn't.

He stepped into the drawing room just as Charlotte let out a horrified gasp.

"What happened to you?" she demanded, springing to her feet as if she could somehow fix him through sheer indignation alone. "You look dreadful."

Alistair raised a brow, too exhausted to offer anything but dry sarcasm. "Your concern is touching."

"Were you attacked?" Charlotte approached him quickly, her sharp eyes scanning his bruised jaw and torn jacket. "Did you even fight back?"

He winced—not because of the insult, but because the effort of replying hurt his ribs. "Must we do this now?"

Without waiting for his consent, Charlotte reached up to touch the dark swelling on his jaw and he caught her hand and guided it away. "After the doctor," he said. "Please."

To his surprise, she didn't argue further. She only gave him a look—part frustration, part worry—and returned to her seat with a huff.

Alistair turned to the doctor. "I hope you haven't been waiting long."

"Not at all," Doctor Wentworth said as he rose, his spectacles perched low on his nose. "Though I fear I will regret asking what brought you to this state."

Alistair exhaled slowly. "I was attacked."

Another gasp from Charlotte. "I knew it! London is a cesspit of crime. I need a muff pistol immediately."

"You most certainly do not," Alistair replied, but she was already halfway to the door.

"I shall begin practicing now," she called over her shoulder.

"Charlotte!" he barked, but the only answer was the click of the door closing behind her.

The doctor gave him a look of wry amusement. "Would you like to chase after her?"

Alistair dragged a hand down his face. "It wouldn't help. Once she's made up her mind, she's worse than a general leading a siege."

The doctor chuckled knowingly. "Ah. I have a daughter like that. Now then, let's have a look."

The examination was unpleasant. Every touch of the doctor's fingers sent bolts of pain through Alistair's side. He clenched his jaw and bore it.

"Bruised, possibly cracked ribs," Doctor Wentworth finally concluded. "I'll leave you with bandages to wrap your chest. You'll need rest and patience."

Neither of which I possess in abundance, Alistair thought grimly. "Thank you, Doctor."

Just as the physician reached into his bag to hand him the bandages, a *crack* echoed through the townhouse.

A pistol shot.

Alistair closed his eyes in weary resignation. "Good gads, Charlotte," he muttered.

"I shall leave you to it," the doctor said, gathering his things.

Alistair strode through the back hallway and out onto the veranda. The scent of gunpowder hung faintly in the air. Targets had been set up on the back lawn, and there was Charlotte, standing with far too much pride and far too little skill, her muff pistol still smoking.

She handed it to a footman, who began the delicate task of reloading.

"Charlotte, what in heaven's name are you doing?" Alistair demanded.

Without looking at him, she replied, "Preparing myself, of course."

"You missed the target entirely."

"My attacker won't know that," she retorted. "All I need is confidence and an intimidating glare."

Alistair retrieved a second pistol from the table and took aim. He fired once, hitting the target dead center.

Charlotte did not look impressed. "Yes, yes, I'm well aware you're a former soldier. Must you always be so smug about it?"

"I was trained to shoot. You, on the other hand—"

"—have just as much right to defend myself," she cut in.

He started to reply, but she was already lifting the pistol again. "Perhaps if you had carried a pistol, you wouldn't have come home looking like you lost a tavern brawl."

Alistair ignored the sting of that and tried to remain calm. "Charlotte, you are not in danger."

"Because I refuse to be in danger," she replied, as she pulled the trigger again. The shot scraped the edge of the target. She let out a triumphant cheer. "Did you see that?"

He gave a slow blink. "You clipped the side."

"Progress is progress."

He shook his head. "Shouldn't you be inside? Resting? Reading? Anything that does not involve weaponry?"

"I'm finished with pistols for the day," she announced, passing the weapon to the footman. "Now I shall practice with my knife."

From the folds of her gown, she produced a small blade.

Alistair stared, stunned. "Why do you have a knife on your person?"

"That's hardly the point."

"It is very much the point."

"I am eight and ten years old," she said grandly. "I can handle a small knife."

She hurled the blade. It missed the target entirely, sending it in the direction of the trees.

Alistair looked to the heavens as if they might send him strength. "That was dreadful."

"It was my first attempt," she said with unwavering optimism. "I only just got the knife at the market yesterday."

"Enough. Please. Come inside before you hurt yourself or someone else."

Charlotte hesitated, then gave a shrug. "Very well. I could use a biscuit. Or perhaps two."

Alistair watched her walk towards the house, knife forgotten, utterly undeterred by failure.

He could survive the beating. He had endured worse during the war—a French bayonet to the leg and fevered nights in makeshift field hospitals. But surviving his sister?

That was an entirely different matter.

Charlotte, for all her charm, was unrelenting. Stubborn as a mule, sharp as a bayonet, and wholly unconcerned with his fraying patience.

Pressing a hand gingerly against his bruised ribs, Alistair exhaled through his nose. Pain flared across his chest like fire licking at every breath. He was done. Whatever resilience he'd summoned earlier had evaporated. All he wanted now was a dark, quiet room and the oblivion of sleep.

He made his way slowly down the corridor towards his bedchamber, his steps deliberate and strained. Each movement sent a fresh throb through his side, but he gritted his teeth and bore it.

Halfway to his room, a familiar figure appeared—Danvers, his valet and former batman, walking towards him with brisk efficiency. The moment Danvers saw his condition, he halted mid-stride, his eyes widening with alarm.

"What the devil happened to you, my lord?"

"I was attacked," Alistair said hoarsely. "I need your help binding my ribs. The doctor left a bandage."

"Of course. Right away." Danvers moved ahead and opened the bedchamber door, holding it for him. "Malone told me you were injured, but I see now his description did not begin to do your state justice."

Alistair stepped inside and immediately began shrugging off his jacket. Each tug at the fabric sent a spike of pain through his torso, and he couldn't suppress a grunt as he finally peeled it away.

Danvers was already at the washbasin, pouring fresh water. "We should clean those scrapes on your face."

"Later," Alistair muttered. "I just want the bandage on and this day behind me."

He pulled the long white strip of cloth from his coat pocket and handed it over before beginning the slow process of undoing his cravat and unfastening his shirt.

Danvers took one look at the bruising and gave a low whistle. "You took quite the beating today."

"Thank you for stating the obvious," Alistair said, exhaling as he lowered himself into the chair. He held up his arms slightly, allowing Danvers access to begin wrapping.

As the first tug of the bandage cinched around his ribs, he hissed. "Easy."

"I am being easy," Danvers replied. "Do you know why you were attacked?"

Alistair stared at a scuff on the floorboards, jaw clenched. "Most likely because I was an easy mark. I've grown… complacent. Life in London has dulled me."

"That doesn't sound like the captain I used to know," Danvers said, winding the bandage with care.

Alistair gave a rueful smile. "That captain didn't need to worry about sisters with muff pistols or invitations to dreadful soirees."

Danvers smirked faintly but asked, "Still… if they jumped you in an alley, how are you still breathing?"

Alistair's smile faded. "Because someone intervened. Lady Jane."

The bandage paused mid-wrap. "Lady Jane? *That* Lady Jane?"

"Yes. She told them to stop." He shook his head slightly, still baffled by the absurdity of it. "She shouted at them. Distracted them long enough that a constable passed by and sent them running."

"That took considerable courage on her part."

"It did," Alistair agreed.

"But why was she even there?" Danvers asked, finishing the wrap and securing it tightly. "I thought she was to marry the Duke of Brackenford today."

"She was," Alistair said. "But she changed her mind. She left him."

Danvers looked genuinely impressed. "Well, I'd say her presence saved your life."

Alistair nodded slowly. *She saved me.* He hadn't let himself dwell on it earlier—too distracted by the pain, the chaos, Charlotte's theatrics—but now it landed hard and cold.

If that constable hadn't walked by... if those men had turned on her...

Botheration.

The thought twisted like a blade in his gut.

How close had Jane come to dying?

He ran a hand over his face. "She risked her life for me. And I did nothing to protect her."

"You did what you could," Danvers responded. "It was her choice."

Alistair gave a slight nod, though guilt weighed heavily on his chest. "I just... I need to rest. Leave me in peace for one—perhaps two—days. And if Charlotte comes looking for me with any more weapons, tell her I've died because of her antics."

Danvers chuckled. "Yes, my lord." He moved to the windows, drawing the heavy drapes to block the fading light.

"Shall I bring you anything before I go? A brandy? A pistol? A biscuit?"

Alistair didn't even open his eyes. "Silence. That is all I need."

"As you wish."

The door closed softly behind him, and at last, Alistair let his body sink fully into the mattress. The pain dulled, the guilt throbbed, and through it all, one name echoed in his mind.

Jane.

3

Jane hesitated before closing the door to her bedchamber, her hand lingering on the handle a moment longer than necessary. Three days had passed since she'd arrived at Olivia's townhouse, and she'd barely seen a soul outside of her maid and the occasional footman delivering meals to her room. She had told herself she needed time to recover, but she knew she could not avoid the world forever.

This morning, she would be brave. Or, at the very least, she would be present.

She smoothed down the soft folds of the borrowed pale pink gown, grateful that Olivia and she were close enough in size. It was a small mercy, though it did little to ease the ache in her chest. Her father still hadn't responded to her letter. A part of her had expected it, but the reality still hurt. Being disowned was one thing. Being forgotten was another entirely.

The smell of fresh bread and tea drew her down the corridor towards the dining room. She paused just outside the threshold, her courage briefly faltering. Through the open door, she spotted Olivia's father-in-law, Lord Everwyck, seated at the head of the table, the morning newssheets held wide before him like a shield. Drat. Olivia was nowhere in sight.

Jane's palms grew damp. She'd spoken to Lord Everwyck only a handful of times, and though he was never unkind, there was something about his manner—so precise, so direct—that left her on edge. Still, she was a guest here. She could hardly remain in her bedchamber forever.

Drawing in a quiet breath, she stepped into the room.

One of the footmen moved to pull out a chair, and she murmured her thanks as she sat, careful to school her expression into something placid. Her hands were steady, though her stomach had begun to knot.

"Lady Jane," Lord Everwyck said, voice dry, his eyes still hidden behind the newssheets.

"My lord," she replied, inclining her head politely.

A footman placed a plate of food before her and she reached for her fork and knife, hoping the simple task of eating might ground her. She had just managed a small bite when Lord Everwyck lowered one half of the newssheets and announced, "You've made the Society page… again."

The food turned to ash on her tongue. She lowered her fork. "I assumed as much."

He glanced over at her then, assessing her with that sharp gaze of his. "Do you regret not marrying the duke?"

She swallowed hard. There were many things she regretted —mostly waiting so long to find her voice—but not this. "No," she admitted. "I don't."

He did not look impressed. "You could have been a duchess. Think of the power and prestige you cast aside."

"I care little about that."

"That is rather foolish to say," he replied. "You threw it all away. For what? And please don't say a love match."

She met his gaze squarely, refusing to cower. "And what if I do?"

Lord Everwyck huffed and flicked the page back into place. "You've been reading too many novels. Love is not something one falls into. It is developed, slowly, and often reluctantly, over time."

"Olivia would disagree."

"She was fortunate," he muttered. "As was my son. But most people of your station can only hope for mutual toleration."

Jane frowned. "That's a rather grim view."

"It's the truth," he said, folding the newssheets and laying them down flat. "You could have had everything. But instead, you've chosen some fanciful notion of affection over security."

Her appetite vanished completely. "The duke is not a good man."

"And you know this how?" he asked, raising a skeptical brow.

She steadied her voice. "I've heard the rumors. Everyone has. His first wife was locked away in an asylum, where she perished some five months later. His second died mysteriously. The third one was run over by a carriage. And the last one, she supposedly fell down the stairs."

"Purely gossip," he dismissed with a wave of his hand.

"Perhaps. But a consistent pattern of tragedy follows him. Too many wives, too many unexplained endings."

Lord Everwyck lifted his glass and took a sip. "Perhaps it was simply a string of bad luck."

"Or perhaps he only wanted me for an heir," Jane said. "What if I had produced another daughter? Would he have cast me aside, too?"

"He has six daughters already. That must weigh heavily."

"And still you defend him," she said, incredulous. "But what of his wives? Of the women who bore those daughters and then conveniently vanished from his life?"

He looked down at the table. "I can't justify it. But life rarely gives us neat explanations. You could have been a duchess."

"At what cost? My life?" she challenged.

From the doorway came an entirely too cheerful voice. "Dear heavens, must we be so morbid before breakfast?"

Jane turned to see Olivia entering the room, radiant in lavender and looking entirely unaffected by the tension hanging in the air. She walked straight to Lord Everwyck and pressed a kiss to his cheek.

"It's good to see you," she said brightly, not bothering to wait for a reply.

A twitch of amusement softened Lord Everwyck's mouth, though his gaze returned pointedly to the newssheets.

Olivia sat beside Jane, placing her linen napkin on her lap with practiced grace. "I'm glad to see you've emerged from your self-imposed exile," she teased.

Jane offered a faint smile. "I thought it was time."

"And I, for one, believe you made the right choice."

Lord Everwyck let out a dismissive sound. "Women," he muttered under his breath.

Olivia laughed. "It must be exhausting being wrong so often."

"I am not wrong," he insisted. "Lady Jane should have married the duke. She'd be on her wedding tour right now—admired by every debutante in Mayfair."

"I believe the word you're searching for is pitied, not admired," Olivia said. "She was handed to the duke like a sacrificial lamb."

"Why do I bother debating with you?" he asked.

"I don't rightly know," Olivia replied, sipping her chocolate. "I'm usually right."

Lord Everwyck pushed back his chair. "Excuse me. I've work to attend to." With that, he left the room, the air relaxing slightly in his absence.

Jane exhaled and looked down at her plate.

Olivia returned her cup to the saucer, then gave Jane a sideways glance. "His bark is worse than his bite, I promise."

Jane bit her lower lip. "He wasn't wrong. At least… not entirely. I've read the newssheets. The *ton* is outraged. They don't understand how I could humiliate a duke."

"Well," Olivia said, "the duke will no doubt rebound soon and select another bride."

The words stung, though Jane didn't know why. "He never cared about me. We'd only spoken a handful of times before the ceremony."

"Then you did the right thing."

"I know. But I still can't seem to escape the consequences."

Olivia tilted her head. "Then perhaps we don't venture to Hyde Park this afternoon?"

Jane laughed weakly. "Heavens, no. I'd be stared at like a two-headed calf."

"So, your plan is to hide out here indefinitely?"

"Yes."

"An admirable strategy," Olivia said with mock solemnity as she reached for her chocolate.

Jane turned her gaze towards the window, watching the light pour across the polished floor. "I haven't heard from my father. Or my brother. I told them where I was… but I have heard nothing in return."

Olivia paused. "Would you like Evander to write them?"

"No. I doubt that would help. My father threatened to disown me, and yet… I had hoped—foolishly, perhaps—that he'd understand what I had to do."

"Your father and brother are not known for their compassion," Olivia remarked.

Jane dropped her gaze to her lap, her fingers tightening in the folds of her borrowed skirt. The pale pink muslin was soft and lovely, but it felt borrowed in more ways than one—like everything in her life now. Nothing truly belonged to her anymore. Not her home. Not her future.

"Should I go see them?" she asked, though she already knew the answer. Still, the question gnawed at her.

Olivia didn't hesitate. "Why? So they can turn you away to your face?"

Tears pricked the corners of Jane's eyes. She blinked rapidly, refusing to let them fall. She'd cried too many times over the past three days, and it had to stop. Grief would not fix her circumstances.

It was time to move forward.

Or at least pretend to.

She looked up, heart hammering, and asked, "Do you still require a companion?"

There. She'd said it. It was mortifying for a woman of her station to work for an income, but what choice did she have?

But the slight pause before Olivia responded made her stomach sink.

"Not at this time," her friend replied.

The words hit harder than she expected.

Before the silence could settle too heavily between them, Olivia reached out and clasped her hand. "I require a friend more."

Jane's throat tightened. A friend. It was a generous thing to say. A kind thing. But even kindness, when one felt adrift, could sting like a wound.

"I can't live off your generous graces forever," Jane said, trying to keep her voice steady. "You've already done more than most would."

"Don't worry about that now," Olivia said with a small, firm shake of her head. "You are more than welcome here, Jane. This is your home for as long as you need it to be."

As she went to respond, Lord Westmere's voice echoed from

the doorway. "My lovely wife is right. We're happy to have you here."

He entered the room and crossed to Olivia, placing a kiss on her cheek. He lingered just long enough that Jane's chest ached with something sharp and silent. They were so clearly in love. It radiated from them in every small gesture—the comfortable banter, the easy affection, the warmth in Olivia's eyes when she looked at her husband.

And for a moment, Jane couldn't breathe.

Would she ever have that? That sort of certainty? That comfort? That love?

Perhaps Lord Everwyck had been right. Perhaps she'd consumed too many books, too many fanciful stories that had convinced her love could be more than duty and toleration. Had she built her expectations on illusions?

"Thank you," Jane said. "Truly. But I must begin to think about my future... or what little of it remains."

Olivia sat straighter. "Not so long ago, I was in a similar place. And everything worked out."

Jane glanced at her, wondering if her friend truly believed that—or if she was simply offering hope because that's what friends did.

Lord Westmere gave Olivia's hand a gentle squeeze before taking his seat. "I'm afraid I have work to tend to this afternoon, but I'm free this evening. Would you care to accompany me to Vauxhall Gardens?"

Olivia's face lit up instantly. "I'd love that." She turned to Jane with a hopeful smile. "Will you join us?"

Jane stiffened, almost recoiling from the idea. Her hand lifted automatically in protest. "I don't think that's a good idea."

"You can't hide out here forever," Olivia said, the gentle note in her voice sharpened by concern. "It would be good for you to get some fresh air. It might lift your spirits."

"I... uh..." Jane faltered. She didn't want to be ungrateful, but the thought of Vauxhall Gardens—of being seen, whispered about, recognized—was enough to send her heart racing. "I appreciate the invitation, but I just don't know..."

Lord Westmere spoke up. "We don't want to pressure Jane into anything she isn't ready for. Do we, Olivia?"

Olivia sighed, relenting. "No. Of course not."

Jane sent Lord Westmere a grateful glance. "Thank you. I shall think on it."

"What if we simply take a tour of the gardens after breakfast?" Olivia asked.

"That I can agree to." It wasn't much, but it was something. A first step.

She knew Olivia meant well. She was doing her best to draw Jane out from under the weight of shame and uncertainty—but the truth was, Jane wasn't even sure what she needed. Every option seemed equally terrifying. Every path forward felt uncertain, unsteady.

But at least she wouldn't have to face it alone.

Not yet.

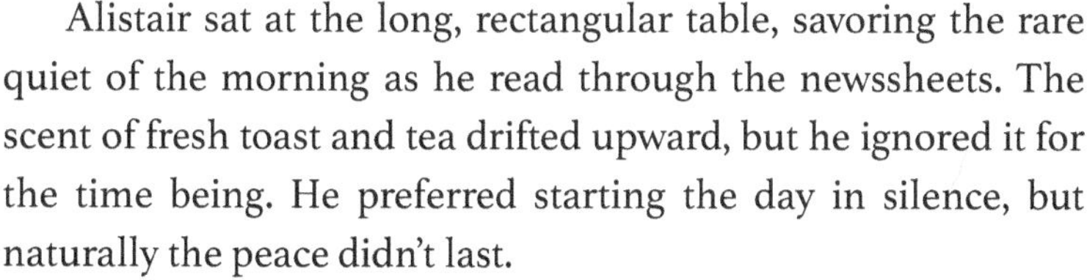

Alistair sat at the long, rectangular table, savoring the rare quiet of the morning as he read through the newssheets. The scent of fresh toast and tea drifted upward, but he ignored it for the time being. He preferred starting the day in silence, but naturally the peace didn't last.

The moment his sister swept into the dining room, the air shifted.

"Good morning," Charlotte greeted, far too cheerfully for any reasonable hour. That alone made him lower the newssheets. She was never this lively before noon.

"What do you want?" he asked, leveling her with a flat look.

Her eyes went wide with faux innocence. "Nothing."

He didn't believe that for a second. "Hmm," he muttered and resumed reading, though he kept one ear trained on her.

Charlotte settled across from him and reached for the teapot. "Although…"

There it was.

"… I was hoping you would accompany me to Vauxhall Gardens this evening," she said.

"No," came his quick response.

Unperturbed, she lifted her teacup and gave a demure shrug. "I figured you would say that, so I shall ask Mrs. Glasner."

He snapped the newssheets down. "Absolutely not. Mrs. Glasner is half-blind and has a foot that turns inward. She is not an adequate chaperone."

Charlotte sipped her tea as though his rising temper was of no concern. "Then I suppose you have no choice but to come with me," she said sweetly, batting her lashes.

Alistair looked heavenward. He was weary of this game. She asked, he refused, she manipulated, and he ultimately relented. Every time. She was maddening. Worse, she knew it.

He preferred evenings at home, a quiet fire, a novel, and perhaps a brandy. Charlotte, on the other hand, seemed determined to go to every social event in High Society, and Vauxhall Gardens was the place to be seen. Anything could happen there. He'd be mad to allow Charlotte to go with Mrs. Glasner.

"I'll take you," he grumbled.

She clasped her hands together and beamed with triumph, though the act was too perfect to be genuine. She'd planned this from the start. "Thank you, Guildford."

He sighed heavily at that name. She only used it when she wanted to annoy him, tease him, exasperate him. While it was his given name, he had chosen at the age of five to use Alistair, his middle name, because his father's name was Guildford. And he didn't ever want there to be confusion about who was who. "I've asked—no, demanded—repeatedly that you stop calling me that." He shook his head as she chuckled at him.

He raised the newssheet again, determined to retreat behind its pages, but one heading caught his eyes and made him freeze.

Former Lieutenant Mark Austen found dead in alleyway.

A sharp breath caught in his throat.

"What is it?" Charlotte asked, her voice suddenly serious.

"A member of my company," he said quietly. "Mark Austen. He's dead."

Her brow furrowed. "How did he die?"

Alistair scanned the article again, his mouth going dry. "He was stabbed. Found in an alleyway yesterday. They suspect a robbery gone wrong."

She set down her teacup. "How awful."

He folded the newssheets with stiff fingers and lowered them to the table. "He survived the war. Was a good soldier and a better man. He deserved more than to die in some godforsaken alley."

Charlotte's eyes softened. "I'm sorry."

"He lived through battles most men couldn't fathom. And this... this is how it ends for him."

She was quiet for a moment, then added, "Is it not strange that two people in the same company were attacked in a similar fashion?"

"I thought the same thing, but it is probably just a coincidence." At least he hoped it was a coincidence.

With a wave of her hand, she responded, "It is a good thing that I carry a muff pistol in my reticule now."

"That is reckless. You'll injure yourself—or worse."

"'Oh, ye of little faith,'" she quipped.

He gave a half-laugh. "Quoting scripture now, are we?"

"I attend church," she said with a shrug. "Why shouldn't I?"

"It's better than those dreadful novels you devour. I'll never understand the mania women have for reading lately."

She gave him a look. "I've always loved reading. It's far more entertaining than stabbing myself with embroidery needles."

He shook his head. "Women are supposed to enjoy needlework."

"Says who? I think it's a conspiracy devised by men to keep women docile and occupied, so they don't start voicing their opinions."

He arched a brow. "Is that what you truly believe?"

"I don't know what I believe anymore," she said, then met his gaze with unflinching resolve. "But I do know I won't have my voice silenced by you. Or anyone."

Alistair took a bite of his food, chewing thoughtfully. "I'm glad you have opinions. I only wish you weren't so stubborn. It's a dangerous combination."

Her teasing expression faded, and she grew quiet. "I worry I'm too much like Father."

He set down his fork. "You are nothing like him. He was cold. Distant. And entirely too cruel for my liking."

"I wouldn't know since I was ignored entirely."

Alistair's stomach twisted. "Being ignored might've been better. At least you were spared the brunt of his wrath."

"One of my old governesses, Miss Wilde, told me Father was disappointed from the moment I was born a girl."

He winced. "That may be true," he admitted, "but it says more about him than it ever said about you."

Charlotte glanced down at her lap. "You had a way out. You could leave. You bought a commission into the Army and escaped."

"I did escape," he said grimly. "And he tried to drag me back. Ordered it, in fact, but I refused."

Alistair hadn't spoken of it in years—how unbearable the

house had become after Mother died. How suffocating. The grief, the rage, the expectations.

Charlotte moved her food around her plate. "At least you have memories of Mother."

"She adored you," he said. "Dotingly so."

Her voice dropped to a whisper. "Father said I killed her."

He froze. "You did not."

"Her health declined after giving birth to me. If not for me—"

"Charlotte, stop." His voice was firm. "She wanted a daughter more than anything. She was happy when you were born. You were not the cause of her death."

She tried to smile, but it faltered. "It doesn't change what happened."

"Charlotte…"

"It's all right," she said, pushing her plate away. "Can we speak of something else?"

He nodded, but the heaviness in his chest remained. So much of her fire, her wit, her need to prove herself—it all made sense now. And he refused to let anyone, even the memory of their father, diminish her worth.

Alistair shifted in his chair, wincing as the dull ache in his side flared again. The bruises along his ribs were persistent devils, stubbornly refusing to fade, unlike the fading yellow and green mottling along his jaw and cheek. He was tired of hurting. Tired of being reminded—every breath, every twist—that he'd been bested.

Charlotte studied him across the breakfast table, her expression uncharacteristically thoughtful.

"You look better," she said at last. "The swelling's gone down, and the bruises are lightening—at least somewhat."

He grunted, not entirely comforted. "My ribs didn't get the message. The doctor said it will be weeks before they're fully healed."

"You should be resting more."

"I rest plenty," he lied, setting down his teacup with exaggerated care. He hated the weakness. The way his body betrayed him every time he coughed or laughed or bent too quickly.

Charlotte, of course, wasn't finished. "Have you spoken to Lady Jane since the... incident?"

He stiffened. There it was. The question he'd been avoiding.

"No," he said. "And I think it best I stay away. For now."

Her brow arched. He knew that look. It was the same expression she used before pulling apart one of his arguments like unraveling a loose thread.

"And why is that?"

"I must think of your reputation." It was flimsy, but it was all he had.

Charlotte scoffed. "What poppycock! Lady Jane saved your life. You owe her."

"I do owe her," he agreed. "But how does one repay a debt like that? There's nothing sufficient—"

"You could marry her."

His fork paused mid-air. "I beg your pardon?"

Charlotte folded her hands primly on the table, her tone infuriatingly calm. "She's ruined. No one will marry her now. You could save her, just as she saved you."

The fork clattered against his plate as he set it down, the weight of her words pressing against his temples. "That is absurd."

"Is it?" she asked, too mildly. "You could do far worse."

He snatched the linen napkin from his lap and tossed it onto the table. "The idea is preposterous. I need a wife who is above reproach."

Her chin lifted. "Why?"

"Because marriage is not a whim. A man of my position must choose carefully."

"Lady Jane has always been kind to me," Charlotte shared. "Even when others were not."

Alistair rubbed a hand across the back of his neck. "There are many factors to consider in selecting a wife. Her family, her reputation, her dowry—"

"And love?"

He blinked. "What?"

Charlotte met his gaze evenly. "And what of love?"

He barked a humorless laugh. "Love? I said nothing about love."

"But why not?" she asked, brows drawing together. "Do you not want to love your wife?"

"I don't believe in love," he said, sharper than he intended. "But I do believe in affection."

Charlotte stared at him, stunned. "*What*? How is that even possible?"

He rose from the table, shoving his chair back more forcefully than necessary. The pain lanced through his side, but he ignored it. "I'm not having this conversation with you. Whom I marry is my decision."

She leaned back, her arms crossed. "What if you choose someone awful?"

"I won't."

"You might. Many debutantes hide their true natures just to secure a man with a title."

He turned and narrowed his eyes at her. "And you know this how?"

Charlotte pressed her lips into a thin line. "Trust me. Everyone wears a mask. Even you."

That gave him pause. "What are you hiding?" he asked.

"More than you could ever know," she murmured. "I have to."

The vulnerability in her tone tugged at something inside

him—something too tangled to name. But he didn't press. Not now.

Instead, he reached for his tea and took a final sip, letting the warmth of it clear away the chill her words had left behind.

"As informative as this conversation is," he said, "I have work that requires my attention."

Charlotte nodded once. "Very well. But we're still set for Vauxhall this evening?"

"Yes," he said tightly, "but I have no intention of staying until dawn."

"We shall see," she replied with a glint of mischief.

"I'm being earnest, Charlotte."

She gave him a pacifying smile. "I know. That's what makes it so amusing, Guildford."

Alistair muttered a curse word under his breath and turned towards the doorway, trying not to limp. Charlotte was, without question, one of the most exasperating people he had ever known. Obstinate. Unrelenting. Entirely too clever for her own good.

And yet, he loved her—deeply, fiercely, without condition.

4

Jane pulled the needle through the embroidery hoop with more force than was strictly necessary, nearly tearing the linen. She stared at the nearly invisible flower petal she'd just stitched. It was her third failed attempt at getting the shade of blue right. It hardly mattered. Her mind wasn't on the design. Or the thread. Or the needle pricking her fingertip.

Her mind was consumed—haunted, even—by the weight of her family's silence. Silence that had stretched on for days now, thick and suffocating, broken only by the distant tick of the clock and the occasional creak of the townhouse's wooden frame. Her father. Her brother. What were they saying about her behind closed doors? Or worse—had they stopped speaking of her entirely?

She tried to swallow the ache that lodged itself in her throat. It was easier to stitch than to think. But the fabric blurred as unshed tears welled in her eyes.

"You did the right thing," Olivia said gently.

Jane paused mid-stitch. Her eyes lifted to the woman seated

across from her, poised with a book in her lap and a quiet steadiness that Jane envied. "Did I?" she asked.

"You did," Olivia said again, more firmly this time. "Your family will come around."

Jane arched a brow. "Do you truly believe that?"

Olivia winced, folding the edge of her book closed. "No," she admitted with a sheepish sigh. "But I'm trying to be optimistic. Someone in this room ought to be."

Jane dropped her embroidery hoop into her lap with a sigh. "I must be a dreadful bore," she murmured. "I can't seem to think of anything but... well, everything I wish I could forget. And this needlework is dreadful."

Olivia smiled faintly. "Is anyone's heart ever truly in embroidery? Come with me to the circulating library instead. We could get a French romance novel, or two."

Jane shook her head. "I'm not sure I can bear the stares. Or the whispers. The shame follows me everywhere. Even in my thoughts."

"I understand," Olivia responded. "But you are still coming to Vauxhall Gardens this evening, aren't you?"

"I don't know..."

"You must!" Olivia interrupted. "I won't accept excuses. You need air. And light. And music. And perhaps a tart or two from the pastry vendor."

Before Jane could form a reply, the butler appeared in the doorway and announced, "Lord Barkley has come to call for Lady Jane."

Jane's head snapped up. "My brother is here?" she asked, her heart leaping with a confused mix of hope and dread.

"Yes, my lady."

She shot to her feet, smoothing her skirts with trembling hands. "Please send him in." She turned to Olivia with wide eyes. "This is a good sign. Don't you think?"

But Olivia's expression had gone guarded. "Let's hear what he has to say first."

Jane barely had time to brace herself before her brother strode into the room—tall, broad-shouldered, and stone-faced. His jaw was clenched, and his eyes were hard, unfeeling.

"Jane," he said curtly, no warmth in his tone.

She forced a smile to her lips. "Adam."

He gave Olivia a brief, stiff nod. "Lady Westmere." His gaze returned to Jane. "I brought your trunks."

"You did?"

"Yes. I believe that concludes our business." He turned towards the door.

"Wait!" she called out.

He stopped, one hand on the doorframe. "Yes?"

"That's it?" Her voice wavered. "You have nothing else to say to me?"

He turned fully, his eyes narrowing. "What would you like me to say? That you've disgraced the family name? That you made a spectacle of yourself and dragged us all into scandal?"

"I couldn't marry him," she whispered. "I just—couldn't."

"You could have been a duchess, Jane." His voice grew cold. "Instead, you chose humiliation. You should be ashamed."

"I—" Her throat tightened. Words failed her.

He advanced a step. "You are a worthless chit," he seethed. "And I'm ashamed to call you my sister."

Tears stung her eyes. Still, she stood her ground. "I don't expect you to understand my reasons—"

"Oh, I understand," Adam snapped. "You humiliated one of the most powerful men in England at the altar. You've ruined your prospects, and ours."

"The duke struck me," she said, her voice breaking.

Adam's lip curled. "And perhaps you deserved it." His fists clenched at his sides. "Frankly, I'm struggling not to do the same."

"No," Olivia said, rising to her feet. "We do not permit violence in this home."

Adam barely acknowledged her. "You permit scandal, though. This whole house is a festering pit of impropriety."

"Enough," came a deeper voice from the doorway. Lord Westmere entered the room with a stern expression. "It is time for you to leave, Lord Barkley."

Adam didn't flinch. "Gladly. But know this—Jane is no longer welcome in our family. Father sent me to deliver that message along with her trunks. As far as we are concerned, she is dead to us."

A cry burst from Jane's throat as she lowered herself onto the settee. "How could you say that?"

"It's no more than what you've earned," Adam stated. "Enjoy your life among ruined women and spinsters."

Lord Westmere stepped forward, his voice commanding. "You've said your piece. Now get out."

Adam turned his scorn towards him. "You've made enemies of us and of the Duke of Brackenford."

"Excellent. My list of enemies was woefully short," Lord Westmere said dryly.

"You'll regret this," Adam growled. "She'll bleed your coffers dry and then you'll cast her out, too."

"Your sister will remain here as long as she wishes," Lord Westmere declared. "She is welcome in our home. Always."

Adam's voice was full of venom. "Why would you protect this worthless girl?"

"Get out!" Lord Westmere exclaimed.

Adam spun and stormed out. Moments later, the front door slammed hard enough to rattle the windows.

Jane rose shakily and rushed to the window. She caught sight of her brother entering his coach, not once looking back.

And somehow... she felt relief.

Olivia stepped beside her. "Your brother is awful. Just awful."

"I know," Jane whispered.

Lord Westmere's voice joined theirs. "Forget what he said."

Jane rested her head against the cool glass of the window. "He wasn't wrong."

"He was," Olivia asserted. "He had no right to speak to you that way."

Jane's lips trembled. "He's always spoken to me like that. Since we were children. Quite frankly, it wasn't the worst conversation that we have had."

"That doesn't make it right," Olivia replied softly, resting her hand on Jane's sleeve.

"No," Jane agreed. "But he spoke for my father. That much I know."

"Then I'm glad you are here, and not with them. You deserve better."

Jane straightened. "No, I don't. I've nothing. No money. No future. One day you will tire of me and cast me out. What will I do then?"

Olivia's expression softened with compassion. "Jane…"

"Excuse me, but I need to be alone," Jane said, her voice tight as she turned from the drawing room. She didn't look back, didn't dare meet their eyes. Not Olivia's, not Lord Westmere's. Not even the sympathetic footman who quietly bowed as she passed.

The moment she entered the entry hall, her steps faltered. There, positioned neatly beneath the wide arching windows, stood her trunks—her life reduced to two battered cases and a few hatboxes. The sight of them struck her like a blow to the chest. They were a symbol of what had been done. She was nothing more than a burden to be packed off and delivered.

For so long, she had been the good daughter. The obedient one. The one who smiled at the right time, curtsied just so, and bit her tongue when it ached to speak. All of it—every silent sacrifice, every forced smile, every carefully measured step—had been for their approval.

And in the end, none of it mattered.

She would never be good enough for them.

The realization landed not with despair, but with clarity—sharp and almost blinding in its honesty. Tears flooded her eyes, but these were not the same tears she had wept over the past few days. These tears were laced with fury.

They had never seen her—not truly. Not as someone with thoughts and feelings and desires of her own. Just a vessel for ambition. A bargaining chip. A means to an end.

Footsteps echoed behind her on the marble floor.

"Jane?" Olivia's voice came gently. "Are you all right?"

Jane did not turn around. She stared straight ahead at the trunks and the life she no longer lived. Still, her voice came out steady. "For the first time... in a long while, I think I am." She paused. "No matter what I did my family would never have truly accepted me. They never did."

"No," Olivia agreed. "They wouldn't have."

Jane turned to face her. "I made the right decision."

Olivia's lips curved into the barest smile. "Yes, you did."

"I don't know what comes next," Jane admitted. "I don't even know who I am beyond them. But I do know... I have a future. It just looks nothing like I once imagined."

Relief brightened Olivia's face. "I know that look. You aren't giving up."

Jane reached up and wiped the tears from her cheeks. "No, I am not," she said with determination. She glanced towards her trunks. "At least they didn't toss my clothing into the street with yesterday's rubbish."

"Shall we begin preparing for Vauxhall Gardens?"

Jane gave a nod. "Yes. And I already know the gown I mean to wear."

With a graceful pivot, Olivia turned towards the butler. "Will you see that Lady Jane's trunks are taken up to her bedchamber?"

The man bowed. "At once, my lady."

Olivia looped her arm through Jane's as they began to ascend the grand staircase together. "Out of curiosity, can you draw?"

"I can. Why do you ask?"

A mischievous grin formed on Olivia's lips. "I was thinking... perhaps you might sketch your brother's face, and we could use it for target practice the next time we shoot."

A laugh escaped Jane's lips. "That may be the best idea I've heard in days."

"I thought you'd like it."

Jane glanced over at her friend. "Thank you... for everything. I know I haven't exactly been pleasant company."

Olivia waved the words aside. "That's utter nonsense. Everyone is allowed to break down now and then. But do you know what I think?"

"What?"

"You're already stronger than you were. Because strength isn't about always doing what's expected. It's about doing what you thought you couldn't."

Jane held on to that as they reached the top of the stairs. She didn't know what the world held for her now—who she'd become, where she'd go. But for the first time, she was no longer afraid to find out.

Alistair strode along the main path in Vauxhall Gardens with his sister on his arm, dodging clusters of chattering patrons like a soldier maneuvering through battlefield smoke.

Candlelit lanterns hung from trees and pavilions in flickering tiers, their light soft and romantic. They were meant to enchant, no doubt. And yet all he could think about was how many blasted people there were.

He hated crowds. Always had. Too many people, too many variables, too many eyes.

Charlotte smiled up at him with practiced ease. "Could you please pretend to be enjoying this?"

He grunted. "Why are there so many people here?"

"Because it is the place to be," she replied with a smug sort of patience, "and more importantly, the place to be seen."

She gasped suddenly and tugged on his arm, pointing ahead. "We must go to the Rotunda!"

Alistair followed her gaze and groaned inwardly. A snaking line of patrons wound towards the domed building like a parade of sheep queuing for slaughter.

"No," he said flatly. "We've seen it before."

"But not tonight," she pressed. "There's always something new."

He narrowed his eyes at the unmoving crowd. "There's nothing new about standing shoulder-to-shoulder with other patrons for half the night."

"A line won't kill you."

"It just might," he muttered under his breath.

She huffed in exasperation. "You are no fun."

"I am very fun," he corrected. "I simply have refined tastes in how I spend my evening." He gestured towards one of the other buildings in the distance. "We could listen to the orchestra or visit any of the other pavilions."

Charlotte slipped her hand from his arm. "You can do what you like, but I am going to stand in line for the Rotunda."

His jaw tensed. "Be serious."

"I am," she said, lifting her chin in that infuriating way of hers. "And really, your aversion to lines is quite absurd. You must've stood in line often enough during your time in the Army."

"I did," he replied, "but I always stood at the front."

"Of course you did," she muttered.

"There are so many sights to enjoy at Vauxhall. Why choose the dullest one?"

"Because I want to explore it."

He exhaled sharply through his nose. "What if I brought you back during the day? You'd have the place to yourself."

Charlotte rolled her eyes. "Must we go through this entire song and dance again? We'll argue, you'll eventually concede, and by then, the line will be longer."

He glared at the line like it had personally offended him. "Fine," he said, defeated. "Lead the way."

She beamed and darted towards the end of the line, practically glowing with victory.

Alistair followed at a slower pace, muttering a familiar refrain. "Blasted lines."

They had not moved more than a foot when a familiar voice called out behind him. "Alcott."

Alistair turned, recognizing Lord Westmere immediately. Beside him stood his wife, Olivia, and—his gaze caught—a familiar figure in blue silk.

Lady Jane.

He bowed to the women, offering a polite greeting. "Good evening, ladies."

Westmere dipped his head towards Charlotte. "Miss Winslow."

His sister barely acknowledged the greeting, too focused on watching the motionless line with the vigilance of a hawk.

Not that there was any movement to note.

Alistair's eyes found Jane again. The blue of her gown framed her shoulders beautifully and drew out the startling clarity of her eyes. There was something subdued in her expression, a tension she tried to hide behind a smile that didn't quite reach her eyes.

"How are you faring?" he asked.

"I am doing well," she replied quickly.

He studied her. "The truth, please."

Her gaze dropped to the ground. "The whispers and stares follow me wherever I go. It's been relentless."

Olivia linked her arm through Jane's. "And she is handling it all with grace."

"I am trying," Jane murmured.

Charlotte turned around then. "Have you seen the Rotunda?"

Jane nodded. "Yes. It's spectacular. I love how your voice carries inside. It's like speaking into an echo."

Charlotte rose on her toes and peered forward. "I hope we make it inside before the fireworks begin."

Alistair sighed. "I hate lines."

Westmere chuckled. "Yes, I remember. At Eton, you'd cause a proper uproar in the dinner line."

Alistair shrugged, unapologetic. "It was the only way to stay entertained."

Westmere turned to his wife. "Alcott used to bring frogs in his pockets and drop them down the backs of other boys. Chaos would ensue, and he'd march right to the front."

"That is terrible," Olivia said, grinning. "And something I could absolutely see myself doing."

Jane blinked in horror. "I would never do such a thing."

Alistair smirked. "I know. But a little mischief never hurt anyone."

"My father would disagree."

He leaned a bit closer. "You're not under his thumb anymore, are you?"

She hesitated. "Well, no… but—"

A sudden idea bloomed in his mind, playful and absurd.

And it would be a far better use of his time than standing in this blasted line. "There's a stream nearby and I'm certain there are frogs there. You should hold one in your hands."

Jane stared at him like he'd lost his mind. "Surely you jest."

"I do not," he said, extending his hand. "Come with me."

"I'm not sure this is a good idea."

"It will be fun," he coaxed, wiggling his fingers. "Unless you're afraid of frogs?"

"I'm not afraid," she protested. "I just don't think they want to be touched."

"They've never complained before."

"That's because they can't *talk.*"

He grinned. "You're protesting far too much."

Her eyes dropped to his outstretched hand. Then, slowly, she placed hers in his. "All right," she said. "But let's be quick about it."

He turned to Charlotte. "We'll be back shortly."

His sister waved him off without even turning around. "Go on."

They moved away from the crowd, weaving through clusters of trees and laughing patrons. He felt the tension in Jane's posture—rigid, uncertain—but she didn't pull away.

They reached the stream, its banks glinting faintly in the moonlight. Frogs croaked cheerfully from the reeds.

He crouched, scanning the stones. One small frog rested atop a mossy rock. He removed his gloves, tucked them into his coat, and reached out.

In one swift motion, he had the frog cupped between his palms.

"Take off your gloves," he instructed, turning to Jane.

She recoiled slightly. "I don't dare."

"You don't want to ruin them, do you?"

With visible reluctance, she began peeling the gloves from

her hands, looking as if she were preparing to face a firing squad.

"Ready?" he asked.

She held out her hands in a cupped shape. "I suppose."

He placed the frog gently into her hands.

She grimaced. "It's slimy. And smells like… pond."

"But now," he said, "you can say you've held a frog."

A reluctant smile crept across her lips. "I did, didn't I?" She studied the creature with growing fascination. "It isn't as awful as I expected."

"Very few things are."

She tilted her head. "I think I'll call him… Mr. Frog."

Alistair chuckled. "That's a terrible name. What if it's a lady frog?"

"How would I know?"

"Flip it over," he said. "A dark stomach means it's male and a plain stomach means female."

She squinted at him. "Are you making that up?"

"No, I assure you that it is true."

Carefully, she turned the frog over. "It has a dark stomach," she reported. "Mr. Frog, it is."

He watched her cradle the creature, her eyes lit with amusement. In that moment, her troubles faded from her expression —if only for a little while. And he found he would gladly endure a hundred lines for the chance to see her smile like that again.

Jane leaned forward and gently placed the frog back onto the flat rock beside the stream. It paused for the briefest of moments before giving a single strong hop and disappearing into the reeds.

"I don't think it liked being held," she remarked.

Alistair crossed his arms and cocked a brow. "If it had an issue, I'm sure it would have said so."

Jane let out a light laugh. "You seem to forget that frogs cannot speak English."

"That we know of," he replied with mock solemnity. "For all we know, they may be more eloquent than Lord Byron and simply choose to keep their linguistic talents hidden from the masses."

She gave him a sidelong look and rose to her feet. "I daresay you might be bottle-weary," she teased.

"Possibly. Shall we return to the others?"

He offered his arm, and she accepted it without hesitation. Her fingers settled against his coat sleeve with a warmth that stirred something in his chest—something dangerously pleasant.

As they strolled back towards the ever-present line, Jane said, "Thank you."

He glanced at her. "For what?"

"I never imagined I would hold a frog," she said, a smile playing at her lips. "It was... freeing. I feel almost rebellious."

"That was hardly rebellion, Jane."

"For me it was," she insisted, her voice laced with vulnerability. "I've always done what was expected. And proper young ladies—so I was told—do not touch frogs."

"Says who?"

"My father. And my brother."

His amusement faded, replaced by a heaviness that settled in his chest. "They were wrong," he said. "I know for a fact Charlotte's handled more than her share of frogs."

Jane turned her face away slightly, but not before he saw the flicker of pain in her expression. "My brother came to see me," she revealed. "He said I was dead to him. And to my father."

His jaw tensed. "I'm sorry, Jane."

"I suppose I expected it," she continued. "But part of me still hoped I was wrong. I don't know why."

Alistair came to an abrupt stop and turned towards her

fully, gently guiding her to face him. Her eyes remained downcast, her lashes casting shadows over her cheeks.

"There's nothing wrong with hoping," he said.

Her voice was barely above a whisper. "Hope is for fools. At least, that's what my father used to say."

"Then your father was wrong."

"Perhaps," she said, still avoiding his gaze. "But in this instance, I was foolish to believe they might understand my reasonings."

He waited until she finally looked up at him. When her eyes met his, full of unshed hurt, he spoke with certainty. "They wanted you to throw away your future, not theirs. And it was cruel of them to expect such a sacrifice."

Her chin lifted with defiance, but he saw the tremble at the corner of her mouth. Her strength was admirable, even when it faltered.

"I need to move forward and be strong," she said.

"I know you can."

"You do?"

He gave her a half-smile. "You survived growing up with them. That alone proves your strength. But now, for the first time, you get to choose your own fate."

Her lips parted, but no words came immediately. At last, she said, "I wish I had a magic ball that could tell me what my future holds."

"Where's the fun in that?" he teased.

"No one likes uncertainty, Alistair."

"Maybe not," he said, "but that's what makes life interesting."

She gave him a dry look. "You and I have very different ideas of what's interesting."

"Perhaps. But I think you'll surprise even yourself, Jane."

And if he had anything to say about it, her future would not be one of exile and loneliness. Not if he could help it.

5

Dressed in a pale pink gown, Jane stepped out of her bedchamber and quietly closed the door behind her. The soft click echoed louder than expected in the stillness of the upper corridor. She paused, her hand lingering on the brass doorknob. Her limbs were heavy, and her mind clouded with fatigue. They had arrived home just as dawn crept across the horizon, and though she had slept, it had not been restful. The events of the past week haunted her dreams, and her waking hours, too.

She had considered requesting a breakfast tray be brought to her room; the thought of facing anyone felt too exhausting, but she had dismissed the idea just as quickly. She needed to be braver than that. If she hid away every time she felt overwhelmed, she would never recover her place in the world. Her future might be uncertain, but she would not cower from it.

Gripping the banister, Jane descended the grand staircase, its polished mahogany gleaming in the soft light that filtered through the stained-glass window above the landing. She had only reached the halfway point when a sharp knock echoed through the foyer, startling her slightly. Her gaze flicked towards the front door, just as the butler crossed the marble floor to answer it.

She had not expected company. Certainly not at this hour. Certainly not—

"I am here to speak with Lady Jane."

The voice. That voice. It was unmistakable, even after all these years.

Aunt Cosima.

Jane's breath caught. Her slippered feet paused on the final step as the butler swung the door open. In walked a petite, elegantly dressed woman with dark hair that was now streaked with silver, her bearing still as regal as Jane remembered.

"Aunt Cosima?" she managed.

Her aunt's sharp eyes brightened. "Jane," she said with a smile that crinkled the corners of her eyes. "Good heavens, you look just like your mother did at your age. It's uncanny."

Jane's heart twisted at the mention of her mother. "Why are you here?"

"I read the newssheets, my dear. I would have come sooner, had you written me. I was ready to leave immediately, but the driver refused to travel through the night—safety and all that. He was right, of course, but I was dreadfully impatient."

Her aunt removed her straw hat, revealing more silver than Jane remembered. She stepped forward, eyes roaming over her. "Let me have a proper look at you. Turn around, if you please."

"Pardon?"

"Turn," Aunt Cosima repeated with a flick of her fingers.

Flustered, Jane did as instructed, turning in a slow circle, suddenly aware of every imperfection.

Her aunt clucked her tongue. "You are far too thin. But that can be remedied. Now"—her eyes darted around the hall—"why haven't you invited me into the drawing room yet? I assume they serve tea in this house."

Jane opened her mouth, but nothing came out. She looked helplessly at the butler.

With a knowing dip of his head, he said, "I shall see to it, my lady," and slipped away to do her bidding.

"Would you care to join me in the drawing room?" Jane asked, feeling as if she were no more than a guest in her own life.

"I would," Aunt Cosima replied grandly, lifting her chin like a queen granting an audience.

Jane led the way, still disoriented by her aunt's sudden arrival. Once seated across from her, she said cautiously, "I must admit that I didn't expect you to come. Father always told me you wanted nothing to do with me."

"That is absolute poppycock," Aunt Cosima said, scoffing. "Did you receive none of the letters I sent you?"

Jane shook her head. "No. And I wrote to you... but Father showed me letters returned, unopened."

Her aunt's expression darkened. "I never received a single one."

For a moment, Jane couldn't speak. "I thought you hated me."

"Absolutely not, Child. I knew he had poisoned you against me. I could hardly blame you since you were under his thumb," Aunt Cosima said. "I must assume that he disowned you for your little... indiscretion."

"Yes, my brother informed me that I was dead to both of them."

"Your father and brother are cads."

Jane nodded slowly. "You aren't wrong. My father made me promise never to speak to you. He said it would ruin our family's reputation."

"Yes, because I married a merchant," Aunt Cosima said with a snort. "A very wealthy one, mind you, but none of that mattered to your father. In his eyes, I married beneath me."

"Didn't you?"

A faraway smile softened her aunt's features. "I married for love. And I would not trade that for all the titles in the realm."

"I'm… I'm glad you're here," she admitted.

Her aunt's smile widened. "Good, because I've come to take you home with me."

"Now?"

"Well, perhaps after a cup of tea and something to eat. I'm starving." She snapped her fingers. "Yes, a boiled egg and toast will do nicely."

Right on cue, the butler appeared in the doorway. "Yes, Ma'am?"

"Will you bring me a boiled egg and toast?" Aunt Cosima declared. "And don't be stingy with the butter. There is nothing worse than dry toast."

With a dutiful bow, he vanished.

"I've secured a townhouse just a few blocks away," Aunt Cosima continued. "You may visit your friends as often as you like. But you're coming with me."

Jane stared. "How did you manage that so quickly?"

"Never underestimate the power of a well-placed gold coin," she said with a smirk. "Now, we must make a plan to restore you to Society."

"That's impossible," Jane replied.

"I daresay that nothing is impossible when you're as rich as I am," her aunt declared. "People tend to listen when I speak."

Jane tried to look hopeful but failed. "I rejected a duke. At the altar. I'm ruined."

"Yes, you are," Aunt Cosima said matter-of-factly. "But that doesn't mean we can't make you the most desirable heiress in London."

"My dowry won't tempt a man in good standing."

Her aunt leaned forward, eyes gleaming. "I am worth ten

times what I inherited, Jane. I've invested wisely. I can make you a princess if I so choose."

Jane's voice trembled. "Why would you do this for me?"

"Because I promised your mother I would watch over you."

Emotion welled in Jane's chest. "Thank you... but—"

"No buts," her aunt snapped. "We'll transform you into the woman every man will be clamoring to marry."

"It won't be easy."

"It shouldn't be," her aunt countered. "Are you afraid of hard work?"

Jane straightened. "No, but I am being realistic."

"Realism is overrated. Besides, I didn't marry for title—I married for love. Do you want the same?"

"I do," Jane said. "I've always wanted that."

A reflective look came into her aunt's eyes. "I remember. You used to act out those ridiculous plays where the princess always married for love."

"They weren't ridiculous," Jane said with a small smile. "And they always had happy endings."

"They still can."

"I want to believe that is true, but things are different now."

A maid entered and placed a tray before Aunt Cosima, lifting the lid with a flourish. Her aunt picked up the toast, took a bite, and grimaced. "Well, that is a disappointment. It is dry. Utterly dry."

Jane laughed under her breath. She hadn't realized how much she'd missed this.

"You should go pack," Aunt Cosima said, setting the toast down with disdain. "We'll leave as soon as I finish nibbling this travesty."

"I can't just leave."

"Why not? You should be with your family. Your real family. And not your father or brother—they're both halfwits."

Jane giggled. "You don't think very highly of them."

"I think they're fools who abandoned you. Family should stick by one another, no matter what."

"But—"

A look silenced her. "What did I say about 'but'?"

"What if my father finds out? Or the Duke of Brackenford?" Jane asked. "You are risking both of their wraths."

"Good," Aunt Cosima said, taking up her fork. "I like having enemies. It keeps things much more interesting."

Jane smiled despite herself. "You truly want to be associated with me?"

"What's the point of having money and power if I can't use it for my favorite niece?"

"I'm your only niece."

"All the more reason." Her aunt took a bite of egg, made a face, and stood. "Yuck. I suppose I will need to eat at home. How have you survived this food? Even an incompetent fool can cook an egg."

"I find the cooking to be more than tolerable here."

Looking unimpressed, her aunt replied, "We need to get you out of here before it is too late."

"I must say goodbye to Lord and Lady Westmere," Jane said. "They've been very kind."

"I'm glad to hear it."

As if the mere mention of her name conjured her up, Olivia appeared in the doorway. "Oh, I didn't realize you had company, Jane."

Jane turned towards her friend. "Lady Westmere, may I introduce my aunt, Lady Cosima Farmonth?"

Olivia curtsied. "My lady."

"A pleasure, Lady Westmere," her aunt replied warmly. "Thank you for caring so diligently for my niece."

"She's always welcome in our home."

"And what a charming home. It is so quaint," Aunt Cosima said, glancing around. "Shall we, Jane?"

"I need to pack," she responded.

"Where are you going?" Olivia asked, her brows furrowed.

Jane knew an explanation was in order. "My aunt invited me to come live with her, at least, for now."

"Yes, and what fun shall we have. I'll have my footmen retrieve your trunks." With a flick of her wrist, her aunt was already heading towards the door. "Come along, Jane."

Jane hesitated, still dazed by it all. But something inside her stirred—something that had been dormant for far too long.

Hope.

And, cautiously, she followed.

Alistair sat hunched over his desk, elbows planted on either side of the open ledger, his quill motionless in his hand. He'd been working through estate accounts since early morning. It was an endless parade of columns and numbers that refused to align. His shoulders ached from sitting too long, and his patience was growing thin.

The rhythmic tick of the mantel clock was the only sound in the study until the door creaked open.

He didn't even bother to look up. "Unless someone is bleeding, this interruption had better be worth it."

His sister's voice floated in. "There you are."

Raising his head, he replied, "Indeed. Here I am—doing something terribly trivial, like working."

Charlotte waltzed in, looking wholly unrepentant, and dropped into the chair across from him with a dramatic sigh. "I'm bored."

Alistair pinched the bridge of his nose. "So naturally, you've come to torment me."

She smiled sweetly and tucked a strand of blonde hair

behind her ear. "We should go to Gunter's for lemon ice. It's far too fine a day to waste it with figures."

"I'm busy."

"I can see that," she replied, her tone infuriatingly light. "But you could take a small break to spend time with your devoted sister. Couldn't you?"

Alistair sighed and closed the ledger. His eyes stung from squinting at columns. "What if we go in an hour?"

Charlotte shook her head. "We mustn't go too late since we're expected at Lady Devon's ball this evening."

He sat up straighter. That could not be right. "Pardon?"

"I told you about it."

"No, you did not."

"I'm quite certain I did," she said with a vague wave of her hand. "You probably just forgot."

He leaned back, glaring. "Convenient."

Charlotte's eyes twinkled. "You never listen when I speak of such things."

"Because I don't want to go to such things."

"You must. I've already confirmed our attendance. It would be beyond rude to decline now." She paused, then added slyly, "Besides, what if Lady Jane attends?"

His entire body stiffened. "What of it?"

"She saved your life, Alistair. You would let her walk into a ball alone, with no ally in sight?"

He frowned. "I doubt Jane would attend."

"You don't know that for certain," Charlotte replied. "And are you really willing to take that chance?"

He resisted the urge to groan aloud. This was a trap, and he was walking into it. "I suppose I could send a message to Lord Westmere's townhouse and inquire if they will be in attendance this evening."

Charlotte grinned. "That would be pointless. She's no longer there."

"She's not?"

Her expression turned smug. "Her aunt arrived this morning and whisked her away. She's now residing in Mayfair, at a townhouse let out by Lady Cosima."

"Lady Cosima?" Alistair repeated, startled. "*That* Lady Cosima?"

"The very same," Charlotte replied with relish. "The townhouse once belonged to Lord Wollet. It's one of the grandest in London. Fitting, considering Lady Cosima is rumored to be wealthier than the king."

He stared at his sister. "How do you know all this?"

Charlotte lifted one shoulder. "You'd be amazed what one learns by listening to the servants."

"Eavesdropping, you mean."

She sniffed. "Is it eavesdropping if it's within your own home?"

"Yes."

"Well, we shall have to agree to disagree."

Alistair closed his eyes for a moment, praying for patience. "Back to Lady Devon's ball, then."

Charlotte perked up. "So we're going?"

As much as he hated to concede, he thought it was for the best. "Very well. But we are not staying until dawn."

"Of course not. You need your beauty sleep."

He reached for the quill again. "I should like to finish another ledger before we depart for Gunter's."

"What if we went now?"

He looked at her. "You won't leave until I agree, will you?"

"You know me so well."

With a reluctant smile, he stood. "We can go now, but only because I need a reprieve from numbers."

Before she could reply, Malone stepped into the room. "Lord Warwicke would like a moment of your time, my lord."

"I need to speak with you," Warwicke said, striding into the study without waiting for permission.

Alistair nodded. "Of course."

Warwicke turned to Charlotte. "Miss Winslow."

She dipped into a graceful curtsy. "My lord," she murmured, then cast Alistair a knowing look. "I shall wait in the entry hall."

As soon as she exited, Warwicke's jovial expression faded. "The men who attacked you have been apprehended. They're in Newgate."

Alistair's attention sharpened at once. "That's excellent news."

Warwicke's face remained grim. "Not quite. They've refused to confess. The magistrate says there's little evidence to hold them. We need you—and Lady Jane—to make a positive identification."

Alistair's heart sank. "I remember pieces. But it all happened so fast."

"Exactly," Warwicke said. "That's why we need Lady Jane. Between the two of you, we might make a case strong enough to press them harder."

He braced his hands on the desk. "Surely there's another way since I don't want Jane to set foot in a place like Newgate."

"There isn't. They're only being held out of courtesy to me. The magistrate is running out of patience."

"How did you even find them?"

Warwicke's mouth curved into a half-smile. "Someone was bragging about roughing up a war hero turned viscount. Didn't take long to make sense of things."

"Did they say why they did it?"

"No. They've been maddeningly quiet. That's why we need more. A clear identification will give us cause to press them harder."

"You mean torture?" Alistair asked.

Warwicke's face grew solemn. "We don't like to use that word." He paused. "Did you hear about Mark Austen?"

"I did. Did you serve with him?"

"No, but I know you did."

"For a few months. He was a good man."

Warwicke's arms folded. "His death occurred within days of your attack. That doesn't feel like a coincidence."

"I considered a connection myself," he admitted, "but I could not see one. So I dismissed it."

"You're sure of that?"

"I am," he said firmly.

Warwicke didn't look convinced. "Then think harder. Something's afoot."

He turned to leave, but Alistair called after him, "Is that all?"

"Did you expect more?" Warwicke asked.

"Not really." Alistair glanced at the doorway. "Charlotte and I are going to Gunter's. Would you care to join us?"

Warwicke opened the door. "No. I'm going home to my wife." He tipped his head. "Miss Winslow."

Of course, she was there, hovering just outside the room. Eavesdropping, as always. "You may come in, Charlotte," Alistair said.

She stepped in, looking entirely unashamed. "You must convince Lady Jane to go to Newgate. She's the key."

Alistair gave her a long, exasperated look. "Truly, eavesdropping?"

Charlotte only lifted her chin. "I maintain that it isn't eavesdropping if it's in one's own home."

"You would be wrong," Alistair said. "Come, let us go to Gunter's."

Charlotte beamed, victorious. "A wise decision. It is a good thing I instructed Malone to have the coach brought around ten minutes ago."

Alistair gave her a sidelong glance. She was always two steps ahead when she wanted something.

As they stepped out into the warm afternoon sun, the sounds of the street greeted them—clattering hooves, distant shouting, the hum of London's pulse. Their coach waited at the curb, glossy and dark, with the family crest discreetly painted near the door. But before they could reach it, a man stepped forward from the edge of the pavement.

He was tall and broad-shouldered, his presence solid and deliberate. Alistair's instincts, honed on battlefields and in officers' tents, immediately prickled.

"Lord Alcott, a word, if I may."

Alistair stopped, his eyes narrowing at the unfamiliar man. "Who are you?"

The stranger adjusted the leather satchel strap on his shoulder. "Lord Luca Dexter," he replied. "I wished to speak with you regarding your recent attack."

Every muscle in Alistair's body tensed. "No."

He turned towards the coach, intent on ending the conversation, but Lord Luca stepped closer, unruffled.

"I understand you served with Mark Austen," he continued, his tone calm but probing. "A man who, as you may know, was found dead in an alley only days ago."

Alistair froze mid-step, jaw tightening. Mark Austen. The name stirred a mixture of grief and guilt in his chest. "What is it that you want?" he asked, voice clipped.

"Do you think there's a connection between his death and your assault?"

"No," Alistair replied curtly.

The man pressed on. "Then why is Lord Warwicke investigating both incidents?"

Alistair's head snapped towards him. "How would you know that?"

Lord Luca merely smiled. "I have my ways. I assure you, I am not your enemy."

Before Alistair could respond, Charlotte interjected. "You're the man who purchased *The London Gazette*."

Lord Luca turned his attention to her and dipped into a courtly bow. "I am indeed. And you must be the lovely Miss Winslow who has the *ton* so enamored."

A faint scoff escaped her. "Flattery, my lord?"

"It is not flattery if it's true," he replied.

Charlotte raised her chin. "Well, I do believe I will wait in the coach." She turned on her heel, but not before casting Lord Luca a final, appraising glance.

Alistair's eyes followed her into the coach, then cut back to Lord Luca. The man's gaze lingered a fraction too long on Charlotte's retreating form, and Alistair felt a flare of protectiveness rise in his chest.

"Good day, Lord Luca," he said, his tone brooking no argument.

But the infuriating man wasn't done. He reached into his coat and pulled out a calling card, extending it to Alistair. "Should you remember anything—anything at all—I'd be grateful to hear from you."

Alistair accepted the card, more out of habit than intention. "I wouldn't hold your breath," he muttered.

Without waiting for a response, he climbed into the coach and shut the door behind him with a firm click.

6

Jane moved slowly through the grand townhouse, her steps quiet against the polished black and white marble floor that gleamed beneath her slippers. Her eyes traced the towering white columns that lined the hall and the ornate gold sconces affixed with precision between floor-to-ceiling mirrors. Crystal chandeliers glittered from above, catching the sunlight and scattering it in delicate rainbows across the walls.

It all felt so surreal.

She had heard whispers—rumors, really—of her Aunt Cosima's wealth, spoken in hushed tones at family dinners or behind fans in drawing rooms. But they had always sounded exaggerated, embroidered tales meant to pass an idle hour. Her father had refused to speak of his estranged sister-in-law, his mouth pinched and voice curt whenever her name arose. It had pained her mother, Jane had no doubt of that, though she had never said so out loud. She simply wore that smile of hers—a smile that tried too hard, one that never quite reached her eyes.

Jane reached out and brushed her fingertips against a tapestry hanging in one of the parlors. The colors were still vibrant, the scene exquisitely detailed—a pastoral countryside with fine embroidery that must have taken someone years to complete. She wondered who had created it, what story it told, and how it had come to hang here.

"Impressive, isn't it?" came a familiar voice behind her.

Jane turned to see Aunt Cosima standing in the doorway, her dark brows arched in amusement. "I was taken by that tapestry as well," her aunt added, gliding into the room with effortless elegance.

"How were you able to let out this place so quickly?" Jane asked, genuinely puzzled.

"I told you that it all comes down to money," Aunt Cosima said with a wry smile. "And I have plenty of it."

Jane lowered her gaze. "Thank you for coming to help me... but it wasn't necessary."

"Nonsense," Aunt Cosima replied, waving off the sentiment with a dramatic flick of her hand. "I suspected your father had disowned you the moment I read you were staying with Lord and Lady Westmere. He's always been as predictable as he is arrogant."

Jane swallowed hard. "He told me he would if I didn't go through with marrying the duke."

Her aunt's features stiffened. "Distasteful. Though not unexpected. And Adam? Does he feel the same?"

Jane's voice faltered. "He... he sided with our father."

"Spineless little man." Then with restrained fury, she asked, "And how did the duke respond when you refused him?"

"He slapped me. My father stood by and did nothing."

Aunt Cosima went rigid. "I would have punched the duke. I don't care who he is. No man has the right to strike a woman—least of all you."

"That's why I ran," Jane admitted. "I couldn't stay after that."

Closing the distance between them, Aunt Cosima placed her hands firmly on Jane's shoulders. Her touch, though steady, held surprising warmth. "I am *so* glad you did. Though I wish you'd come straight to me."

"I didn't have any money," Jane admitted, shame warming her cheeks. "My reticule was stolen the moment I stepped into the square after leaving the chapel."

"Well, it matters not now. I am here and I will fix this."

Jane's brow furrowed. "I don't think you can, but—"

"Ah!" Cosima held up a finger. "What did I say about the word '*but*'?"

Jane managed a faint smile.

"Let's look at you," her aunt said, stepping back and giving her a critical once-over.

Jane bit her lower lip, acutely aware of the state of her gown—clean, but plainly cut and showing the signs of too many wearings. Still, she lifted her chin, prepared to defend it.

"You're a pretty enough thing—no doubt there—but your wardrobe is entirely uninspired," Cosima declared. "We must dress you in colors that bring out your beautiful blue eyes."

"My gowns are sufficient," Jane replied.

"Yes, and bread is sufficient, but one tires of it quickly. I want you to walk into a room and be the envy of every simpering debutante."

Jane shook her head. "I have no desire to be noticed in that way. I'm quite content remaining a wallflower."

Her aunt arched a brow. "Your mother said the same once. But even she stepped into the light on occasion. It's good to surprise people." She paused thoughtfully. "And you need diamonds. And pearls."

"I was given a diamond bandeau for my wedding, but I suspect my father will ask for it back when he realizes I still have it."

Aunt Cosima's eyes narrowed. "What of your mother's jewelry collection? Did you not inherit it?"

Jane's heart sank. "No. My father never mentioned it."

"Why am I not surprised?" She frowned. "Your mother insisted those pieces be yours. Fortunately for us, I inherited your grandmother's collection, and I see no reason you shouldn't wear them."

"Thank you, but—"

"*No buts,* Jane."

Jane gave a tiny nod.

Her aunt turned and strode to the doorway. "The dressmaker is already en route. I've commissioned an entirely new wardrobe for you. No arguments."

There was little Jane could say. "Thank you," she murmured, following after her aunt, unsure whether she felt grateful or overwhelmed.

"We should begin dressing for the ball this evening," Cosima said over her shoulder.

"Ball?"

"Lady Devon's," her aunt replied, as if it were obvious. "I informed her I was in Town. She insisted I attend and that I bring you."

Jane stopped short. "She must be mistaken. No one wants me at their events... not after what I did."

Aunt Cosima turned, her expression unreadable. "Then why did Lady Devon write me personally?"

"Perhaps... perhaps to laugh at me."

Her aunt's voice went firm. "No one will dare laugh at you—not with me there."

The conviction in her voice sent a strange feeling rushing through Jane's chest. Could it be... safety? Still, she whispered, "You cannot stop the gossip."

"No," Cosima agreed. "But we can make them gossip about something else."

Just then, the butler appeared, his slicked-back black hair as perfectly in place as his decorum. "Forgive the interruption, my lady, but Lord Alcott has arrived. He asks to see Lady Jane."

Her aunt's brow lifted. "Well, this is interesting."

"It's not," Jane said quickly. "We've been friends for years."

Aunt Cosima's eyes sharpened. "Is he anything like his father?"

"No," Jane rushed out. "He's nothing like his father."

Cosima gave a small, satisfied nod, a smile tugging at the corner of her mouth. "Good. That man was dreadful," she said. "Why don't you go greet your Lord Alcott and give him a tour of the gardens?"

"Lord Alcott is not my anything," Jane replied.

"Yes, of course," Aunt Cosima said airily, but the sparkle in her eyes betrayed her amusement—and her meaning.

Jane pressed her lips together as she turned towards the entry hall. Alistair was not hers. They were merely friends. Whatever girlish fancy she'd once had for him had long since been locked away and forgotten. She had buried it years ago—hadn't she?

Still, her breath caught for the briefest of moments as she spotted him standing just inside the doorway, looking devilishly handsome.

He bowed as she approached. "Lady Jane. You are looking well."

"As are you," she responded. "Would you care for a tour of the gardens?"

"I would be delighted," he said, offering his arm.

She placed her hand lightly in the crook of his elbow, and they began their walk through the corridor that led to the rear of the townhouse. Jane's gaze flicked to the walls, where dozens—perhaps hundreds—of antique mirrors hung in deliberate asymmetry.

"Quite the collection," Alistair remarked, glancing around. "I've never seen so many mirrors in one place."

"My aunt claims they reflect light and fortune," Jane said.

"Though I suspect she also likes the idea of being surrounded by her own likeness."

A nearby footman opened the rear door, and they stepped out onto the stone veranda. The scent of blooming roses rose to meet them, carried on the breeze. The gardens' path stretched ahead, lined with perfectly trimmed rose bushes in soft blush, ivory, and deep crimson.

Jane gently slipped her hand from his arm but remained close as they began to walk. "What is it you wished to speak with me about?"

Alistair's expression sobered. "Warwicke visited me this morning. He said the men who attacked me have been captured and are currently in Newgate."

Jane stopped short, a gust of relief sweeping through her. "That is wonderful news!" she exclaimed.

Alistair nodded, though his smile was subdued. "It is. But Warwicke asked if we might go to the prison and identify them."

Her heart stuttered as she turned to face him fully. "Surely there is another way?"

"I'm afraid not," he said. "Do you believe you could recognize them if you saw them again?"

She looked away, down the rose-lined path that suddenly felt too narrow. "I remember their faces every time I close my eyes," she admitted. "And the way they looked at me..." Her voice caught. "Like I was prey. I have no desire to ever see them again."

"I understand," he said. "And I wouldn't ask you if there were any other way. But—Jane—I didn't get a clear look at them. Everything was blurred. I need your help."

She clasped her hands together, her fingers tightening as dread curled in her stomach. She knew what he was asking of her—knew how much it mattered—but even the thought of stepping foot in Newgate made her feel ill.

"I'm sorry," she whispered. "I don't think I can."

Alistair took a step closer. "I know you're afraid. I would be, too. But I'll be with you the entire time. No harm will come to you—I swear it."

Her eyes searched his. "What you're asking is... difficult."

"I know," he said, his voice sincere. "But if anyone has the strength to do it, it's you."

She gave a small huff, shaking her head. "You think too highly of me."

"No, I don't," he said. "Or have you forgotten that you walked into that alleyway alone and saved my life? If not for you, I'd be dead."

Her throat tightened. "Those men would've killed me, too, if the constable hadn't walked by when he did."

"Which only makes your actions braver," he said. "You didn't know help was coming."

She looked up at him then and saw the honesty in his eyes. Flecks of warm brown glinted in the green, and there was something else in his gaze, something pleading and earnest and very nearly tender.

With a slow, reluctant breath, she exhaled. "Very well. I'll go with you. Only because I want those men to be held accountable for what they've done."

Alistair's relief was palpable. "Wonderful. I will inform Warwicke." He glanced over his shoulder towards the townhouse, and a boyish grin touched his lips. "I hope I haven't come at an inconvenient time."

"Why would you think that?" she asked.

"Because your aunt is very obviously watching us from that window on the main floor."

Jane turned her head and there was Aunt Cosima, her face pressed unapologetically against the glass, watching them with all the subtlety of a hawk eyeing its prey.

Jane sighed, already imagining the teasing she'd receive later. "She's... invested in my affairs."

"I rather gathered that," he said with amusement. "Are you attending Lady Devon's ball tonight?"

"I only just learned that I am," Jane replied.

"Then may I beg the honor of a dance?" he asked, offering his arm once more.

Jane tilted her head. "Are you quite sure you wish to be seen with me?"

"Yes," he said without hesitation.

"And what of your sister? Does she feel the same?"

He leaned a fraction closer. "Who do you think demanded I ask you?"

Jane laughed. "In that case... I shall save you a dance."

"Wonderful," he said, smiling down at her. "I have something to look forward to."

"So it begins," Alistair grumbled under his breath as his boots touched the pavement. He stared up at the flood of carriages spilling onto the gravel courtyard. The *crush* outside Lady Devon's townhouse was as dense and glittering as one might expect from the event of the Season.

His sister's delighted laughter cut through his thoughts. "Your aversion to crowds is quite humorous, Brother."

Alistair didn't look at her. "I fail to see the humor in suffocating among preening strangers."

"Lady Devon's ball is *the* ball," Charlotte said, nearly bouncing with excitement as she came to stand beside him. "Everyone who is anyone will be here tonight."

He flicked his eyes towards the main entrance. "All the more reason I would rather be at home. With a good book. And a locked door."

She grinned. "And that is precisely where we differ. I want to be out in Society and enjoy myself."

He turned to her, finally. Her eyes sparkled, cheeks already flushed from the cold air or the anticipation. She looked so young. Too young. "Do not have too much fun."

She scoffed. "Is there such a thing?"

"Yes," he said firmly. "There is. This is your first Season, Charlotte. You are very naïve in the ways of the world."

Her smile faded slightly. "I know more than you think."

"That is not something to be proud of," he replied, not unkindly. He offered his arm. "Come. Let's get this night over with."

She slipped her hand into the crook of his arm, a grin returning. "That's the spirit."

As they stepped closer to the entrance, Alistair could feel the press of bodies tighten around them. The heat from torches and lamps clung to the air, mingling with perfume and the chatter of overlapping conversations. His spine went stiff. It always did in crowds. He needed space. Visibility. Control. These tightly packed gatherings reminded him too much of the battlefield—not in chaos, but in unpredictability.

At least tonight, no one is armed, he thought. *Not that I can be sure.*

They stepped inside the townhouse, the marble floors echoing beneath their feet as they followed the throng down the corridor to the ballroom. Gold chandeliers glittered overhead, casting warm light over silk gowns and tailored coats. Laughter and music filled the air.

"Champagne," Charlotte gasped, her eyes darting towards a liveried footman holding a tray.

"You may have one glass," Alistair responded.

She rolled her eyes. "You are no fun."

"One should always keep their wits about them," he said. "Especially when dealing with the *ton*."

"Again, no fun."

He patted her gloved hand. "You will thank me later when you are happily married with a horde of children running underfoot."

Her expression shifted. The corners of her mouth lowered, and her grip on his arm slackened. "What if I don't want that?" she asked softly.

Caught off guard, he asked, "Why wouldn't you?"

Charlotte looked away, tension tightening her jaw. "Because I can do more than be a wife and breeder."

The word landed like a blow. *Breeder*. It sounded so harsh on her tongue.

"I never suggested you couldn't," he responded.

"No, but Society has," she said. "I must be perfect. Perfect wife. Perfect mother. But what if I want more out of life?"

He studied her, brow furrowed. This wasn't the giddy sister he had escorted moments ago. This was a woman—restless, thoughtful, and quietly simmering.

"Where is this coming from?" he asked.

"It's been on my mind for some time now."

"And you thought now was the best moment to bring it up?" he asked with a wry twist of his lips.

She waved her hand dismissively. "Forget I said anything."

"I won't forget," he said. "And we'll discuss it tomorrow. Privately. At home."

"Wonderful," she muttered under her breath.

Before he could respond, a voice rang out behind him.

"Alcott."

He turned and inclined his head at the approaching couple. "Lord Wilton. Lady Wilton."

Lord Wilton smirked. "I'm surprised to see you here tonight given your well-known distaste for crowds and all that."

Alistair gestured towards his sister. "Charlotte wished to attend."

"Well, who could blame her?" Lady Wilton interjected with a warm smile. "It's the event of the Season."

Charlotte beamed. "It is, though my brother would much rather be home with a book and a brandy."

Lady Wilton laughed. "As would mine, but he agreed to escort me."

Alistair's attention was stolen by a sudden shift in the atmosphere. A hush rippled across the ballroom like a breeze rustling through tall grass.

His instincts sharpened. He turned his gaze to the entrance.

Lady Jane.

She had entered on the arm of her aunt, Lady Cosima. She looked radiant in a sapphire gown, the black netting catching light with each step. Her golden hair had been swept up elegantly, two curls left to soften her face. Diamonds glittered at her throat and ears, but none of it could distract him from the tightness in her posture. Her chin was raised, but her eyes held barely concealed vulnerability.

She was putting on a brave face while a ballroom full of jackals prepared to feast on gossip.

Charlotte nudged him. "Go help her."

He didn't hesitate. That was all he needed.

He stepped away from the group, ignoring the murmurs, and moved towards Jane. The crowd parted without effort and he came to stand in front of her, offering his hand. "Lady Jane, would you be kind enough to share this dance with me?"

Relief shimmered in her gaze. "I would be honored, my lord."

Her fingers settled into his, warm and trembling. As they walked towards the dance floor, he leaned in slightly.

"You were brilliant," he said.

"Was I?" she asked with a nervous laugh. "I felt anything

but. I've spent the past ten minutes hoping I wouldn't trip over my hem."

"I would never let that happen."

"You're kind, but you don't need to keep rescuing me."

He stopped walking, pulling her gently to a pause. "I do need to," he said, meeting her eyes. "You saved my life, Jane. I'm only returning the favor."

She offered a small smile, but her voice was hushed when she said, "I shouldn't be here. I can feel their eyes on me. Judging me."

"Let them judge," he said evenly.

"That's easy for you to say," she replied. "You're a viscount. A war hero. And I… I'm just Jane."

He held her gaze. "I happen to like *just* Jane."

Before she could respond, the music began. Alistair took his place opposite her on the dance floor, ignoring the whispers and the stares. Tonight, he would be her shield—if not in war, then in dance.

They stepped into the opening positions just as the music began, and Alistair immediately noted how stiff Jane's posture was. Her chin was held a touch too high—as though defying anyone to pity her. She moved with the grace of someone well-trained, but it was rigid, rehearsed.

Still, he matched her steps easily, instinctively adjusting his pace to guide rather than lead too forcefully. It wasn't the finest waltz he'd ever danced, but he found he didn't care. He was more focused on her. And then—there it was—a smile. Small. Faint. But real. A glimpse of the girl she had been before Society decided to destroy her.

When the music came to its inevitable close, he bowed with the rest, but unlike the others, he remained close. Straightening, he stepped towards her and said softly, "You dance splendidly."

Her eyes sparked with dry humor. "I daresay you need spectacles, my lord."

He allowed a rare chuckle to escape. "No, truly. I usually make it a firm rule to avoid dancing altogether. But I must admit… I rather enjoyed our dance."

"You are kind."

"I'm honest." He offered his arm again. "Shall we?"

She placed her hand lightly on his arm. "I just wish everyone wasn't staring at me."

"*Us*," he corrected. "They are staring at *us*, not just you."

That earned him another smile—this one more private, more grateful. "Thank you," she responded. "It's nice to know I'm not entirely alone in this. Most of my friends vanished the moment the scandal touched me."

"Then they were never truly your friends."

"No, they weren't. But if I'm being honest… I suppose I deserved it. I did the same once—to others. I was so afraid of stoking my father's anger that I stayed silent when I should have spoken. I wasn't brave."

"Hindsight is everything. And regret is a heavy burden. But that doesn't mean you're beyond redemption."

She didn't respond to that, but the way she held to his arm a little more firmly told him she'd heard it.

They had almost reached Lady Cosima when a very familiar giggle drifted above the hum of conversation. His head snapped around, and his stomach sank.

Charlotte.

She stood across the ballroom, a flute of champagne in hand, surrounded by a half-circle of eager young men all vying for her attention. One leaned in far too close. Another touched the edge of her sleeve. Charlotte laughed again—charming, radiant, and oblivious to the fact that Alistair was growing increasingly bothered.

"Botheration," he muttered under his breath.

Jane followed his line of sight. "What is it?"

"Charlotte."

"Oh," Jane murmured. "You must go to her."

"I will. As soon as I see you safely to your aunt."

But Jane withdrew her hand from his arm. "I'll be fine. Truly. Your sister needs you more than I do at the moment."

He paused. He didn't want to leave her—not like this. But Charlotte...

"Thank you," he said.

He turned on his heel and stalked across the ballroom, jaw clenched, ready to peel each of those fawning dandies off his sister one by one.

As he approached, he attempted to nudge one particularly bold gentleman aside, but the man stood his ground with a smirk.

"Shove off," the man said with a laugh that grated on Alistair's nerves.

Alistair raised a brow. *Enough.*

He cleared his throat and said, with crisp authority, "Charlotte."

His sister turned at once, eyes widening as she took in his expression. "Brother."

The pack of men turned and shifted to make room for him. That was more like it.

"Let's go," he said, extending his arm.

Charlotte arched a brow but allowed him to lead her away from the group, her steps graceful and unbothered. She didn't speak until they reached a quieter corner near the rear of the ballroom.

"That was poorly done on your part," she said, not even looking at him.

"Was it?" he asked, not feeling the least bit apologetic.

"They were only asking to fill my dance card."

He turned to face her fully. "What were you thinking, standing alone among a group of unchaperoned men?"

"I was thinking I was being friendly," she replied.

He groaned. "Why didn't you remain with Lady Wilton while I was dancing with Lady Jane?"

"I didn't want to."

"Charlotte, this is not a game," he chided. "Your reputation is at stake."

She smiled faintly, and he knew that look. It was her smug I-know-what-I'm-doing expression. "I assure you, I'm more aware of my reputation than you are. Besides, we were surrounded by people."

"All it takes is one rumor," he snapped. "One careless whisper of impropriety and you are ruined."

She placed her champagne—untouched, thankfully—on a passing footman's tray. Then she looked at him, her expression unreadable.

"There's talk the queen may name me the diamond of the Season," she said.

He stilled. "Is that what you want?"

"It's what every debutante is meant to want."

"Then be careful, Charlotte."

She met his gaze squarely. "I am careful. I know what I'm doing, Alistair. You must trust me."

Trust. It was such a small word for such an enormous risk. He gave a tight nod, though he wasn't sure he meant it. Not yet.

"Then don't give me a reason not to," he responded.

7

Jane stood at the edge of the ballroom, her gaze drifting towards the rear where Alistair was speaking with his sister. There was a tension in his shoulders she recognized all too well. He was enduring something unpleasant and doing his best to hide it. She wished there were something she could do to help him, to return the kindness he had shown her by asking her to dance. That moment had not gone unnoticed. In fact, it had been the subject of considerable attention.

She could feel the stares pressing into her skin even now. The rustle of silk, the faint gasps behind gloved fingers, the subtle but unmistakable flick of fans snapping open—none of it escaped her. No matter how much she tried to hold her head high, she knew she was still the scandal of the evening. The fallen woman who had dared to show her face at a proper ball.

Her aunt leaned close and murmured above the music, "You danced wonderfully with Lord Alcott."

Jane barely had time to form a reply before a hand clamped around her arm.

"What do you think you are doing?" a voice hissed.

Her stomach dropped.

Adam.

His grip was bruising, and she instinctively tried to wrench herself free, but he only held tighter. "What do you want?" she demanded, keeping her voice low to avoid creating a scene—even as her pulse pounded with dread.

"I want you gone," he growled, leaning in so close she could feel his breath against her cheek. "You don't belong here. Not anymore."

Jane straightened her spine, refusing to cower before him. "I am not going anywhere."

"Oh, yes, you are," he said. "Even if I have to drag you out myself."

Before she could respond, her aunt's voice sliced through the tension. "Release her, young man."

Adam's head snapped towards their aunt. "You shouldn't be here either. You married a merchant."

"Ah," Aunt Cosima said with an arched brow. "But a wealthy merchant."

He sneered. "Is there such a thing?"

Her aunt smiled knowingly. "Indeed. Wealthier, in fact, than you and your entire family combined."

"And how would you know that?"

"I have my ways." Her voice was light but laced with steel. "Now, I'll ask again. Release your sister."

A flicker of hesitation crossed Adam's face before he finally let go. Jane cradled her arm, resisting the urge to rub it. He had no doubt left a mark.

"You both need to leave," he spat. "You're not welcome here."

"Actually," Aunt Cosima said, "we were both personally invited. And we intend to stay until the final dance is over."

Adam's lip curled. "Jane is an embarrassment to this family. As are you."

"Curious," Aunt Cosima said with an indulgent tilt of her head, "considering I've just made her my heir."

Jane's breath caught. "Are you... quite certain?"

Her aunt lifted her chin proudly. "I am. That should make the *ton* reconsider their opinions of you."

"You cannot be serious," Adam spluttered. "Jane is hardly qualified to be anyone's heir. She knows nothing of estate management—"

"And you do?" Cosima countered.

"I know more than she ever will. She's just a... a useless female."

Jane felt the insult like a slap, but before she could retort, her aunt stepped in.

"Then it is fortunate," Aunt Cosima said, eyes gleaming, "that I am a useless female as well. I shall place my stock in Jane."

"You're making a mistake."

"Perhaps," she conceded, "but it is my mistake to make."

Adam's nostrils flared with rage. "You risk making an enemy out of me and of the Duke of Brackenford."

Cosima gave a delicate shrug. "An enemy or two might keep me young."

Before Adam could explode, a familiar voice broke the standoff.

"May I have the privilege of this next dance?" Lord Luca asked, his tone light, though his eyes flicked between her and her brother with quiet calculation.

Relieved by the interruption, Jane slid her hand into his. "You may."

As he led her onto the floor, he leaned closer and said under his breath, "I thought you might need rescuing."

She gave him a weary smile. "Was it that obvious?"

"To me, yes," he replied, voice dry. "No offense, but I'm not especially fond of your brother."

"Then you are in good company, my lord."

He grinned. "Lord Barkley was a tyrant at Eton. We were at odds more often than not."

"I cannot say I am surprised."

They took their places in the quadrille, and Jane tried to prepare for the dance, but her mind still reeled from the confrontation. And from her aunt's declaration.

Lord Luca gave her a sidelong glance. "I must say, I'm glad you didn't go through with the wedding."

"As am I," she admitted. "Though I am living with the consequences now."

He nodded, his expression turning solemn. "It is still better than being shackled to the Duke of Brackenford, I imagine."

"It is," she admitted.

A beat of silence passed before he asked, "Did he ever speak to you about his first wife?"

Her brow furrowed. "Only that she was mad."

"Did he ever say what made him believe that?"

She shook her head. "No. He rarely spoke of her... or of any of his wives, for that matter. Only that they had failed him by not giving him a son."

He gave a wry smile. "That sounds about right."

"Why do you ask?"

"Merely curious."

She studied his face. "By the way he spoke of her, I never believed he had any affection for her."

"He didn't. It was an arranged marriage. They were second cousins."

The music began, and they moved through the figures of the dance. But even as Jane smiled and curtsied and turned about the floor, her mind was racing—not just with the weight of what had transpired, but with the knowledge that she was no longer a castoff.

She was an heiress now.

It all seemed like a dream.

The music came to a graceful end, and Jane dipped into a final curtsy. She was still catching her breath when Lord Luca approached once more, his expression polite but thoughtful.

He offered his arm. "Thank you for the dance."

She placed her gloved hand on his forearm. "It was my pleasure."

As they crossed the floor, weaving through murmuring guests, Jane felt the glances again—less scandalous than before, perhaps, but still curious. Still uncertain.

Lord Luca leaned slightly towards her. "I understand," he said quietly, "that you are the reason Lord Alcott is still alive."

Her steps faltered. "I… uh…" She couldn't quite look at him.

He patted her hand in a gesture that was unexpectedly kind. "Do not worry, Lady Jane. Your secret is safe with me. I only wished to say… what you did was brave."

"I was merely at the right place at the right time," she said. It was the truth—at least in part—and she hoped it would be enough.

"It was more than that," he said, stopping beside her aunt. His gaze held hers, solemn and sincere. "And we both know it."

Then he released her hand and bowed. "Until later, my lady."

Jane watched him walk away, his tall frame disappearing into the crowd.

Her thoughts were broken by her aunt's voice behind her. "A dance with a viscount and now a duke's son?" Aunt Cosima's tone was teasing, but not without pride. "You are making quite the impression tonight, my dear."

Jane turned to face Cosima, the humor in her aunt's words lost beneath the swirl of emotions in her chest. "Did you truly mean it?"

"Mean what?" she asked. "You must be more specific

because I say a lot of things, most of which I cannot remember."

Jane swallowed. "What you said earlier... about making me your heir."

For a brief moment, her aunt's sharp features softened. "Yes, darling. I meant every word. There is no one more deserving of managing what I've built."

Jane felt the truth of it settle over her like a warm shawl... and yet, the weight of it was dizzying. "Adam was furious."

"Good," her aunt replied. "I know he is my nephew and I am supposed to love him, but he makes it so dreadfully difficult."

Jane gave a breathy laugh, equal parts disbelief and relief. "I can't believe this is happening."

Her aunt stepped closer. "Believe it. This changes everything. Your future. Your choices. But—" She held up a finger. "There is one condition."

"Which is?"

"I must approve of whomever you marry. I won't have you throwing yourself away on some dandy or a fortune-hunting scoundrel. I want you to marry for love."

Jane blinked at her, stunned. Of all the possible conditions, she had not expected that. "For love?" she echoed, her voice almost a whisper.

Her aunt's expression grew more serious than Jane had ever seen it. "I married for love, and it made me wealthy in more ways than coin ever could. I want the same for you."

Emotion swelled in Jane's throat, and she struggled to find the words that might possibly convey the gratitude she felt. "Thank you," she managed. It felt too small, but she meant it with her whole heart. "Truly... thank you. This feels like a dream."

"And so it is," her aunt said, touching her arm. "Now that

you are an heiress, you may marry whomever you choose. Tell me—do you have someone in mind?"

The question hung in the air, innocent and yet dangerously pointed.

Before she could stop herself, an image leapt unbidden into her mind: Alistair.

His broad shoulders. The gentleness in his eyes. The way he had stood beside her when no one else dared.

She shook her head quickly, willing the thought away. Why had she thought of him? He was her friend. That was all. He had always been kind to her—even as a boy—but there had never been more than that. Had there?

Her aunt raised a brow at her silence. Jane forced a smile, brushing away the thought like one might swat at a persistent moth.

"No one," she lied. "Not at present."

But even as she said it, her mind betrayed her—and there he was again, in the corner of her memory, looking at her as though she mattered.

As though she had always mattered.

"The worst thing ever just happened!"

Alistair looked up from his breakfast as his sister burst into the dining room, her cheeks flushed with the sort of theatrical distress that would have sent most brothers into alarm. He, however, merely dabbed his mouth with his white linen napkin and braced himself. Years of Charlotte's dramatics had taught him the wisdom of measured reactions.

"What happened?" he asked, taking another sip of tea.

Charlotte flung herself into the nearest chair with a sigh

worthy of the stage. "I was named the diamond of the Season by the queen."

He paused mid-sip. That, he hadn't expected. "Isn't that what you wanted?"

"Yes," she said emphatically, leaning forward as if daring him to challenge her. "But in the same article, Lady Jane was mentioned as Lady Cosima's heir."

Now Alistair was baffled. "I'm afraid I don't see what the problem is."

Charlotte huffed in irritation. "No one will talk about me now. They will talk about Lady Jane and her newfound fortune."

"And that is a problem because...?"

"Because Lady Jane was ruined," Charlotte said with relish, lowering her voice as though scandal might seep through the very walls. "And now she is not only rehabilitated but a staggering heiress. Compared to her, we are beggars."

His brow furrowed. "We are not beggars."

"Perhaps I should offer to sweep her chimneys," Charlotte muttered.

"I daresay you are exaggerating... again," Alistair remarked, setting down his cup. "You got what you wanted. You are the diamond."

Charlotte's fingers curled around her teacup. "But not like this."

He studied her for a moment. "Are you upset with Lady Jane?"

She shook her head immediately. "Heavens, no. I'm happy for her. I truly am. I just..." Her voice faltered. "I don't know what I feel, honestly."

Alistair pushed back his chair. "Well, as illuminating as this conversation is, I have matters that require my attention."

"How can you leave when my whole life is falling apart?" she demanded.

He chuckled as he rose. "Your life is hardly falling apart."

Her eyes darted to the long clock in the corner. "And where, pray tell, are you going at this hour?"

His expression sobered. "To visit the family of my fallen comrade."

Charlotte's vexation melted into quiet sympathy. "I suppose my complaining can wait, then."

"Thank you," he murmured, leaning down to press a brief kiss to the crown of her head before striding from the room.

As he crossed the hall, his thoughts returned to Charlotte's earlier words. Jane... an heiress. The transformation of her circumstances was extraordinary, and he would need to pay her a visit—if only to offer congratulations and see for himself whether the shadow of her scandal had truly faded.

The coach rocked gently as it joined the morning traffic, but his mind drifted far from Lady Jane. He rehearsed, silently and without satisfaction, what he might say to Lieutenant Austen's family. Words always seemed inadequate when standing in the wake of grief.

The streets narrowed as the coach entered a less fashionable part of Town. When it halted, he stepped down, the air here tinged with coal smoke and damp stone. He mounted the steps of a modest building and knocked.

A white-haired housekeeper opened the door, her lined face polite but cautious. "May I help you?"

He offered his calling card. "I was hoping to speak with Mrs. Austen."

Her eyes widened almost imperceptibly as she read his name. "Yes, my lord. Please come in." She led him through a plain but tidy hall into a drawing room where a dark-haired matron sat beside a young woman who so closely resembled her that she could only be Mark's sister. Both were dressed in mourning black.

Alistair bowed. "Mrs. Austen."

The older woman smiled faintly. "My lord. Allow me to introduce my daughter, Miss Mary-Ann Austen."

He inclined his head to the young lady. "A pleasure, Miss."

Mrs. Austen gestured to a chair. "Please, sit with us."

He did so, folding his long frame into the proffered seat. "I wanted to extend my most sincere condolences on the loss of your son, Lieutenant Austen."

Tears welled in her eyes. "He fought so hard on the Continent... to return home only to die here—it is a cruel twist of fate."

"It is," he agreed. "Which is why I would like to pay for his funeral."

"That is not necessary—" she began.

"I know," he interrupted gently, "but it is the least I can do. If I can lift even a single burden, I will."

Her composure faltered and tears spilled freely. "Mark spoke highly of you."

"And I of him. You raised a fine son."

Miss Austen, who had been silent, spoke up. "We had a visitor—Rosalie—who said we should expect you."

The name struck him like a blow to the chest. Rosalie.

He kept his expression neutral, though the air seemed to thin around him. Surely it could not be the same woman. The one he had left behind on the battlefield.

Miss Austen crossed to a writing desk. "She left a note for you."

Mrs. Austen smiled faintly. "A most charming young woman."

"Did she say how she knew Lieutenant Austen?" Alistair asked, careful to keep his voice even.

"She said they met during the war. Weren't you acquainted?" Mrs. Austen asked.

"Yes," he forced out, stretching a smile over the unease coiling in his gut. "Of course."

Miss Austen returned and handed him a folded scrap. "Here is the letter."

He opened it and read the note silently to himself, "*The Shewrock Tavern. Room 2.*"

He resisted the urge to crush it in his fist. What was she doing here? She was supposed to be part of his past—buried, forgotten, never spoken of again.

"Is everything all right, my lord?" Miss Austen asked.

He summoned the same false smile. "Yes, I was merely... surprised. I haven't heard from Rosalie in some time."

"Charming young woman," Mrs. Austen repeated.

Alistair rose abruptly, bowing over Mrs. Austen's hand. "It was an honor to speak with you both. I will be in touch regarding the funeral."

"Thank you, my lord," Mrs. Austen said.

He saw himself out, giving brisk instructions to his driver before climbing into the coach. The door shut, and he let his head fall back against the seat.

Rosalie. Here.

Had they made a grave mistake in letting her live?

The coach lurched to a stop outside The Shewrock Tavern, its weathered sign swinging in the brisk wind. Alistair pushed open the door, the smell of stale ale and damp wood seeping inside. He reached beneath the bench and slid out the small wooden box, flipping the latch with practiced precision, and retrieved the pistol from within.

He tucked it into the waistband of his trousers, the familiar weight pressing against his hip. He wasn't certain he would need it today, but uncertainty was a luxury he could not afford. Better to walk in ready than to leave in a coffin.

The moment he stepped inside, the tavern swallowed him in noise—loud laughter, tankards slamming on tables, the rasp of boots scraping the floor. His eyes flicked over the crowd, cataloguing faces without lingering. No one here mattered except the one he had come for.

He cut across the room, moving along the side wall towards the narrow staircase. Each step groaned beneath his boots, the old timber complaining under his weight. He ascended quickly, pulse steady, senses sharp, until he reached the upper corridor. The air here was warmer, quieter, the floorboards creaking faintly with every shift of his stance.

He stopped before room two.

His fingers brushed the butt of the pistol as he drew it free, the smooth wood and cool steel grounding him. Raising his hand, he knocked once—firm, deliberate.

The door opened almost at once.

Rosalie.

She stood there—a young woman with dark hair tied loosely at the nape of her neck, freckles dusting her pale cheeks. The very same girl he had left behind on the Continent… alive. She regarded him with unnerving calm, not a flicker of fear in her gaze.

"Why are you here?" His voice came out hard, clipped. The pistol was aimed squarely at her.

Instead of flinching, she took a measured step back, holding the door open. "Do come in, my lord."

Alistair hesitated, then stepped inside. He closed the door behind him without lowering his weapon. "How do you know who I am?"

Her lips curved in something between a smile and a grimace. "After you left… that night, sparing me," she began, faltering for just a moment, "I made it my mission to discover your identities. Yours, and your comrades'."

"For what purpose?"

"You let me live. That was a mistake." Her voice dropped lower. "My brother forced me to tell him who killed our father, and I came to warn you that he will not rest until you are all dead."

His grip on the pistol tightened. "It was not personal. It was our assignment."

"My brother doesn't care." Her chin lifted. "He will hunt you down, one by one."

"Did he kill Lieutenant Austen?"

"Yes," she replied. "And he tried to kill you in the alleyway. He failed, and he does not take failure well."

Alistair lowered the pistol slowly, though he kept it at his side. "How do I know this isn't a trap?"

"You don't," she said. "But I had to do something. He was on his way to kill John Wiley when I slipped away."

He stepped towards her, closing the space between them. "Tell me where your brother is."

Her jaw set. "I may have betrayed him by warning you, but I will not let you kill him. He's all the family I have left."

"He is killing innocent men."

Her eyes sharpened. "Are any soldiers innocent? They kill, then return home as if nothing weighs on their conscience."

"Not me. I feel the weight of every man I killed," he said, and was surprised to hear the truth in his own voice.

"Then you are one of the rare ones, my lord." She brushed past him and placed her hand on the door. "I wish you luck."

He caught her arm before she could leave. "I could have you arrested."

"You could." She met his gaze, unblinking. "But you won't."

"How did you arrive in England?"

"It doesn't matter."

"It does to me."

She tugged at her arm, and he let her go.

"Be on your guard, my lord. My brother is a vicious man who will have vengeance for our father."

"Your father was responsible for the slaughter of thousands of our troops."

"Then you know exactly the kind of man my brother is."

With that, she slipped out into the corridor. He did not follow.

Alistair stood there for a long moment, listening to her footsteps fade. Finally, he turned his attention to the room—bed neatly made, no belongings in sight, not even a stray cloak or valise. She had never intended to stay.

Only to warn him… and to disappear.

Blast it!

A sharp curse tore through his mind as the weight of Rosalie's words settled in. John Wiley. If her warning was true, the man's life was hanging by a thread.

Alistair strode for the door, his pulse quickening with every step. The din of the tavern seemed to fade into a dull roar in his ears, replaced by the pounding of his own heartbeat. He pushed through the crowd, shoving past a drunken man and ignoring the slurred protests that followed.

The air hit him like a slap—cold, damp, bracing. "Driver!" he bellowed, striding towards the waiting coach. The startled coachman straightened at once.

"To King's Street, near the river—make haste!" Alistair barked, his voice edged with command. He yanked open the door and climbed inside, slamming it behind him.

The wheels lurched into motion, rattling over the cobblestones, and Alistair gripped the edge of the bench to steady himself. Every second felt stolen. If he was too late…

No. He couldn't afford to think that way. He would reach Wiley in time.

He had to.

8

Jane sat curled into the corner of the drawing room settee. The pale afternoon light caught in the motes of dust drifting lazily through the air, and she let her gaze wander to the windows now and again, enjoying the rare luxury of perfect stillness. A book lay open on her lap, and she had been wholly absorbed in its world—far more appealing than her own—until the spell was broken.

The peace ended abruptly.

From the entry hall came the unmistakable sound of raised voices, shuffling boots, and the creak of the front door opening and closing more than once. Jane froze, finger marking her place in the book as she listened. That was far too much activity for an ordinary caller.

The butler entered, his expression hovering between apology and unease. "There are many gentlemen here to see you, my lady," he said with a bow.

A sinking feeling tightened her chest. "Many? *How* many?"

"Ten."

Her lips parted. Ten. Ten determined gentlemen, who only yesterday would not have crossed the street to greet her, and now they were lined up at her door. She had no doubt it was because news of her inheritance had spread like wildfire through the gossiping circles of Mayfair.

"I... I..." Her voice trailed off. What could she say? That she had no intention of meeting them? That she wished they would all go away and leave her to her book? The truth was, she did not trust a single one of them.

Before she could answer, there was a sudden click and a section of the wainscoting slid open. A narrow panel revealed her Aunt Cosima, standing with a conspiratorial smile.

"I knew these servants' tunnels would come in handy," Aunt Cosima said with satisfaction. "Come along, dear. Make haste."

Jane did not hesitate. She crossed the room in an instant and slipped inside the narrow space, the panel closing firmly behind her. Darkness wrapped around them until her aunt struck a match and lit a stubby candle, casting a warm, flickering glow on the close brick walls.

"Now that we are hiding," Aunt Cosima said, "what would you like to do?"

Jane exhaled, only now realizing how fast her heart had been beating. "I don't know. Anything that doesn't involve ten fortune hunters in the hall."

"You will have to face them sooner or later," Cosima reminded Jane, the corners of her mouth twitching in amusement.

"Yes, but today is not that day," Jane replied firmly. "They are not here for me, only for what they believe I can give them. Every one of them turned his back when I was ruined so why should I trust them now?"

Her aunt's eyes glimmered with approval. "A sensible answer. Come—we shall take a turn in the gardens instead. I have not yet perfected my route through these tunnels, but I shall try not to get us lost."

As they began their slow progress through the narrow passage, Jane asked, "How did you even know those men were here?"

"I saw them from my bedchamber window," Aunt Cosima replied with relish. "Two of them were already engaged in fisticuffs on the pavement. I'm surprised you didn't hear them."

Jane shook her head. "I heard nothing. I was reading."

"A fine pastime."

"My father would disagree."

"Of course he would," her aunt said with a snort. "He disapproved of anything that might encourage a woman to think."

Jane smiled faintly. "He always warned of *reading mania*."

"If men said anything that was at least somewhat informative, perhaps women would not need to read so much," her aunt quipped.

A laugh escaped Jane before she could stop it.

Finally, Aunt Cosima pressed another hidden panel and pushed it open. They stepped into a back corridor, where a waiting footman opened the door to the veranda. Cool air greeted them as they descended into the gardens' winding gravel paths.

The relief in Jane's chest was so profound she had to speak. "Thank you for everything."

Her aunt gave a dismissive wave. "Stop thanking me, Child. It is plain to me you are used to going without."

"I wouldn't say that," Jane protested. "I had gowns and ribbons aplenty."

"That is not what I mean. I speak of affection freely given, without condition."

Jane's gaze dropped. "My father loved me… in his own way. At least, I hope he did."

"There is only one way to love," her aunt said. "The way your mother did, freely and unconditionally."

Tears welled in Jane's eyes at the mention of her mother. "I miss her every day."

"So do I. And she loved you dearly, without exception."

"I sometimes wonder how different life might have been if she had survived. Would Adam have been less cruel?"

"Perhaps. Or perhaps not. Your father's influence runs deep."

"I have always wondered what it would be like to belong to a happy family," Jane murmured, "one where love was not withheld the moment you displeased them."

Her aunt squeezed her arm. "You are safe here. You may be whoever you wish to be."

Jane let out a breath that felt heavy with years. "But I am not certain who that is."

"That, my dear, is for you to discover. But you will be loved no matter what you decide."

Their moment was interrupted by the butler stepping out onto the veranda. "My lady, Lord Ketteridge demands to speak to his daughter."

Jane's entire body went rigid. "My father is here?"

Aunt Cosima spoke up. "Inform Lord Ketteridge that I will see him in the study—alone. He forfeited the right to address his daughter when he cast her off."

"Are you sure?" Jane asked.

"I am," her aunt responded. "Enjoy the gardens."

Jane watched her aunt stride away, feeling her own legs weaken. She sank onto a bench, trying not to dwell on the inevitable day when she would have to face him herself.

When had life grown so complicated? For years, she had done exactly as expected, bending under the weight of her family's demands. Here, with her aunt, there was no such weight. She was free.

A familiar voice broke her thoughts.

"I thought I might find you here."

She turned and saw Alistair approaching, his stride purposeful. "Alistair! What are you doing here?"

"I hope I'm not intruding. I came to see how you were faring."

"You are never intruding," Jane said with a small smile. "I'm glad you're here."

"The butler turned me away, as were many other of your gentlemen callers," he said, his tone light.

From the townhouse came muffled shouts—her father's voice among them. Jane glanced towards the sound. "My father came to see me but my aunt is contending with him."

"That would explain the shouting," Alistair said dryly, lowering himself onto the bench when she shifted to make room.

His smile didn't reach his eyes, and Jane sensed the weight he carried. "Something troubles you," she prodded.

"Another one of my comrades has died," he admitted, leaning forward. "One murdered in a robbery... another, they claim, took his own life. But I don't believe it. Not for a moment."

Her heart tightened. "I'm so sorry."

The pain in his eyes was undeniable. "When did life become so complicated?" he murmured.

"I was just asking myself the same thing."

"And your answer?"

"I haven't one yet."

"Neither do I," he muttered. "At least you are an heiress now, and your scandal is in the past."

How she wished it were that simple. "Yes, but now I must deal with fortune hunters."

Straightening in his seat, he advised, "Be cautious, Jane. You deserve better than that."

"Fortunately, my aunt must approve any suitor before I inherit."

"A wise condition."

"She helped me escape a hallway full of them earlier," Jane said with a soft laugh. "Through the servants' tunnels."

"I'm glad you have someone looking out for you."

"I have two people," she said, nudging his arm. "You've always been kind to me, even when I was a straggly little girl trailing after you."

"You were never that bad," he said, and this time his smile almost reached his eyes.

A thought came to Jane. A dreadful, chilling thought. "Were your comrades' deaths... and your attack... somehow related?"

Alistair's expression changed in an instant. Whatever flicker of warmth had been in his eyes vanished, replaced by a grim hardness. "It has everything to do with my attack."

Before she could draw breath to ask more, he abruptly stood. "I'm sorry," he said, his voice clipped. "I shouldn't have come here. I've no right to burden you with this."

Jane rose quickly, the urgency to keep him from leaving stronger than she'd anticipated. "You are not burdening me."

"But I am..." His voice cracked with emotion. "My friends are dead because of me."

"I do not believe that to be true."

"It is," he stated.

"Alistair..."

He turned away, but not quickly enough to hide the sheen of tears in his eyes. That small, unguarded glimpse broke something in her.

"Excuse me," he murmured, his voice rough, "but I should go. I won't intrude on your time any longer."

She could have let him walk away—perhaps that would have been the polite thing, the easy thing. But every instinct in her resisted. Her heart told her to stop him. She reached for his arm, fingers curling into the sleeve of his coat.

"Jane..." His tone held warning, yet he didn't pull away.

"I am so very sorry about your friends. Truly," she said, willing him to hear the sincerity in her voice. "But you are not responsible for their deaths. You cannot be."

He finally looked at her, and the façade he wore so often—his calm, charming smile—was gone. In its place was a sorrow so deep it unsettled her.

"I wish," he began, "that I had been the one who died."

The words struck her like a blow. Before she could think better of it, she closed the small space between them, sliding her arms around his neck and holding him. "Well," she whispered, "I am glad that you are here... with me."

At first, he went rigid in her embrace, as though startled by the contact. But then she felt the shift—his breath eased, his shoulders lowered, and his arms came around her, drawing her close.

They stood together like that, wrapped in a silence that was not awkward but weighted with unspoken things. She could feel the steady thud of his heart beneath her cheek and found herself wishing he might trust her enough to share the whole of his burden.

After what felt like both a moment and an eternity, his hands loosened, and he stepped back.

"We shouldn't have done that," he said, looking down upon her.

"No," she admitted. "But I do not regret it."

He attempted to smile, but it was tinged with sadness. "Neither do I."

Jane's gaze drifted to his mouth as he spoke. She became suddenly, acutely aware of how little distance there was between them. They were close enough that she could catch the subtle scent of spice and leather clinging to him.

She ought to step back— propriety demanded it—yet the thought did not stir her feet. Instead, she found herself holding her ground, her pulse quickening for reasons that had nothing to do with surprise and everything to do with the man before her.

And to her quiet astonishment… she found she didn't mind at all.

Alistair felt a subtle, near-imperceptible shift in the air between them. Something had changed, though he could not have named it if his life depended on it. All he knew was that he liked being this close to her. The delicate fragrance of her perfume—something soft and floral—drifted towards him, teasing his senses. For one dangerous moment, he considered leaning closer, letting himself bask in her nearness.

Sanity, however, reasserted itself with a hard grip.

He cleared his throat, forcing himself to take a deliberate step back. The loss of warmth was immediate. In the brief glance he caught of her eyes, he thought he saw disappointment. Could that truly be there? Or was it simply his own foolish longing inventing what he wished to see?

"I should go," he said, the words tasting like retreat.

"Before you go, will you tell me what is troubling you?" she asked. "I might be able to help."

Temptation pressed at him. But he shook his head. "Thank you for the kind offer, but I must go about this on my own."

Her brows drew together. "And why is that?"

"I do not wish to burden you with my troubles."

"I daresay it is too late for that," she countered, her tone soft yet stubborn. "We are friends, are we not? And friends lift each other up."

He knew what she was doing. She was trying to help him, and he valued her all the more for it. "It is not that simple."

"Why can't it be?"

Because, he thought, the truth could cut her as deeply as it cut him. But some part of him—worn down by the weight of secrets—wanted to trust her. Wanted to let her in.

Gesturing towards a nearby bench, he asked, "Shall we sit?"

Only when she lowered herself gracefully onto the seat did he join her. She regarded him expectantly, yet refrained from pressing further. That patience—uncommon and oddly disarming—made the confession come easier.

"In the war," he began, "I was given an assignment. My team was tasked with crossing enemy lines and killing a French general. We all suspected it would be a one-way journey, but we were willing to pay the price for the greater good."

The old memories unspooled—dark, jagged things. "There were four of us. We traveled deep into enemy territory, and fortune favored us at first. We ambushed French soldiers, took their uniforms, and slipped into their camp under the cover of night. The general's tent was easy enough to find."

He took a steadying breath. "He was sleeping. I clamped my hand over his mouth, drew my knife, and slit his throat before he could make a sound." His jaw tightened. "What I did not see—until it was too late—was the young woman in the corner. She saw everything."

Jane leaned forward slightly. "Did you kill her?"

"I tried," he admitted, "but I couldn't. She reminded me too much of my sister. None of us could do it. So we took her with us."

"Did she cry out?"

He shook his head. "I kept her close, knife to her stomach to ensure she stayed silent. The night guards were our only obstacle. In our distraction, we forgot to change back into our British uniforms."

Her breath caught. "Oh, no."

A wry smile tugged at his mouth. "By some miracle, we

weren't shot on sight. We explained ourselves and we were eventually allowed through to our camp."

"What did you do with her?"

"We rode for an hour before letting her go. Far enough that it would take half a day for her to reach the camp. She was still in French-occupied territory, but... it was the only way to keep her safe from our own army's interrogation. She would have been tortured and killed."

Jane's voice was firm. "Then you did the right thing."

"Did we?" His gaze fixed on some distant point. "Our orders were to kill the general and leave no witnesses. We failed."

"You saved her life."

"At what cost?" he asked bitterly. "We swore never to speak of Rosalie again. For her sake... and for ours."

She offered him a weak smile. "You acted honorably."

He rose abruptly, restless. "No. The honorable thing would have been to obey my orders. She saw our faces. And she found me again."

Jane's eyes widened.

"I saw her earlier. She told me her brother is hunting me—and the others—down."

"She warned you?"

"She did. I don't know how she reached England, and she wouldn't tell me."

"That was... kind of her."

He tipped his head back, staring at the gray sky. "If we'd killed her, my two comrades would still be alive. I failed them."

"No. You all chose to let her live," Jane insisted.

"I led the mission. It was my choice. I was weak."

"I think you were brave."

"I respectfully disagree," he grumbled. "Their blood is on my hands."

Jane cocked her head. "You said there were four people in your team. What of the fourth man?"

"Lord Rupert Milnes. Third son of a marquess."

"Then he is in danger, too."

Alistair frowned. "I sent word to his townhouse that he was in danger, but I doubt he will believe me. He is rather cocky in his abilities."

"Then you must go to him."

"I will… I just had to see you, even for a moment." Blazes. Why had he just admitted that? He dragged a hand through his hair. "This is all my fault."

Her hand touched his sleeve—light, steady. "What's done is done. You must move forward."

"I should have killed her, but Rosalie reminded me so much of Charlotte," he murmured.

"You did your best."

"My best wasn't enough."

Jane's voice softened. "I disagree."

"That's because you don't know what soldiers must do," he said, his voice fraying. "Because of this, I went somewhat mad, shattered in private, and wore a smile that lied better than any mask."

"Alistair…"

He couldn't bear that look in her eyes—the one that saw him as damaged. "I should go."

"Did I say something wrong?"

Now he felt like a jackanapes. "No. This is not about you. It's me."

"Very well," she said at last, stepping back though her eyes lingered on him. "I will not keep you here. You should go to Lord Rupert and ensure he is safe."

He nodded once, the decision solidifying in his mind. "I should go." A pause stretched between them before he added, "Thank you for listening."

"Always, Alistair," she replied.

He was on the verge of saying something else—something

that might have been dangerous to admit—when a voice cut through their fragile moment.

"Good heavens, what has you both looking so grim?"

Alistair turned, schooling his features, and saw Lady Cosima approaching with an expression that seemed equal parts curiosity and amusement. He inclined his head. "My lady."

"One minute I see you two embracing, and the next, you look as though someone has died," she remarked.

Jane answered before he could. "Two of Lord Alcott's comrades have died."

Lady Cosima's hand flew lightly to her chest. "How awful. I wouldn't have said something if I suspected that was the case." Her gaze shifted to him, appraising but kind. "How are you faring?"

He drew on the mask he had worn so often since returning from war and forced a small smile to his lips. "I am all right."

"Would you care for a cup of tea? Or something stronger? Brandy, perhaps?" Lady Cosima offered.

"No, thank you," he said. "I need to keep a clear head at the moment."

"Smart thinking, young man. But do refrain from embracing my niece. You are fortunate no one else saw, or there might have been consequences to your actions."

A blush flared across Jane's cheeks. "It was my fault. I was the one who embraced him."

"No, it was entirely my fault," he countered immediately, unwilling to let her shoulder the blame alone.

Lady Cosima's eyes glimmered with mischief. "You both seemed to be active participants in the embrace."

Heat prickled along the back of his neck, and he stepped back. "If you will excuse me, I need to see to a few things."

"Would you care to join us for dinner?" Lady Cosima asked.

His instinct was to decline since he had no appetite for

company. But the thought of another evening in Jane's presence proved difficult to resist. "I would enjoy that. Thank you."

"You are more than welcome to bring your sister," Lady Cosima added with a wave of her hand. "The diamond of the Season."

"That is kind of you," he said with a bow. "Good day."

He turned and began walking away, his thoughts already shifting towards Lord Rupert and the warning he must deliver, when Jane's voice called softly after him.

He stopped and looked over his shoulder. She crossed the distance quickly. "Be careful, Alistair," she said in a hushed tone.

Feeling an uncharacteristic urge to lighten her worry, he teased, "Are you worried about me?"

"I am," she admitted, lowering her gaze to the lapels of his jacket.

Something warm and strange unfurled in his chest at the confession, chasing away the cold edge that had lingered since speaking of the war. "You need not worry about me. I will be safe."

"I truly hope so," she murmured, stepping back.

He watched her walk away and briefly admired the way the light caught in her hair. The quiet conviction settled in him like a vow—he would do anything to return to her.

But first, he had to find Lord Rupert and warn him. Time was not on their side, and danger was already moving closer.

9

Alistair's boot tapped a sharp rhythm against the coach floor, the sound loud in the cramped space. The short distance to Lord Rupert's townhouse felt interminable, the streets clogged with carriages moving at a snail's pace. Every jolt of the wheels grated on his last nerve. Rupert was in danger, and he could not afford a delay.

This was his fault.

He stared hard at the opposite bench, seeing not the worn leather but the face of a frightened young woman—Rosalie. He'd spared her life, and in doing so, had unwittingly condemned his comrades. The alternative—cold-blooded murder—would have haunted him for the rest of his days, but knowing he had chosen the path of mercy offered him no comfort now.

The coach lurched to a halt. Before the footmen could even dismount, Alistair wrenched the door open and stepped down. The crisp air bit his lungs as he strode up the walk, but he stopped short at the sight of the townhouse's main door—ajar.

Every muscle in his body tensed.

He drew his pistol, holding it low against his thigh, and

eased the door open with the other hand. His eyes dropped to the white-haired butler sprawled motionless on the polished floorboards.

His stomach dropped. Too late.

A sudden crash from above snapped him into motion. He took the stairs two at a time, the wound in his ribs screaming with each stride. As he reached the landing, silence slammed down like a curtain. The only sound was the pounding of his own pulse in his ears.

He moved down the corridor, every sense straining. A door stood ajar ahead, warm light spilling into the dim hallway.

With his pistol raised, he stepped through the threshold.

Relief loosened the iron band around his chest when he saw Lord Rupert was on his feet, towering over a man crumpled on the carpet, his broad shoulders squared in triumph. Blood streaked Rupert's knuckles.

"You're all right," Alistair exhaled, lowering his weapon slightly.

Rupert turned, his brows drawn low. "What are you doing here?"

"I came to warn you that your life is in danger."

Rupert snorted, retrieving a jagged knife from the floor. "A little late for that. This wretch tried to kill me in my own home. He took me by surprise, but I've dealt with worse."

Tucking his pistol into his waistband, Alistair's voice dropped. "Lieutenant Austen and John Wiley weren't as fortunate. They're both dead."

Rupert's eyes flickered. "I read about Austen, but Wiley—?"

"They're saying he took his own life."

"John would never—"

"I know. It's all tied to Rosalie." He let the name hang heavy between them.

Rupert inhaled sharply. "I had hoped never to hear that name again."

"As had we all. But she found me," he revealed. "She warned me her brother wants us dead for killing their father."

Rupert's jaw hardened. "Let him come. I can handle any mercenary he sends."

"I nearly died," Alistair said, rubbing the bruised ribs where pain pulsed with every breath. "An alleyway attack, but Lady Jane intervened, or I wouldn't be standing here."

Rupert's gaze sharpened. "Lady Jane Lyttelton? I read her name in the newssheets this morning. It seems fortune's been kind to her." He cocked his head. "How did Rosalie find you?"

"I don't know, and she did not share that information. But suffice it to say, both of our lives are in danger."

Rupert frowned before he bellowed for his staff. A lanky servant appeared.

"Where is Wilcox?" Rupert asked.

"The intruder knocked him out, but he is awake now," the servant informed him.

"Send for the doctor and constable."

When the servant left, Rupert hauled the attacker upright, slapping him until his eyes snapped open.

"Who hired you?" Rupert demanded.

A cruel smile came to the man's lips. "No one. I just wanted the pleasure of killing you."

In a swift motion, Lord Rupert pulled the man up and shoved him into a chair. "You think you are clever? But you will most likely spend the remainder of your life in Newgate, and that is assuming you don't get transported."

The man's eyes spewed with hate. "It would be preferable to talking to you."

Alistair stepped forward, retrieving his pistol again, the click of the cock echoing in the room. "That's the wrong answer."

The man's bravado wavered.

"You think I won't pull the trigger?" Alistair asked in a steely voice. "You've left me with nothing to lose."

The man cracked. He shifted in his seat, glancing between Rupert's bloodied fists and the barrel of Alistair's pistol. With a muttered curse, he reached into the inside pocket of his jacket and produced a crumpled scrap of paper, his fingers trembling as he held it out.

"This note was slipped under my door. Came with some coin," the man said.

Rupert snatched it and read it. No words were needed; the weight in his expression confirmed what Alistair already suspected. It was from Rosalie's brother.

"Can I go now?" the attacker asked, hopefully.

Rupert let out a dry laugh. "Yes, when the constable drags you away to prison."

The man shrugged, as if the idea were a minor inconvenience. "It's not like I killed anybody."

"You would have slit my throat, given half the chance," Rupert responded.

"True," the man allowed, rubbing at his reddened jaw, "but you did beat me to a bloody pulp. That's worth something, isn't it?"

Rupert shook his head, disgust flashing in his eyes. "Just shoot him. I doubt we'll get anything else useful."

Before Alistair could respond, the door opened and a dark-haired, matronly woman stepped inside, her crisp white apron tied around her waist. "The constable is on his way, my lord," she announced. "I have brought some footmen to deal with this miscreant."

"Thank you, Mrs. Henderson," Rupert said without looking away from the prisoner. "You may take him away."

Two broad-shouldered footmen entered, each seizing an arm. The man snarled and twisted, but their grip was iron.

They marched him out, his boots scraping along the floorboards, his curses fading down the hall.

"Will there be anything else?" Mrs. Henderson asked.

Rupert flexed his bloodied hands and winced. "Bring me some ice and something to wrap my hands."

"I shall see to it," she said, before disappearing into the corridor.

Silence settled over the room again.

Alistair slid the pistol back into his waistband, its weight a cold reminder of how close this had come to another death. "I'm sorry," he said. "I wish I'd gotten here sooner."

"It was nothing I couldn't handle," Rupert said, his voice laced with that brand of arrogance Alistair had known since the Peninsula. "Now tell me more about Rosalie."

Alistair leaned a shoulder against the wall. "Not much to tell. She left a note with Lieutenant Austen's family, instructing me to meet her at a tavern. That's where she warned me… and then promptly vanished."

Rupert crossed the room and dropped into the chair his attacker had only just vacated, the leather groaning under his weight. "You shouldn't have let her leave without telling you everything she knew."

Alistair's jaw tightened. "It wasn't that simple." He had replayed that meeting enough times in his head to know he wouldn't have pried another word from her without a blade to her throat—and he was unwilling to try.

"Did she at least tell you how to contact her?" Rupert pressed.

"No." The single syllable tasted bitter.

Rupert raked a hand through his dark hair, leaving it in slight disarray. "So we have someone trying to kill us and no more than scraps to go on."

"Perhaps you should go to your family's country estate until I sort this out," Alistair suggested.

"And leave you alone to fight this madman? Never."

"This isn't your fight," Alistair countered.

Rupert's look was steady, the sort that cut through excuses. "I made it my fight when we all decided not to kill Rosalie, Captain."

The old title hit its mark—reminding Alistair of the decision they had all agreed to in that fateful moment, and the consequences now circling them. Slowly, he crossed the room and sank into a chair opposite. His ribs complained with the motion. "If you feel that way..."

"I do," Rupert responded.

Alistair gave a short nod. "Then we will root out Rosalie's brother... together."

A faint smile tugged at Rupert's mouth. "Good, because I've no wish to retreat to my father's estate. He'd ask why I'd abandoned London during the Season, and I've no desire to trouble him with the truth."

"How is your father doing?" Alistair asked, though he already suspected the answer.

Rupert's expression sobered at once, the faint humor of their earlier exchange vanishing. "He is well enough for now," he said, the clipped tone and the way his gaze slid away making it clear that this was not a subject he intended to entertain further.

Alistair took the hint and rose from his chair, his ribs giving a dull throb with the movement. "Then I suggest you carry a pistol on your person for the time being."

"That won't be a problem." Rupert reached towards the bed and drew a pistol from beneath the pillow. "I usually have one within arm's reach at all times."

Alistair's brow lifted. "Then why beat the man with your fists when you could have ended it with a single shot?"

A smug smile touched Rupert's mouth. "No need to waste a

bullet—not when I've been putting in hours in the boxing ring."

"Just be careful."

Rupert inclined his head in mock solemnity. "I will."

Crossing to the door, Alistair paused with his hand on the knob. "I'll send word if I learn anything or if Rosalie makes contact again."

"She had better not," Rupert muttered.

Alistair stepped out of the bedchamber and walked down the corridor, its carpet muting his footsteps. His comrade was safe—for now—and the knowledge brought a fleeting measure of relief.

But relief was quickly swallowed by the gnawing churn of uncertainty. Too many questions, too few answers. Why had Rosalie risked seeking him out? How much did she truly know? And how far would her brother go to exact his revenge?

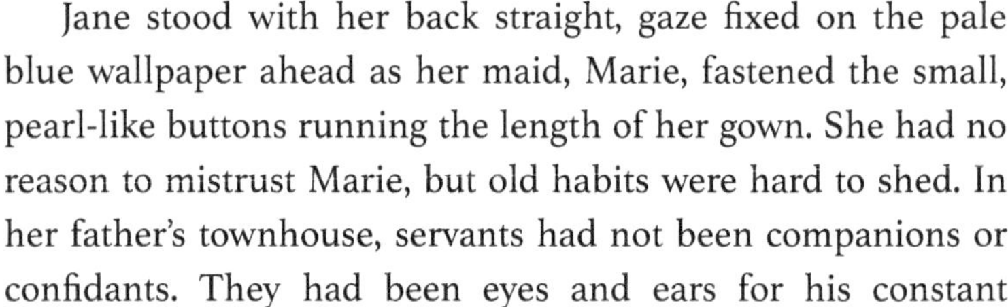

Jane stood with her back straight, gaze fixed on the pale blue wallpaper ahead as her maid, Marie, fastened the small, pearl-like buttons running the length of her gown. She had no reason to mistrust Marie, but old habits were hard to shed. In her father's townhouse, servants had not been companions or confidants. They had been eyes and ears for his constant scrutiny.

The final button was secured, and Marie stepped back. "Will there be anything else, my lady?"

Jane reached for the gloves laid neatly upon the table. "No, thank you," she replied.

She let herself out into the corridor, and at once saw her aunt advancing towards her, a knowing smile in place.

"You look beautiful," Aunt Cosima said warmly. "Now, do you like Marie? I personally selected her to be your maid."

"She is... fine," Jane replied, adjusting her gloves.

Aunt Cosima's brow arched. "Just fine?"

"I do not know her well enough to make a sound judgment," Jane admitted. "I prefer not to speak much to the servants."

Her aunt's expression softened, but curiosity lingered in her eyes. "Is there a particular reason why?"

Jane cast a glance at her bedchamber door and lowered her voice. "They are not to be trusted. At least, not in my father's house. They would report every detail of my comings and goings to him."

"I see. And you think I have them spying on you?"

"No... but—"

Aunt Cosima's gloved hand touched her sleeve in gentle interruption. "Marie is a kind soul. You may trust her to keep your secrets."

Jane's lips curved in a faint, self-conscious smile. "I am not accustomed to opening up to anyone."

"I hate how your father treated you," her aunt said. "But here, you are free to be who you wish to be. No one is spying on you. I give you my word."

Jane winced, knowing how ridiculous she sounded. "I am sorry."

"For what?" her aunt asked. "You did nothing wrong so there is no need to apologize."

"It is a habit."

"Well, break it," Aunt Cosima said briskly, though her smile was fond. "Shall we go spy on our guests?"

"Why would we do that?"

"Why not? Or we could hide in the tunnels and jump out to frighten them."

Jane gave her a bemused look. "For what purpose?"

"For fun."

Jane's lips twitched despite herself. "You and I have very different definitions of fun."

"You are no fun."

"I am fun," Jane protested.

"Then prove it. Slide down the iron banister."

Jane's mouth fell open. "I am not ten years old."

"I challenge you most emphatically."

"That means nothing to me."

Aunt Cosima's eyes gleamed. "I should think you have not the courage... unless you prove me wrong."

Jane sighed. "Only if you do it with me."

"Was there any doubt?"

As they walked towards the grand staircase, Jane found herself half-amused, half-appalled. A lady sliding down a banister—it was absurd. But her aunt was already positioning herself at the top, mischief in her posture.

"Shall we race?" Aunt Cosima asked.

"This is ludicrous," Jane murmured, eyeing the long stretch of black iron.

"Stop overthinking it and live in the moment." And with that, her aunt was gone, gliding down with an unladylike laugh.

Jane sat gingerly, bracing herself, then loosened her grip. The air caught at her skirts and the polished iron hummed beneath her. By the time she reached the marble floor, she was smiling—truly smiling.

"That was atrociously undignified," she said, trying to school her features.

"Was it so bad?"

"No," Jane admitted. "It was actually... quite fun."

"See? It is the little things that make life worth living," Aunt Cosima said, looping an arm through hers. "We should see to our guests now."

They entered the drawing room where Alistair and Charlotte sat on opposite settees. Alistair rose immediately, bowing with courtly ease.

"My ladies."

Jane curtsied. "My lord." She turned to Charlotte. "Thank you for coming to dinner."

"It is far better than being trapped at home," Charlotte said.

Alistair's lips quirked. "You must excuse my sister. She craves constant social engagement. She would prefer it if we went out every night."

Aunt Cosima nodded in approval. "I see no harm in that."

"I do," Jane said frankly. "I would rather stay in with a book than endure the *ton*."

"You and Alistair are two peas in a pod," Charlotte murmured.

"Charlotte dislikes opposing views," Alistair teased.

"That is because I am always right," she replied primly.

"Not always," he countered.

"I am right more often than not."

Alistair chuckled. "We shall have to agree to disagree."

"Don't we always?" Charlotte asked with amusement in her voice.

Turning back to Jane, Alistair asked, "How are you faring?"

Jane met his gaze. She wanted to know far more than politeness allowed in company. "Would you care to take a turn about the room?"

"I would be delighted," he said, offering his arm.

Once they were out of earshot, Jane lowered her voice. "Did you arrive in time to save Lord Rupert?"

"In time, yes, but he had already subdued his attacker."

"That is most fortunate."

Alistair's tone held a touch of wry admiration. "Rupert's arrogance has always been matched by his skill. It served him well in battle."

"What did he say when you told him Rosalie warned you?"

His mouth pressed into a line. "He was not pleased. We both believed she belonged to our past."

"Do we still need to go to Newgate to identify your attackers?"

"Yes. Tomorrow morning, if you are still willing."

Her aunt's teasing voice drifted over from the settees. "Can you speak up, dear? Miss Winslow and I cannot hear you."

Jane stopped mid-step, slowly turning towards Aunt Cosima. "I thought you said you weren't spying on me."

"This is a drawing room," her aunt replied with a playful glint in her eyes. "If you wanted privacy, you should have taken Lord Alcott on a tour of the gardens."

"She is right," Alistair remarked, a hint of amusement in his voice.

Jane narrowed her gaze at him, though her lips curved in a smile. "Traitor."

Before Alistair could respond, the butler entered and bowed. "Dinner is ready to be served."

Aunt Cosima sprang to her feet with more enthusiasm than elegance. "Wonderful. I am starving. I haven't eaten since I had a biscuit nearly two hours ago."

Jane bit back a smile. Only her aunt could make two hours sound like a harrowing fast.

They moved towards the dining room in companionable silence, the rich scent of roasted meat and freshly baked bread greeting them before they even crossed the threshold. Alistair stepped ahead to pull out the chairs for the ladies before claiming the seat beside her.

The footmen moved with precision, placing steaming bowls of soup before each guest. The delicate aroma of herbs and slow-simmered stock rose up, reminding her how little she had eaten herself.

Aunt Cosima lifted her spoon but paused midair, as though

making a toast. “Please, enjoy. My cook is phenomenal. I stole him away from the Duke of Clarence.”

Jane was about to take her first sip when Charlotte’s voice cut in. “Congratulations on being the talk of the *ton*.”

Jane lowered her spoon. “I am hardly the talk of the *ton*.”

Charlotte made a show of stirring her soup. “Did you hear that I was named the diamond?”

“No, I hadn’t heard that yet,” Jane replied.

“That is because everyone is talking about how you are an heiress now,” Charlotte muttered. “No one cares about me.”

Jane’s brow lifted in mild disbelief, but before she could respond, Alistair glanced heavenward in exasperation. “Please excuse my sister... again. She is in high dudgeon over nothing at all.”

“That is not the least bit true,” Charlotte insisted. “But I am not angry at Jane. I am rather happy for her.”

Jane offered her a small, sincere smile. “Thank you, Charlotte.”

Charlotte pouted faintly. “I wish I were an heiress.”

Alistair let out an exasperated sigh. “You have a dowry of fifteen thousand pounds. That is nothing to scoff at.”

“I suppose not,” Charlotte conceded, though her expression said otherwise.

Jane lowered her gaze to her soup, grateful for the distraction. Some women might have basked in being the diamond of the Season or in attracting whispers and admiring glances. But not her. She had no desire to be the glittering centerpiece of the *ton*’s attention. If anything, she dreaded it. The more eyes on her, the more likely someone would see past the surface and wonder at the truth she preferred to keep to herself.

Her aunt’s voice broke through Jane’s thoughts. “Why, pray tell, do you need to go to Newgate tomorrow?”

Jane’s lips parted, but before she could form a reply, Alistair's deep, steady voice filled the pause. "Jane needs to identify the men who attacked me."

Aunt Cosima's gaze snapped to her. "My niece was there?"

"Yes," Alistair said, his tone unwavering. "She is the reason I am still alive."

"Jane is a hero," Aunt Cosima said, her voice filled with pride.

Jane tried to shake her head, ready to deflect such praise, but Alistair was already looking at her. His gaze caught hers and held it fast, as though neither of them could quite look away.

"Yes," he said quietly, his voice meant for her alone. "My hero."

It was a simple phrase, but the weight of it settled in her bones. There was warmth in his eyes, yes, but also something deeper—something that made her breath catch and her heart quicken. In that moment, Jane was uncomfortably aware of how close he sat, of the faint scent of sandalwood that clung to him, and of the truth she dared not name: she liked the way it felt to be his hero.

10

Jane sat before the dressing table, the soft morning light filtering through the drapes, as Marie styled her hair. She wanted to trust the maid—truly, she did—but trust had become a rare currency, not easily given after years under her father's watchful, condemning eyes.

In a careful voice, hesitant so as not to sound intrusive, Jane ventured, "How do you like being a maid?" The moment the words left her lips, she winced inwardly. Foolish question. What maid would dare say she disliked her position, especially to her mistress?

Fortunately, Marie merely smiled at Jane's reflection in the looking glass. "I enjoy it tremendously, my lady. My mother was a lady's maid, and she taught me her ways from the time I could walk."

"That is good." Her voice was polite, but her mind scrabbled for something else to say, some topic that wouldn't feel so stilted. Conversation had never been her strongest suit since years of being silenced had made her tongue wary.

Marie stepped back and asked, "Do you like your hair?"

Jane turned slightly, studying the smooth coil and artful

arrangement in the mirror. "I do. Thank you," she murmured, and meant it. Marie's skill was undeniable.

"Now, we should get you dressed."

Jane rose and allowed Marie to help her into her gown. She stood still while Marie fastened the endless row of tiny buttons along her back.

As Jane opened her mouth to speak, Marie beat her to it. "Lady Cosima hired me especially for you. She thought we might become friends."

Jane glanced over her shoulder. "I would like that," she said sincerely. Then almost against her will, she added, "And I am sorry if I seem distant. I'm afraid that I am not used to maids who are genuinely interested in me. When I lived with my father, they all reported back to him about everything I said or did."

Marie's hands stilled. "That is awful."

Jane nodded. "It was… exhausting. I never knew who I could trust."

"I can see why," Marie said, fastening the final button with care. "But I promise you, whatever you say to me will be held in the strictest confidence."

Jane turned fully to face her, touched by the sincerity in the young woman's expression. "That means a great deal to me."

Before Marie could respond, the door swung open and Aunt Cosima swept in, bringing with her a faint whiff of lavender and brisk efficiency. "Good, you are ready. Lord Alcott is waiting for you in the entry hall."

At the mention of Alistair's name, Jane's heart made an unexpected leap. Heavens, why did his name alone stir such a reaction?

Aunt Cosima's sharp gaze shifted to Marie. "You will be accompanying Lady Jane to Newgate for propriety's sake."

"I don't think that is necessary—" Jane began, but her aunt cut her off with a raised hand.

"It is more than necessary," Aunt Cosima said firmly. "You are going to a prison. We must maintain some decorum."

Jane conceded the point with a small nod. Her aunt reached into her reticule and produced a small, gleaming object. Jane blinked at it. "What is that?"

"It is a muff pistol," Aunt Cosima said, as if it were the most ordinary thing in the world.

Jane stared. "Why are you giving it to me?"

"So you can protect yourself. I assume you can shoot?"

"Yes, but—"

"What did I say about the word 'but'?" her aunt chided, her tone lightly teasing but her eyes entirely serious. "Now, slip this into your reticule and be on your way."

Jane hesitated. "What if I… accidentally shoot myself?"

"Do you truly think you will?"

"Well, no, but—"

Her voice trailed off as Aunt Cosima pressed the cool metal into her palm. "Trust me. You are an heiress now, and a pistol may come in handy."

The determined set of her aunt's jaw brooked no further argument. Jane inclined her head. "Thank you," she said, meeting her aunt's gaze.

"You must hurry," Aunt Cosima urged. "Do not keep Lord Alcott waiting."

Slipping the pistol into place, Jane looped the reticule over her right wrist and left her bedchamber, Marie following close behind. At the top of the staircase, she spotted him—Alistair—in the entry hall below. Their eyes met, and before she could stop herself, a smile softened her lips.

She descended, her hand gliding along the iron banister, every step measured and graceful. "Good morning," she greeted.

He bowed. "You are looking especially lovely this morning."

"I hope not," she replied. "I wore one of my simpler gowns. It seemed more fitting for a visit to Newgate."

Leaning closer, he murmured, "You could outshine anyone in a sack."

Heat bloomed in her cheeks. "That is kind of you to say, my lord."

"It is merely the truth."

The way he looked at her—admiring, unapologetically so—made her almost believe it. Her brother's voice, calling her plain, echoed faintly in her memory, but for once, she began to wonder if it had always been one of his many lies.

Alistair offered his arm. "Shall we?"

Jane glanced back as Marie reached the bottom of the stairs. "My aunt insists my maid accompany me."

"I assumed as much," Alistair said, leading her to the door.

Outside, the morning air was brisk. A footman opened the door to the open-air carriage, and Alistair's gloved hand closed warmly over hers as he helped her inside.

Once seated, the carriage lurched forward into the bustling street. Jane's gaze drifted to the vendors calling out their wares, to ragged children darting through the crowd, and to the swirl of London life she was still learning to navigate.

Alistair's voice drew her back. "Thank you for agreeing to this."

"I was hesitant at first," she admitted. "But I don't want those dangerous men to be released."

"Nor do I."

She studied him. "The bruising is almost gone."

"My ribs are another matter entirely," he said with a faint grimace. "But I would rather not speak of injuries."

"What would you prefer to speak of?"

He settled back. "How are you adjusting to life with your aunt?"

That brought a genuine smile to her lips. "It has been wonderful. No one spies on me or criticizes my every move."

He gave a short laugh. "I know the feeling. My father criticized everything I did. I could never live up to his expectations."

"At least your father had expectations," Jane said. "Mine only told me I was a useless female whose sole purpose was to marry well and bear sons." The bitterness in her tone betrayed her, no matter how she tried to hide it.

"That was wrong of him. You are so much more than that."

Jane lowered her gaze to her lap. The rhythmic sway of the carriage did nothing to ease the knot in her chest. "No matter what I did, I was never good enough for him." The words were quieter than she intended, as if voicing them aloud might somehow make them truer.

Alistair shifted in his seat, angling his broad frame towards her. His voice held the steady assurance of a man who had already walked through fire. "Stop performing for others just to win their approval. Be true to yourself."

Her lips twitched into something between a smile and a grimace. "You make it sound so simple."

He gave a short, dry chuckle. "I do. Yet I ran away and joined the Army just to escape my father."

The thought of Alistair—strong, capable, decisive—being driven away from his home stirred something tight in her chest. "Do you miss him?"

His gaze went distant. "At times, I do. He wasn't always a tyrant, but after my mother died… he changed."

"My father was the same way."

Alistair's brow furrowed, his eyes darkening. "For as hard as he was on me, I wish he had spent more time with Charlotte. He neglected her entirely, leaving the servants to raise her."

Jane winced at the thought. "That must have been hard on her."

"We all have trials," he said. "Some more difficult than others, but that is our lot in life."

Before he turned his head, she caught the pain flickering in his eyes—unspoken, buried, and yet raw.

"I am sorry your father treated you so terribly," she murmured. "I… ran away, too."

His gaze snapped back to hers. "I am so glad that you did."

A lump formed in her throat, but she pressed on. "Some may think that because I keep going, I don't hurt. But let me be very clear. I hurt, and I keep going."

Without hesitation, Alistair reached for her hand. The contact startled her, but she didn't pull away. "We all hurt at times," he said, his thumb brushing lightly against her knuckles. "But it is in those times that we grow stronger than we ever imagined possible."

Jane glanced down at their intertwined hands. "I am glad that we are friends, Alistair."

Something flared briefly in his eyes—something she couldn't name. Before she could figure it out, it was gone, shuttered away.

"I am, too, Jane," he said, releasing her hand. "Forgive me. I should not have been so familiar."

"You can always be familiar with me." The words escaped before she could stop them, and heat crept up her cheeks in a betraying rush.

His mouth curved into a slow, broad smile. "You shouldn't say such things to me."

"I… uh… didn't mean it quite that way…" she stammered, wishing she could gather the words back into her mouth.

He chuckled again, this time with genuine amusement. "I was teasing you, Jane. And I would never take liberties with you. You must know that."

A pang of something—disappointment, perhaps—stirred in her, but she forced a smile. "I trust you."

"And I trust you."

They held each other's gaze for a moment far longer than propriety allowed. The quiet hum of carriage wheels on the cobblestones seemed to fade, leaving only the soft thrum of her pulse and the warm weight of knowing she trusted only a handful of people in the world and Alistair was one of them.

The carriage jolted over a rut, pulling her forward, and she caught herself with one gloved hand against the seat.

Alistair looked ahead. "We are almost there. I feel I should warn you that Newgate is... unpleasant. The stench alone can be overpowering."

She arched a brow, unable to resist a touch of levity. "Do you spend a great deal of time in prisons?"

"No," he said with a wry smile. "Very rarely. But they are not for the faint of heart."

Jane lifted her right arm slightly. "I brought a muff pistol with me."

He gave her a sidelong glance. "I will keep you safe. You must know that."

"I know," she replied, "but my aunt insisted."

Turning her head, Jane saw up ahead a massive block of soot-darkened stone. Newgate. They had arrived.

Alistair noticed the moment Jane's shoulders stiffened. It was subtle—a tightening of her spine, a faint lift of her chin—but unmistakable. The closer the carriage drew to Newgate, the more tension he could feel radiating from her.

His gaze drifted upward as they passed beneath the looming main gate. The stone walls were dark with centuries of soot and weather, the heavy surface pitted with deep grooves where wind and rain had gnawed at it over time. The smell hit next—an unpleasant mix of manure from the street and the stale, acrid reek of the prison itself, pungent enough to creep beyond the walls.

Newgate was no ordinary building. It rose like a fortress, oppressive in its scale, its narrow, iron-barred windows grudgingly offering prisoners the faintest slice of the sky. The air around it felt colder, heavier, as though the place itself breathed despair.

A handful of warders in plain coats lingered near the entrance, their eyes following the carriage with idle curiosity. The street noise clattered faintly in the background, but here, immediately before the gates, there was a stillness that felt almost unnatural.

But his focus wasn't on the building. It was on Jane.

"How are you faring?" he asked, watching the faint crease appear between her brows.

"The smell is rather wretched," she admitted.

"It is," he said, grimly. "That is the scent of hundreds of unwashed prisoners confined together."

She reached into her reticule and withdrew a handkerchief, pressing it to her nose. "Much better," she murmured.

The carriage halted. Alistair exited and turned, extending his hand for Jane. Her gloved fingers slid into his, and he was pleased when she allowed him to guide her down onto the gravel path. He tucked her hand firmly into the crook of his arm, keeping her close—not for propriety alone, but because something in him bristled at the idea of her walking into Newgate without his arm to steady her.

Two armed warders flanked the entrance, rifles resting in their hands. Before they could move forward, the door opened, and Lord Warwicke stepped out.

"Alcott," Warwicke greeted with a curt nod before inclining his head towards Jane. "Lady Jane. It is good of you to come."

"It is my pleasure," she said, though the slight tremor in her voice betrayed her unease.

Warwicke smiled, as though he had not noticed. "Your help in identifying these men will go a long way to securing their conviction."

"It is the least I can do," she replied, the same faint quiver in her tone. Alistair gave her hand the smallest squeeze, a silent promise of reassurance.

"Follow me, and stay close," Warwicke said, holding the door open for them.

Alistair leaned closer, speaking for her ears alone. "You are doing very well."

"Am I?" Her eyes met his briefly. "My legs are shaking, and my heart is pounding."

"We will get through this together," he said.

Her chin lifted a fraction. "I can do this."

"Good."

Inside, the entry hall was dim, the air cooler but no fresher. In one corner stood a long desk, behind which two men sat with the air of officials who resented interruptions.

Warwicke approached first. "Lord Alcott and Lady Jane are here to identify his attackers."

One of the men, dark-haired and sallow-faced, barely looked up. "Stand over there. We will be with you shortly," he said with the dismissiveness of one accustomed to giving orders to those who could not protest.

Warwicke's voice turned sharp. "Perhaps I was unclear. We are not going to wait while you twiddle your thumbs."

A side door opened, and a white-haired man in a red waistcoat emerged. "You heard the man, Stevens. Do your job."

Stevens grudgingly reached for a ring of keys hanging behind him. "Follow me, but remain close, or I'll have no choice but to leave you locked up."

The steel door groaned open on its hinges, releasing a blast of fetid air. Jane's sharp intake of breath was audible.

Alistair bent his head towards her. "Do not worry. I won't let anything happen to you."

"I believe you," she said simply.

They stepped into a narrow corridor as Stevens went to unlock another door ahead of them. Beyond it lay the cell hall —rows of barred enclosures on either side, the dim light leaving much in shadow. The floor was sticky underfoot, coated with layers of grime. The smell was suffocating, the kind that clung to the back of the throat.

A few prisoners whistled at the sight of Jane, but she gave them no heed.

Warwicke gestured towards a white-haired man standing back. "This is Cayser, a Bow Street Runner. Do not let his age fool you. He is among the best."

Cayser dipped his head in acknowledgment. "Warwicke brought me in to make sure your attackers do not escape justice." His gaze swept over the cells. "Take your time. See if you recognize anyone."

Alistair scanned the faces but saw nothing familiar. "I'm sorry. I didn't get a good look."

"I did," Jane said firmly, stepping forward. She pointed towards a cell. "That man, with the dark hair—he was one of them."

"Are you certain?" Cayser asked.

"Positive." She moved farther down the row. "And these two as well."

One of the men gripped the bars, sneering. "You don't know what you're talking about, Lady."

Jane didn't flinch. "I would recognize you anywhere."

The man bared his teeth. "You're lucky I'm not out there with you." He reached for her through the bars.

Alistair was there instantly, placing himself between them. "Do not waste your breath on him. He has no power here."

Cayser was already at the steel door and instructed, "There is no reason to linger here any longer."

But as they began to leave, the dark-haired prisoner Jane had first pointed out called out, "I want to make a deal."

"I'm listening," Cayser said, pausing for a brief moment.

The man leaned against the bars. "We were set up."

"By whom?"

"Don't know. A note was slipped under my door with some coin, giving instructions on who to kill. We were promised more money once the job was done."

Cayser's expression was unreadable. "Not much of a bargaining chip."

"Wait!" the man blurted. "The note was in French. Does that help?"

Turning back towards the man, Cayser asked, "You speak French?"

"My mother was French. She taught me enough."

The Bow Street Runner gave no further reply. He simply opened the door and ushered them through.

The moment the heavy door clanged shut behind them and Cayser turned the key in the lock, the oppressive stench of the prison was cut off. The echo of the bolt sliding into place sounded final, almost like a seal on what had just transpired.

Cayser faced Jane, his tone unexpectedly warm. "Thank you for what you did. I know it wasn't easy."

Jane's posture remained straight, though Alistair could see the faint tremor in her hand as she held her handkerchief. "No, it wasn't," she said. "But it needed to be done."

"That it did," Cayser agreed with a short nod.

Alistair stepped forward, offering his arm. "Come. We should return you home now."

Her gloved fingers slid into the crook of his arm, and he

guided her down the corridor. The warders they passed gave her openly curious looks—some lingering longer than he liked. He supposed he couldn't fault them entirely; Jane was a striking young woman. Still, a sharp protectiveness stirred in him, an instinct to shield her from every stare.

Once outside, he helped her into the carriage, his hand firm beneath hers, then climbed in after and settled into the seat opposite. The door shut, the driver snapped the reins, and the wheels began their uneven roll over the cobblestones.

"With any luck," he said, "those men will be transported soon enough."

Jane gave a small nod, though it carried the weight of hesitation. "I hope so."

He studied her face for a moment before asking, "Are you all right?"

Her hands were clasped tightly in her lap, fingers pressing into her gloves. "Do you think I am weak?"

"Heavens, no," he rushed out.

"Then why," she asked, "am I afraid to face my own father?"

He heard the sadness beneath her question, and something in his chest tightened. "That," he said, leaning forward slightly, "is a complicated question."

"It shouldn't be." A small frown tugged at her mouth. "I think it is time I speak to him."

His brow furrowed. "Whatever for?"

She lifted her chin, though he saw the faint quiver there. "He holds no power over me anymore since he disowned me. And because of my aunt, I will never have to rely on him again."

"Are you quite sure?"

Her eyes met his, steady but not entirely without fear. "I am. But only if you accompany me."

"I would have it no other way."

"My father will no doubt yell at me," she warned. "You should prepare yourself for that."

He moved from his seat opposite to sit beside her, the carriage swaying with the shift in weight. "As long as that's all it is," he said, "I will not tolerate him striking you or speaking to you with disrespect."

Her lips curved into a smile, though it did not quite reach her eyes. "Going to Newgate with you proved I can do hard things."

"I never doubted that for a moment."

"But I did," she said, her voice almost a whisper. "I have been so used to being told what to do, how to act, what to think. It is refreshing to know I have a choice in my life."

He didn't say it aloud, but the thought lodged firmly in his mind: he would do everything in his power to ensure she never forgot that again.

11

Jane sat in the carriage, her back as rigid as the seat itself. Her gaze was fixed on her father's townhouse—tall, imposing, and entirely unwelcoming. She could not say how long she had been staring at it. Perhaps only moments had passed, yet it felt as though she had been sitting there for an eternity, trapped in the quicksand of her own hesitation. Did she truly have the strength to face him?

Alistair's voice broke through her spiraling thoughts. "Are you sure you want to do this?"

"Yes," she replied, her voice firmer than she felt. "It is something I have to do."

"I understand," he said, leaning back in his seat with the kind of calm she envied. "I am ready whenever you are."

She shut her eyes briefly, gathering what little courage she possessed. Alistair had been endlessly patient with her, never pressing her, and never hurrying her along. She knew, without question, that if matters went badly inside, he would protect her. So why did fear still coil so tightly in her chest? Her father could not hurt her—not in the way he once had. Not anymore.

"I am ready," she announced, though her pulse still thudded in her ears.

Alistair tipped his head in acknowledgment. "Shall we, then?" He stepped down from the carriage, then turned back to her and extended his hand.

Jane placed her gloved hand in his and he assisted her onto the pavement. Once her feet touched solid ground, she felt a quiet relief when he tucked her hand securely into the crook of his arm. She had always felt safe with Alistair—safe, cared for, and, in some strange, foolish way, at home.

Nonsense. She could not—would not—entertain such thoughts. Alistair was her friend. Nothing more.

They mounted the steps together, and Alistair's hand hovered near the brass knocker before pausing. "Just breathe, Jane."

She exhaled slowly. "I can do this," she murmured, though the words were meant as much for herself as for him.

"I know you can," came his quiet reply.

The door opened almost at once after his knock, and the butler's eyes widened at the sight of her. "Lady Jane, do come in," he said, stepping aside.

Her boots had barely touched the marble floor when her brother's voice rang down from the top of the staircase, sharp and mocking.

"Ah, the prodigal daughter has finally returned," Adam drawled.

Jane lifted her chin and looked up at him. "I am here to see Father."

"And what makes you think he wishes to see you?" Adam asked, descending with deliberate leisure. "I believe I made our position on that matter perfectly clear."

"If Father turns me away, that is between him and me."

Adam stepped onto the marble floor, his expression narrowing into something darker. "Why is Alcott here?"

"I asked him to accompany me," she responded.

"For what purpose?" he mocked. "If Father did want to see you, this is a family matter. No need to parade outsiders into it."

"Regardless," Jane said, keeping her voice steady despite the trembling in her knees, "I thought it best that Lord Alcott came with me."

Adam scoffed. "I fail to see the logic, but then, I do not expect much from you. You are only a useless female."

Her cheeks burned, but before she could reply, Alistair's voice cut through the air. "That was entirely uncalled for."

"I will speak to my sister however I please," Adam shot back. "I could not care less whether you object."

Alistair stepped closer, his voice edged with steel. "If you insult her again, I will have no choice but to challenge you to a duel."

Adam's brows shot up. "A duel? Surely you jest—over Jane?"

"I am perfectly serious," Alistair said. "And I assure you, I do not miss when I fire my pistol."

Jane's lips curved into a small, grateful smile. His words were a shield, and under their protection, she felt a spark of bravery she had not known in years.

Adam's mouth twisted, but he merely said, "Suit yourself. Let us see if Father will waste his time with you."

As her brother strode away, Jane touched Alistair's sleeve lightly. "Thank you."

He patted her hand. "You are braver than you think."

"With you, I can be as brave as I wish," she admitted in a whisper.

"You don't need me for that," he said. "It's already in you. I've seen it."

She glanced towards the corridor. "Adam is dreadful."

"I don't disagree," Alistair replied. "But he is a bully, and I have never tolerated bullies."

"Well," she murmured, "wait until you speak to my father."

Alistair's lips twitched. "I can't wait." He gestured down the corridor. "Shall we?"

Before she could answer, her father's voice thundered from the study. "Jane! Get in here!"

Her shoulders straightened of their own accord. "Let's get this over with."

"That's the spirit," Alistair teased.

They walked in silence until they reached the study, where her father sat behind his great mahogany desk, Adam lounging near the window.

Her father's eyes narrowed. "What is Lord Alcott doing here?"

"I asked the same thing," Adam muttered.

Jane met her father's gaze without flinching. "He was gracious enough to accompany me."

"Then he can wait in the hall," her father said with a dismissive wave.

"No," Jane replied, her voice calm but resolute. "He stays, or I leave with him."

"I beg your pardon?" her father growled.

She felt the instinct to shrink under the force of his tone, but Alistair's quiet presence anchored her. "You heard me, Father."

Adam's dry chuckle grated against her ears. "Look who found a backbone."

Her father leaned back, studying her as though she were a puzzle he had no patience for. "Your little antic at the chapel has cost me dearly. The duke is suing us for breach of contract."

"I am sorry to hear that," Jane said, though she felt anything but.

"Since you are of age, I expect you to repay every penny I owe him."

Her breath caught. "With what money?"

"I care not how, but you will," her father said coldly. "Perhaps your dear Aunt Cosima will oblige you."

"How much?"

"Ten thousand pounds."

She could only stare. "That is a fortune."

"It is," he responded. "And you brought it upon yourself by refusing to marry him. You should have done your duty."

"I told you I did not want to marry him, and I should not be responsible for that amount since I signed nothing. Only you did, Father," Jane retorted.

"We all have duties in this family," he snapped. "You failed yours and humiliated us in the process."

"Surely there must be another way," Jane said, forcing her voice to remain steady though her stomach twisted in knots. "What about my dowry?"

"That can be accessed only when you are married." Her father's lips thinned. "However, the duke is willing to overlook this—indiscretion—and still take you as his wife."

Her mouth fell open in disbelief. "You cannot be in earnest."

"I am."

Adam interjected. "Do the right thing, Jane—for once in your life."

Her gaze snapped to her brother. "And in what possible way is marrying the duke the 'right thing'?"

"You would be a duchess," Adam said, his tone sharp with condescension. "With your inheritance from Aunt Cosima, you would never have to fret over your future."

A thought struck her—cold, unwelcoming. "Does the duke only wish to marry me now because Aunt Cosima has named me her heir?"

Adam let out a short, derisive laugh. "Well, it certainly isn't for your sparkling personality."

"No," she said, her voice firm this time.

Her father rose from behind his desk, his height and posture meant to intimidate. "You will marry the duke."

"No," she repeated. "I will not. And you cannot force me."

He came around the desk and Jane's heartbeat thundered in her ears. Before he could reach her, Alistair stepped forward, placing himself squarely between them.

Her father halted, his voice low and dangerous. "Step aside, Alcott."

"I don't think I will," Alistair replied. "If you wish to speak to Jane, you can do so from where you are."

Her father's glare sharpened. "And what gives you the right to speak for my daughter?"

Alistair's jaw tightened, his fists curling at his sides. "I don't speak for her. She is perfectly capable of speaking for herself."

The two men locked eyes, their mutual disdain thickening the air. Finally, her father leaned back slightly, conceding nothing. "This is pointless. Jane must do her duty."

Jane stepped from behind Alistair but kept close enough to feel the steady presence of his arm beside hers. "My duty is no longer to this family."

"You insolent, ungrateful little chit!" her father roared. "You owe me everything."

"I owe you nothing," she stated, the words spilling from her lips before fear could stop them.

Adam moved to stand behind their father, his arms rigid at his sides. "You play at bravery, Jane, but we both know this conversation would go very differently if Alcott were not here."

Her brother's words stung—not because they were entirely untrue, but because she refused to let them diminish her resolve. "I think we are finished here."

Her father surged forward a half-step. "How dare you!"

Alistair extended his arm, and she slipped her hand into the crook of his elbow without hesitation. "If you wish to speak to me civilly, you know where to find me," she said.

She did not look back as they left the study. The corridor stretched before her like a path out of some oppressive fog, and she kept her head high, even when the sound of raised voices erupted behind them. No doubt her father was seething over her defiance.

Once outside, Alistair helped her into the carriage. The moment the door shut, the vehicle lurched forward.

"That went well," he said with a wry twist of his lips.

"Quite frankly, it went better than I anticipated," she replied, her voice lighter than she felt.

He was silent for a moment before saying quietly, "I'm sorry."

"For what?"

"I had no idea your father and brother treated you so abominably," Alistair said. "You told me as much, but to see it—" He shook his head. "It is remarkable you survived at all."

She stared down at her gloved hands, twisting them together. "It was hard," she admitted.

Alistair leaned forward, his eyes fixed on hers with an intensity that made it impossible to look away. "Life can be ironic at times because, in the end, some of your greatest pains become your greatest strengths."

She studied his face, searching for any hint of doubt. "Do you truly believe that?" she asked, her voice tinged with both hope and skepticism.

"I do," he replied. "Because you, my dear, not only survived an unbearable situation, but you thrived."

Her breath caught, and she felt the faintest curl of warmth unfurl in her chest. "I did, didn't I?"

His answering smile was gentle, but his gaze held steady, as if he could see through every defense she'd ever built. "And now," he started, "you can put your father and brother behind you. They belong to your past. You, Jane, have an entire future ahead of you—one that they have no claim upon."

She let his words settle around her like a warm cloak, the truth of them sinking in. For so long she had felt tethered to her family's cruelty, as though their disdain defined her worth. But here, with Alistair's steady presence and quiet conviction, she felt the faintest shift—small, but real. Perhaps her past did not have to own her future.

The carriage drew to a smooth halt before Lady Cosima's townhouse, the polished black lacquer of its panels catching the late afternoon light. Alistair stepped down first and turned to offer his hand to Jane. Her fingers rested in his palm as he helped her to the pavement. He kept hold of them a moment longer than necessary before releasing her, telling himself it was simply out of courtesy.

As they walked side by side towards the townhouse steps, the faint rustle of her skirts and the clipped rhythm of his boots on the paving stones filled the space between them. He glanced over at her and asked, "Would you and your aunt care to join Charlotte and me for dinner?" The words left him before he had considered why he was issuing the invitation.

"That sounds wonderful," she replied with a smile.

He returned it—an unguarded, genuine smile—and said, "I will look forward to it then." And heaven help him, he meant it. Why had he invited her? They had dined together only the previous evening.

The main door swung open, the butler standing in silent readiness. Jane ascended the steps, and he stopped short of following. "This is where I leave you," he said lightly, though there was a weight to the moment. "But I shall look forward to you dining with me... er... with us, this evening."

If she noticed his slip, she gave no indication, only saying, "Until later, Alistair," before disappearing inside.

Once she was safely within, he turned away, making the short walk back to the carriage with a curious tightness in his chest. What in the blazes was happening to him? Feelings—real ones—were edging their way past his defenses, and that was dangerous. He had always intended to marry with reason, not affection. His parents had married for love and had lived in mutual misery. He would not repeat their mistake.

He had scarcely settled into his seat before the carriage door jerked open. Lord Warwicke climbed in and dropped onto the bench opposite.

"We need to talk," his friend said without preamble.

Alistair stiffened. He hadn't even seen Warwicke approach. He was slipping, and it was Jane's fault—at least partly.

The driver leaned back. "Is everything all right, my lord?"

"Yes, just drive," Alistair ordered. When the driver turned away, he fixed his gaze on Warwicke. "What is it?"

Warwicke settled in, his eyes keen. "I couldn't help but notice you weren't surprised when that prisoner claimed he'd been set up or when the note was mentioned to be in French."

"I wasn't," Alistair admitted.

One dark brow rose. "Perhaps you will be good enough to explain why."

Alistair exhaled, realizing there was no sense in holding back any longer. "During the war, I led a four-man team into a French camp to kill a general. We expected to die in the attempt, but luck—so we thought—was on our side. The general's daughter saw the deed, and we took her with us to keep her from raising the alarm."

He dragged a hand through his hair, the memory a mix of smoke, shouts, and the metallic tang of blood. "She found me here and warned me that her brother intended vengeance. Two of my men are already dead, and Lord Rupert narrowly escaped an attempt on his life. After which, his attacker confessed about receiving a note under his door with some coin."

Warwicke's expression darkened. "Was the general's name Leclerc?"

Alistair blinked. "It was. How do you know that?"

"This is bad," Warwicke said grimly. "You killed Jules Leclerc's father."

The name meant nothing to him. "And who is that?"

"A smuggler—no, more than that. A man who makes people disappear for a price. The wealthy and desperate pay him to erase them from their enemies' reach. Dangerous. Wanted. I heard his name often enough in the Army and since returning."

Alistair frowned. "His father was a general. It is rather surprising his son chose a life of crime."

Warwicke leaned forward. "Jules isn't merely a criminal; he's a strategist. He's built an empire on disappearance and survival. No one gets close—he's always on the move, surrounded by mercenaries."

"No man is untouchable."

"Perhaps not, but he's as close to it as any I've seen. If I were you, I'd hire more guards and keep to your townhouse."

Alistair tilted his head. "Will this threat pass?"

"Not without effort. I'll ask my contacts at Bow Street to sniff out a lead."

"And if they find nothing?"

"Then we'll find another way. But don't second-guess the past now," Warwicke said. "Focus on surviving it."

Alistair huffed. "That is easy for you to say. Two of my men are dead and it is all because we let someone live."

Warwicke's eyes held compassion. "You let an innocent live. You did the right thing."

The carriage slowed to a halt outside his own townhouse. Warwicke stepped out with a parting, "I'll be in contact."

Alistair sat for a long moment, watching his friend disappear into the street. Every turn of events seemed to knot the noose tighter. And now Jules Leclerc—another enemy of the lethal sort—was added to the list.

"My lord?" the footman prompted, holding the door.

Alistair stepped down, stripped off his gloves as he entered his home, and handed them to the butler. He needed counsel. Not the kind found in a drawing room, but from someone who had seen him through fire before.

He strode up the stairs, down the corridor, and into his bedchamber. Danvers was there, folding linen.

"We need to talk," Alistair said, shutting the door.

Danvers straightened at once. "What has happened?"

Alistair shrugged out of his coat and tossed it onto the bed. "Have you heard of Jules Leclerc?"

Danvers's eyes narrowed. "I have. That's not a name you want spoken in connection with yours."

"Too late. He's the son of the man I killed. He wants me dead."

Danvers's reply was blunt. "Then he won't stop until one of you is."

"Precisely. Which is why I need to end this before he does."

Danvers moved to hang up the discarded coat. "I'll see more guards posted. And you'll stay here until this is resolved."

Alistair hesitated before adding, "I've invited Lady Jane and her aunt to dine with us tonight."

Danvers glanced over his shoulder, a knowing gleam in his eyes. "You're spending a great deal of time with Lady Jane. Any reason for that?"

"No reason," Alistair rushed out.

"She is beautiful."

"She is," he conceded, "but we are friends. Don't overthink it."

Danvers's smile was infuriatingly unconvinced. "If you say so, my lord. I'll inform the cook of your guests."

When the door closed behind his valet, Alistair looked towards his bed. He could rest. Or he could work. There was always work to be done.

Coming to a decision, Alistair crossed the bedchamber in long strides and pulled open the door. The corridor beyond was quiet save for the muted tick of the long clock in the entry foyer. He intended to head for his study, but as he passed the open doorway of the front parlor, movement caught his eyes.

Charlotte sat at the small writing desk near the window, her head hunched over. Her quill flew across the page in quick, decisive strokes, the faint scratch of ink on paper filling the stillness. She was so intent upon her task that she did not notice him until he stepped across the threshold.

"Charlotte," he said.

Her head snapped up. "Alistair! What are you doing here?"

"I do live here."

"Yes, you do," she allowed, with a pointed look, "but what are you doing here?" Even as she spoke, she folded the paper with swift precision and tucked it deep into the folds of her gown, her movements far too deliberate to be casual.

He advanced a step, folding his arms. "What were you writing?"

"Nothing."

"It didn't look like nothing," he said evenly, unwilling to be put off by her tone.

She pushed back her chair and rose. "My, aren't you nosy today," she said with airy indifference. "I think I shall retire to my bedchamber for a rest."

"What are you about?"

A faint, mischievous smile tugged at her lips. "Nothing nefarious, I assure you."

"That didn't answer my question," he countered.

Charlotte only stepped closer and placed a sisterly kiss on his cheek, the gesture light but evasive. "I will be down for supper."

He watched her glide towards the door, every inch the picture of unruffled innocence—except he knew better. Charlotte was hiding something; she always was these days.

As she reached the doorway, he said, "Lady Jane and her aunt will be joining us for dinner."

Charlotte paused, glancing back at him with one perfectly arched brow. "Did we not dine with them just last night?"

"We did," he admitted, aware of the weakness in his explanation, "but I thought it polite to extend another invitation."

Her look suggested she saw directly through him, though she said nothing. That was the problem with sisters—they rarely needed words to voice their suspicions.

12

Jane sat opposite her aunt in the swaying coach, her gaze fixed upon the darkened street beyond the glass. The lamplight fell upon the slick cobblestones, and even at this late hour hawkers still cried their wares, their voices rising and falling in an uneven chorus. The pungent tang of the River Thames clung to the night air, slipping in through the seams of the window.

Beside her, Aunt Cosima lifted a handkerchief to her nose. "The smell is rather potent tonight."

"It is," Jane murmured, though her eyes stayed on the bustling pavement.

The coach bounced over a rut, and for a while, the only sounds were the steady clop of hooves and the creak of the carriage springs. Then, without warning, her aunt asked, "Are you interested in Lord Alcott?"

Jane's head turned, and she met her aunt's sharp gaze. "Heavens, no. He and I are merely friends."

"You two do not act like friends," her aunt observed. "But if that is the case, I have nothing to worry about."

Her brow furrowed. "Why would you worry?"

Cosima gave a nonchalant shrug, but there was calculation in her eyes. "I do not consider Lord Alcott worthy of you. He is only a viscount, and I believe you could do better in the marriage mart."

"I do not care about marrying for a title," Jane said firmly.

"That is good. I simply wish for your happiness," her aunt replied. "And I do not believe you could be happy with Lord Alcott."

Jane studied her. "Why?"

"It is only a feeling I have. Since you claim you do not harbor feelings for him, it is a moot point."

Jane pressed her lips together. She did have feelings for Alistair—ones she had no intention of voicing. At least, not to her aunt. Yet Cosima's quiet certainty left Jane oddly unsettled. What was it she thought she saw in him that could not bring happiness?

"You do not have feelings for him, do you?" her aunt pressed.

Jane summoned her most convincing smile. "No, I don't," she lied.

Her aunt's answering nod was one of approval. "That is good. After all, to remain my heir, I must approve of your husband."

Before Jane could form a reply, the coach slowed and rolled to a stop before Alistair's townhouse. The door swung open, and a footman appeared, offering a steadying hand as they stepped down onto the lamplit pavement.

They had scarcely mounted the steps when the door opened to reveal the butler. "Lady Cosima. Lady Jane. Please do come in."

Inside the entry hall, Jane's breath caught as she saw Alistair descending the staircase. His gaze found hers instantly, and for one impossibly suspended moment, the rest of the world fell away. There was something in his eyes—a glimpse of the future she dared not imagine.

Good heavens, what was wrong with her?

He came to stand before her, bowing slightly. "Lady Jane. You are looking lovely this evening."

Warmth rose to her cheeks. "This is how I always look," she blurted, then wished she could snatch the words back.

His low chuckle sent a ripple through her. "I concur." Turning to her aunt, he inclined his head. "My lady."

"Thank you for inviting us to dine with you and your sister this evening," Cosima said.

"My pleasure," he replied. "Charlotte will be down shortly. Shall we wait in the drawing room?"

They moved into the drawing room, and Jane sat beside her aunt on the settee. Alistair settled into the chair opposite them, only for Cosima to lean forward and ask, "Are you frequently bottle-weary, my lord?"

Alistair blinked. "I beg your pardon?"

"Do you often get deep in your cups?" she persisted. "Brandy? Ale? Port? What is your drink of choice?"

His gaze flicked to Jane, silently appealing for rescue.

Jane shifted towards her aunt. "Why are you asking such a question?"

"I merely wish to know if Lord Alcott is frequently foxed," Cosima said with an air of innocence.

Alistair gave a small, careful smile. "While I may take a drink or two on occasion, I do not overindulge."

"That is good." Cosima's eyes gleamed with satisfaction. "And how do you feel about dogs?"

"I like them," he said, clearly wary now.

"Another good answer."

Jane caught his baffled look and could only shrug in reply. She had no idea what Cosima was attempting.

Charlotte's entrance in a pale pink gown broke the odd

rhythm of the conversation. "I hope you weren't waiting long," she said.

"Not at all. The dinner bell hasn't rung yet," Alistair assured her.

As Charlotte sat beside her brother, she glanced between everyone. "Did I interrupt something?"

"No," Alistair said swiftly.

Cosima smiled. "I was simply learning more about your brother. Did you know he likes dogs?"

"I do," Charlotte said. "We keep hunting dogs at the country estate."

"And his feelings about cats?" Cosima pressed.

"I am not as fond of cats as I am of dogs," Alistair admitted.

Cosima looked faintly disappointed. "That is unfortunate to hear."

The dinner bell spared him further interrogation. "Shall we adjourn to the dining room?" he suggested.

As Cosima and Charlotte left the room, Alistair leaned towards Jane. "Why was your aunt asking such questions?"

"I don't know," she said truthfully. "But it is rather alarming you don't like cats."

"I don't dislike them. It's not as if I'd kick one," he said dryly.

She laughed. "That is a relief."

He offered his arm. "Your aunt is... eccentric."

"That is a word for it," Jane replied with fondness. "She has been kind to me, and I am grateful. She has changed my life."

"That she has. I'm happy for you."

She saw the flicker of pain in his eyes and asked, "Are your ribs still troubling you?"

"They are. The doctor says it will take time. It's been a convenient excuse to avoid Vauxhall Gardens with Charlotte, though."

"I suspect she is disappointed."

"She is, though she keeps herself busy with her writing. She's secretive about it."

Jane suspected she knew the answer since she was privy to the fact that Charlotte wrote for the Society page, under the name "Mr. Fairchild." She had discovered that information when she had searched her uncle's study months ago.

But it was evident that Alistair didn't know that. So she bit her tongue, knowing she didn't want to betray Charlotte. It was not her secret to tell.

They entered the dining room together and Alistair moved ahead to pull out a chair for her—a small courtesy, yet one that warmed her more than she cared to admit. Once she was settled, he took the seat beside her.

Aunt Cosima broke the silence by asking, "Do you believe in ghosts, my lord?"

Jane's gaze flickered to Alistair. His brows drew together, the faintest crease forming between them. "I believe," he said slowly, "there are many things we do not understand."

Her aunt nodded once, as if his answer had merely whetted her curiosity. "Do you sing when taking a bath?"

Jane nearly choked on the sip of water she had just taken.

"No," Alistair replied, his tone clipped but polite.

"Have you ever been chased by a swan?"

"No."

Aunt Cosima leaned forward. "What would you do if a goose followed you home from the market?"

Jane's lips twitched despite herself.

Alistair reached for his glass, his expression unreadable save for the faint glimmer of amusement in his eyes. "Does this goose also grant magic wishes?"

"No, it is merely a goose," Aunt Cosima said in all seriousness.

His smirk deepened. "Then I am afraid we would be having goose for dinner."

Jane, sensing that the next question from her aunt might involve something even more absurd—possibly involving bunnies or runaway milkmaids—intervened. “Has anyone read anything of note lately?” she asked, forcing a brightness into her tone.

Charlotte, who had been quietly buttering a roll, looked up. “Yes, I recently read the gothic romance *The Mysteries of Udolpho* by Ann Radcliffe.”

Aunt Cosima’s gaze shifted back to Alistair with sly interest. “And how do you feel about your sister reading such a book?”

“I have no issue with the books that she reads,” Alistair replied. “I think it is important for a young woman to be able to think for herself.”

Aunt Cosima’s mouth curved in approval as she murmured, almost to herself, “Good answer.”

Jane lowered her eyes to her plate to hide her smile, privately wondering whether Alistair even realized he had just passed one of her aunt’s unspoken tests. But to her surprise, he had a few questions of his own.

“My lady,” he began, addressing Cosima, “do you believe that tea tastes better if it is stirred clockwise?”

Aunt Cosima did not so much as blink. “Only if stirred with a silver spoon by a left-handed footman.”

Jane pressed her lips together to keep from laughing.

Emboldened, Alistair continued. “And if you were stranded on a deserted island with only a trunk of hats, would you wear them all at once or ration them out over the years?”

Aunt Cosima tapped her chin in thought. “I would build a signal tower entirely from hats. One must be resourceful.”

A soft giggle escaped Jane’s lips before she could stop it.

Alistair glanced at her, as though he found her laughter far more rewarding than winning the exchange. “One final question,” he said, turning back to Aunt Cosima with mock gravity.

"If you could invite one historical figure to supper, but they had to be dressed as a badger, who would it be?"

Without hesitation, Aunt Cosima declared, "Julius Caesar. I have a few pointed questions about his choice of friends."

Jane laughed outright, unable to contain herself. "You two are being ridiculous."

"I am glad that you said it," Charlotte remarked primly, though there was a faint sparkle in her eyes. "Perhaps we could have a more civilized conversation."

Alistair leaned back in his chair, both palms raised in mock surrender. "Very well. I concede," he said, his tone one of exaggerated defeat. "What, then, should we discuss?"

Charlotte's entire expression brightened, as though she had been waiting for such an opportunity. "Well, we could discuss what Mrs. Thompson was wearing to Lady Winter's ball. It was rather scandalous, was it not?"

Jane listened politely as Charlotte went on and on about Mrs. Thompson's gown, but her mind drifted back to the lighthearted banter between Alistair and her aunt.

Now, with Charlotte in full gossip, the atmosphere seemed to settle into something quieter, more proper… and far less interesting. Jane found herself glancing at Alistair, catching the faint twitch of his lips as though he, too, might prefer the earlier absurdities. She had to look away before he caught her watching.

Still, a smile lingered on her lips. Perhaps, if she was lucky, the ridiculousness would return before the evening was through.

Alistair remained on the front steps of his townhouse, watching as Jane and Lady Cosima's coach rattled down the street. He lifted his hand in a final wave until the lamps upon the rear panel blurred into darkness. He had enjoyed himself more than he had expected and Jane's laughter still rang in his ears. But it was past midnight, and the weight of weariness pressed down upon him. It was time to retire.

Stepping inside, he was greeted not by silence, but by his sister. Charlotte stood in the entry hall with arms crossed, a mischievous glint in her eyes. "You like Jane," she declared.

Alistair forced a smile and sought to deflect. "Of course I like her. She is my friend."

Charlotte's answering smirk was positively amusing. "No, you *like* Jane. As in, your heart beats faster when she enters a room. It is rather obvious."

He leaned down to brush a brotherly kiss upon her cheek. "Goodnight, Charlotte."

But she fell into step beside him as he mounted the staircase, refusing to be dismissed. "You cannot fool me, Alistair. I have not seen you smile this much in years—perhaps ever. Around Jane, it is as though you cannot contain your happiness."

He kept his voice even. "I do enjoy her company, but that is all it is."

"You are lying to yourself," Charlotte countered, her tone earnest.

At the top of the stairs he halted, turning to face her with a touch of impatience. "Is there a point to this conversation?"

"Yes." She lifted her chin. "I want you to be happy."

"And I want the same for you."

Charlotte stepped nearer, her eyes unflinching. "I can tell that Jane makes you happy and I truly believe you could be content with her."

He let out a long sigh, weariness warring with the stirrings her words provoked. "Jane and I are—"

"Friends," she finished for him, with maddening satisfaction. "But I think you feel more than friendship."

He shook his head. "When I marry, it will be a logical decision, not one born of infatuation. I cannot afford the mistake our parents made. Their marriage began as a love match, and in the end, they despised one another. I will not repeat that folly."

"You are not Father," Charlotte whispered, retreating a step. "Just think on what I said."

She brushed past him, and Alistair lingered in the corridor, her words echoing in his mind. Blast it—she was right. His feelings for Jane ran deeper than he cared to admit. And yet… what future could there be? She was Lady Cosima's heiress, with half the *ton* clamoring for her hand. A woman of fortune could choose among dukes, marquesses, and princes. Why would she ever look to him?

A pang tightened his chest. Was it jealousy that gnawed at him? No—he told himself firmly—it was not. He wanted Jane to be happy. That was all. And yet the thought of her eyes lighting up for another man unsettled him in a way he did not wish to name.

Shaking off the thoughts, he retreated to his chamber. Danvers was there, setting out Alistair's nightshirt with his usual quiet efficiency.

"Good evening, my lord," the valet greeted.

"Good evening," he replied. "I am weary and ready to retire for the evening."

Danvers offered a subdued smile. "Not surprising, considering the hour. Shall I fetch you a glass of brandy?"

Alistair began shrugging out of his jacket. "Yes—" He stopped, recalling Lady Cosima's earlier remark about his overindulgence. "No. I believe warm milk will suffice tonight."

"Very good, my lord," the valet said before departing to do his bidding.

Tossing his coat upon the bed, Alistair moved to his looking glass, fingers working at the knot of his cravat. The familiar creak of a floorboard drew his attention, but before he could speak, a livery-clad footman slipped into the chamber.

Something was wrong.

Alistair stiffened, his instincts honed from years at war. His suspicion was confirmed when the man drew a jagged knife, the candlelight glinting upon its edge.

Without hesitation, the servant lunged.

Alistair twisted aside, the blade missing him by inches. "Who are you?" he barked.

The man sneered. "It does not matter. I am here to kill you."

His gaze darted to the side table where his pistol lay, but the assailant blocked the path. When the knife came again, Alistair caught the man's wrist, holding it in a battle of strength. "I am afraid you will leave disappointed," he ground out.

The would-be assassin yanked free and slashed once more. Alistair staggered back, knocking over his writing desk in the hope that the crash might summon aid. Hatred blazed in the man's eyes as he advanced, forcing Alistair against the wall.

The knife rose—deadly, certain.

Alistair drove his fist into the man's stomach, sending him doubling over. Seizing the chance, he darted for the side table, fingers closing around the pistol.

But before he could cock it, the man rushed him again. Fear jolted through Alistair's veins.

A gunshot split the chamber.

The intruder stopped short, his eyes wide. Blood spread across his jacket. The knife clattered to the floor as he collapsed to his knees.

Alistair turned to the doorway. Danvers stood there, pistol still smoking in his hand, his expression grim.

Alistair strode forward, crouching beside the dying man. "Who sent you?" he demanded.

The footman choked on blood. "I don't know... a note... slipped under my door..." His voice broke, and with a final gasp, he fell still.

Searching the body with grim efficiency, Alistair found two slips of paper. One bore his own address, instructions for his murder. The other—

His blood ran cold.

No. It could not be.

"Good gads, no," he whispered, staring at the second note. "This one bears Lady Jane's address."

Danvers inhaled sharply. "How could he even know of her?"

"I do not know," Alistair said, his voice taut with urgency. "But I cannot allow her to come to harm. You must find Warwicke at once. Tell him I was attacked and that I must speak with him directly."

"At this hour?"

"He will listen to you," Alistair asserted. "He trusts you from the war. I must remain here for the constable."

At that moment, Malone burst in, his eyes widening at the scene. "My lord, are you hurt?"

Alistair shook his head. "I am unscathed. Send for the constable immediately."

Danvers prodded the dead man with his boot and muttered, "We may wish to interview the servants a touch more carefully."

Despite the grimness of the hour, Alistair almost laughed at his valet's dry humor. "Indeed."

"First question might be: do you intend to kill the master of the house?" Danvers quipped.

Alistair allowed himself a brief huff of amusement, though his mind was already fixed elsewhere—on Jane, and the danger that hovered far too close.

Danvers tucked the pistol into his waistband. "I will return as swiftly as possible."

Alistair gave a terse nod. "See that you do."

Left alone, Alistair sank down onto the edge of his bed, his back pressing against the carved post. The footman's lifeless body sprawled on the carpet before him, the acrid smell of discharged powder still hanging in the chamber. His heart was still thudding with the echo of the fight, though outwardly he forced himself into stillness.

Jane.

The thought of her name alone twisted his insides. If one assassin had carried her address, who was to say there weren't others? How was he to keep her safe? He had fought battles, commanded men, stared down French cannon fire—but this? Protecting Jane felt far more daunting.

A gasp cut through his thoughts. He did not need to look up to know who it was.

Charlotte.

She advanced into the chamber, her silk slippers whispering against the floorboards. "What happened here?"

Alistair gestured towards the corpse, his tone dry. "Isn't it obvious? He brought me the wrong drink."

Charlotte stopped short, her lips pressing into a line. "Is this truly the time for humor?"

He exhaled, weary. "Not really."

Her skirts rustled as she crouched beside the body, her brow furrowing. "Is he dead?"

"He is."

"Did you shoot him?" she asked, her gaze flicking from the body back to him.

"No. Danvers did."

A faint smile touched her lips despite the tension in the room. "Then Danvers deserves an increase in his wages." She straightened, eyes sharpening. "Why was this man trying to kill you?"

Alistair's jaw tightened. "It is... complicated."

"Complicated?" Charlotte folded her arms, her chin lifting in that familiar stubborn tilt. "I am no longer a child. Do not treat me like one. Tell me the truth."

He met her eyes. "All you need to know is that someone wants me dead. But I will not let that happen."

Her composure faltered. She stepped closer, her tone breaking with emotion. "You had better not. You are the only family I have left, Alistair. I cannot lose you, too."

His chest tightened at her words. Rising, he placed his hands gently on her shoulders. "You won't lose me. I promise you that. I will take care of myself, and I will see to it that additional guards are stationed around the townhouse to protect you as well."

Charlotte glanced once more at the body, then arched a brow. "Well, when you hire the replacements, perhaps you ought to ask them a very important question."

"And what question is that?"

"Whether they prefer to stab their master before or after supper," she quipped.

A reluctant huff of laughter escaped him despite the grim night. "I shall keep that in mind."

As his sister stood beside him, her trust in his word clear in her eyes, Alistair knew the truth: he was not nearly as confident as he sounded. The danger was too close, too deliberate. And Jane—Jane was in the very center of it.

13

Alistair sat in his study, the fire burning low in the grate and shadows stretching long against the paneling. His cravat hung loose about his neck, a testament to his disheveled state of mind. He had endured over an hour of the constable's endless prying questions, every inquiry striking like a hammer upon his frayed nerves. Yet he had given little away, only vague and evasive replies. The man had left frustrated, muttering beneath his breath about wasting his time, but Alistair cared not. What were the law's petty frustrations compared to the gnawing terror in his chest? Jane's face rose unbidden in his mind—her soft laugh, the brightness of her eyes—and the dreadful certainty that she might be the next target.

He rubbed at his brow, trying in vain to will away the thought.

The door creaked open and Warwicke strode inside, his breathing labored. "I came as fast as I could."

"Thank you for coming," Alistair murmured, holding up the glass in his hand. His voice was hoarse, worn. "Would you care for something to drink?"

"No," came the swift reply.

A humorless smile tugged at Alistair's lips as he set his untouched glass down with a soft clink. "You and me both, then. I had hoped it might steady me, but I find myself too restless even for brandy."

Warwicke lowered himself into the armchair opposite, eyes sharp. "Tell me everything."

Alistair drew in a long breath and let it out in a weary sigh. "There isn't much to tell. A footman—one we had only just hired—attempted to kill me. Danvers shot him before he could succeed." He paused, running a thumb along the rim of his glass. "Afterwards, we found two notes. One bore my address. The other... Jane's."

Warwicke stiffened. "You need to warn her."

"I know," Alistair said heavily. "And I shall—tomorrow. But I would spare her needless fear if I can. I did, however, send over guards to watch her townhouse until I go speak to them."

"Two of your comrades are dead already. The time for sparing feelings is past."

Alistair closed his eyes briefly, conceding the truth of it. "You are right. If only there were a way to guard her every hour of every day."

Warwicke grew silent. "You could marry her."

Alistair's head jerked up. "Be serious."

"I am," Warwicke countered, his gaze unwavering. "You feel something for her—anyone with eyes can see it. Marriage would place her under your constant protection."

The words settled like lead in Alistair's chest. Marriage. The very thing he longed for, yet the last thing he dared claim. His jaw clenched. "The closer she stands to me, the greater the danger she is in. No. She must be far from me." He leaned forward, forcing the thought from his lips before he could falter. "She could marry Lord Whitehill."

Warwicke's brow furrowed. "Have you lost your senses?"

"Think of it. Whitehill has recently lost his wife. By all accounts, he is a decent, honorable man. He would treat Jane kindly." Alistair's voice hardened. "More importantly, he could keep her safe as a former soldier."

"That is absurd."

"I disagree. It makes perfect sense." Alistair's hands gripped the arms of his chair until his knuckles whitened. "If Jane is with me, she will die. But Whitehill can give her safety, stability. I would make him understand what is at stake and he would see that she is guarded."

Warwicke studied him in silence for a long moment. "You would sacrifice her—willingly—to another man?"

Alistair forced himself to meet his friend's eyes. "It is not a sacrifice if it means her life."

"And what of your life?" Warwicke asked. "What of your heart?"

"It doesn't matter," Alistair said, rising abruptly. He strode to the tall window, staring out into the night. The moon spilled cold light over the gardens below, silvering the hedges. "If I die, so be it. I have done deeds I can never atone for. But Jane—Jane is innocent. She deserves a chance at life unshadowed by my past."

Warwicke tried again. "She ran from one marriage already. Do you truly think she would accept this one?"

"That was the Duke of Brackenford," Alistair snapped, his voice sharper than intended. He pressed a hand to the window frame, steadying himself. "A vile man. Whitehill is nothing like him. He is charitable. Kind. He would never hurt her."

Warwicke rose, exhaling slowly. "You were attacked only hours ago. You are in shock. I suggest you get some sleep before you make such a rash decision."

Alistair turned, his expression grim. "Are we any nearer to finding Jules Leclerc?"

"No, but—"

"Then what choice do I have?"

Warwicke frowned. "We will find a way. You are not alone in this."

"If Jules is in London, every hour matters," Alistair bit out. "Jane must be kept safe."

Warwicke shook his head. "And what if she refuses? What makes you think she would agree to your scheme?"

Alistair's shoulders slumped, weariness crashing over him. "I do not know. But I must at least try."

Warwicke laid a hand on Alistair's shoulder, his tone gentling. "I know this is tearing you apart. But do not throw away your chance with her so easily. We will find another way."

"And if we fail?" Alistair's voice broke. "If Jules reaches her first?"

The silence that came next was damning.

Warwicke finally admitted, "I don't know."

Alistair stepped back, dislodging his friend's hand. "I cannot bury her, Warwicke. If Jane dies—" His voice faltered, hoarse with raw emotion. "It would destroy me."

A moment passed before Warwicke said, "Then do what you think you must. I will keep searching for Leclerc. He cannot hide forever."

When Warwicke departed, Alistair sank into his chair, his head falling into his hands. He knew his friend did not understand, but he must do what was right. He could not watch Jane pay for his sins.

And then the realization struck him with brutal force.

He loved her.

Suddenly everything made sense. Every mistake he had made, the paths he had taken, and all the decisions he had made—led him to her.

But he couldn't act upon it. Not now.

"That was conveniently dramatic, Brother," came Charlotte's voice from the doorway.

Alistair lifted his head to find her standing there in her wrapper. "You were eavesdropping," he said flatly.

"Of course I was," she replied with a careless wave. "I always do. And you are a fool if you think giving Jane away is the answer."

His mouth tightened. "You misheard me. I am not abandoning her. I am ensuring her survival."

She drifted farther in, perching on the arm of a chair. "And who is this Jules Leclerc?"

Alistair stared at the ceiling for strength before answering, "A very bad man who wants me dead."

"Why?"

He swallowed slowly. "Because I killed his father."

Charlotte didn't react. "Did he deserve it?"

"Yes." His voice was firm. "He was responsible for the deaths of thousands of our soldiers."

"Thank you for finally telling me the truth."

Alistair winced at his sister's words. "I should have done so sooner," he admitted. "But I was trying to protect you."

"I don't need your protection."

"Yes, you do," he said more forcefully than he intended, his voice rising with conviction. "I have a duty—to you, to this family—"

Charlotte's eyes glinted as she asked, "To Jane?"

The name hit him like a blow, for it was true. He pressed a hand against the desk as if bracing himself. "Yes... to her as well. After all, she saved my life. I owe her everything."

"Even your happiness?"

Her quiet challenge sank into him, leaving him momentarily unable to meet her gaze. "Even my happiness," he murmured at last, the words tasting bitter as they left his tongue.

Charlotte sighed, the sound full of sisterly exasperation.

"Well, I don't need your protection, and I would imagine Jane feels the same way."

"But you are just a wo—"

The sharp look she leveled at him halted the word on his tongue. "I hope," she began, "you weren't about to say it is because I am a woman."

He cleared his throat. "It is a simple fact..."

Charlotte crossed her arms. "I am not some simpering miss in need of coddling, Alistair. Stop treating me as though I am made of glass."

"What do you expect me to say? You are my younger sister. I will always look out for you."

"That is fine," she responded, "but you don't need to shield me from pain, or sorrow, or whatever else life chooses to hurl at me. I am stronger than you think."

Her words struck him to silence. "I don't want to fail you, Charlotte. Not as Father failed you."

Her eyes widened. "You could never do that," she rushed out. "Just being here... caring for me... is more than what he ever did."

A hollow laugh escaped him, though it was tinged with relief. "He did not set a very high standard, did he?"

That earned a genuine laugh from her. "No, he did not. But you will never be like him. He was half the man you are."

Alistair smirked, rising. "What a nice thing to say. You do like me, then."

Charlotte rolled her eyes but her voice softened. "I love you, Brother."

A warmth he hadn't realized he needed spread through him. "Good, because you are stuck with me."

"I suppose that is all right with me," she said with mock solemnity, before stepping into his arms.

Alistair wrapped her in an embrace. For the first time in

hours, he felt some measure of ease return to him. Perhaps, just perhaps, he was not failing her as he so often feared.

After a long moment, she stepped back, her expression thoughtful. "We should be going to bed."

"You go ahead," he encouraged. "I am not quite ready to retire."

Charlotte hesitated, her lips pursed as though wrestling with something. "Alistair... there is something I need to tell you."

He straightened, alert. "Which is?"

A flicker of indecision crossed her face. "Never mind. Now is not the time for it."

"You know you can tell me anything," he said, trying to coax her.

"I do know that ," she said. "But I suppose I want to keep this secret just a wee bit longer."

"*Wee*? I am in trouble if you are speaking like a Scotswoman now."

It earned him the laugh he had intended, the tension breaking. "Goodnight, Alistair," she said, her smile lingering.

"Goodnight, Charlotte."

He watched her leave, the door closing softly behind her, and he wondered what secrets his sister might be keeping from him.

Jane stood straight, her hands lightly clasped before her as Marie fastened the small pearl buttons running down the back of her gown. The silence between them was not uncomfortable, but it carried a weight that Jane knew rested largely on her own reticence. She wanted to confide in her maid, but the years of guardedness made it difficult. Still, she ought to try.

She cast a glance over her shoulder. "You once told me your mother was a lady's maid. But what of your father?"

Marie's nimble fingers paused briefly before resuming their work. "He was a butler. They met when my mother entered service at a grand estate. Alfred was then an under-butler and a widower. His wife had died in childbirth, leaving him with a baby."

Jane's heart gave a tug. "That must have been very difficult."

"It was," Marie responded. "He sent the baby to live with his sister until he could provide a more settled home. Years later, when he and my mother married, little Suzy came to live with us."

The final button slipped into place, and Marie stepped back. Jane turned to face her and asked, "Were you close with Suzy?"

"I was. I was close to all my siblings," Marie replied, a fond light in her eyes.

A pang of sadness swept through Jane. "That must have been very nice. I was never close with my brother. He… he delighted in cruelty."

Marie's gaze was steady. "You cannot choose your family, but sometimes—under the right circumstances—they may become your dearest friends."

Jane shook her head. "My life is simpler without him. I must admit, though, I envy your closeness with your siblings."

Marie's lips curved faintly. "From what I've heard of Lord Barkley, he is not a man I would wish to call friend either."

A grateful smile touched Jane's lips. "Thank you."

"Family is not always blood," Marie said. "It is made up of those who want you in their lives, who accept you as you are."

Before Jane could reply, the mantel clock chimed, reminding her of the hour. "I should go. But… thank you, Marie."

Marie gave a modest shrug. "I did very little."

"You listened," Jane replied, moving towards the door. "And that is more than most people do."

As she stepped into the corridor, she nearly collided with her aunt, who approached with brisk steps.

"Good morning," Aunt Cosima greeted warmly. "You look lovely."

Jane glanced down at her gown, one of her simpler muslins. "This is nothing extraordinary. I had thought to do a little gardening after breakfast."

"I believe I shall join you."

Jane's heart lifted. "I would enjoy that greatly."

They proceeded together down the corridor. Aunt Cosima's voice carried a note of cheer. "Last night was rather enjoyable, was it not?"

"It was," Jane agreed. "Does that mean you have altered your opinion of Lord Alcott?"

"For you? No. But for someone else—perhaps."

Jane's brows drew together. "I am confused as to your reasoning."

Aunt Cosima stopped at the top of the staircase, regarding her with sharp eyes. "Does this mean you are interested in Lord Alcott as a suitor?"

Jane's heart gave a sudden flutter, but she forced steadiness into her tone. "No. We are merely friends."

"Then it ought not matter what my reasoning is," her aunt replied, and descended the stairs.

Jane lingered a moment, wondering why her aunt's disapproval bothered her so much. Alistair was honorable, brave, and far kinder than most men of her acquaintance. Any lady would be fortunate to marry him. Even her.

The thought startled her. She had always considered him a friend. Yet something warmer, something deeper, had been stirring in her breast. Not love—not yet—but something perilously close. And it frightened her.

"Are you coming, Jane?" Aunt Cosima called from below.

"I am," Jane answered quickly, descending after her.

A sharp knock reverberated through the entry hall. Aunt Cosima huffed. "Who can that be at this hour? We haven't even had breakfast."

The butler crossed swiftly to the door and opened it. The Duke of Brackenford stepped inside.

Jane felt her breath seize. She forced her spine straight, reminding herself the man no longer held any power over her.

His sharp gaze found hers. He did not bow. Merely inclined his head a fraction. "Lady Jane, might I have a word? In private."

Every instinct screamed no. She did not wish to be alone with this man ever again. "I would prefer my aunt be present as a chaperone," she attempted.

"That will not be necessary," he said with a dismissive wave.

"I believe it is," Jane insisted.

The duke's frown deepened, emphasizing the creases in his weathered face. He was a man accustomed to obedience, not opposition. "What I have to say will take but a moment. Surely even your aunt can allow me that."

Jane caught Aunt Cosima's quick glance towards the servants' passages—an unspoken signal that she would remain close, unseen. Understanding, Jane inclined her head. "Very well. We may speak in the drawing room."

The duke strode past without acknowledgment of her aunt, as though she were invisible. Jane followed, her chin held high though her pulse pounded in her ears. The last time she had seen him was at the altar, when she had rejected him.

Once inside, he stopped in the center of the drawing room and turned, his thin smile like a crack in old stone. "You are looking well, Jane."

She kept her voice even, despite him speaking so informally to her. "What do you wish to discuss, your grace?"

"I have come to ask for your hand in marriage."

Jane nearly forgot to breathe. "I beg your pardon?"

"Your father informed me that you regretted your hasty actions," he continued, unbothered. "That you would be amenable to correcting your error."

"My father was mistaken. I have no intention of marrying you."

The smile collapsed into a scowl. "You owe me. You humiliated me before my friends and family, before the *ton*. But I am willing to forgive you now that your circumstances have improved."

Realization hit her. "You mean since I became an heiress."

"Yes. With your fortune, I would be richer than the king himself."

Jane's mind raced. He would devour her inheritance, discard her once he had it, as he had his other wives. She lifted her chin. "My position remains unchanged. I do not want to marry you."

"That is because you are thinking too small," he sneered, advancing a step. "Once we are wed, we can have your aunt declared mad. Two doctors' signatures, and the fortune is yours."

"But my aunt is not mad."

"That is irrelevant," he said with a smirk. "Her eccentricities will suffice. After all, what sane woman marries a merchant?"

"One who follows her heart," Jane shot back.

"The heart has no place in marriage. Marriage is a business transaction."

She moved behind the settee, needing the barrier. "I intend to marry for love."

"Love is fleeting," he snarled, shaking his fist. "But power endures. You would be a duchess. No one would ever slight you again."

"My answer is no," Jane said.

He advanced towards her, his breath sour with brandy and tobacco. “Perhaps you do not understand what I am offering.”

“I understand perfectly,” she replied, refusing to shrink back. “And I do not want it.”

His eyes glinted dangerously. “You will not defy me again. We will marry, and your fortune will be mine.”

Summoning every ounce of strength, Jane met his gaze without wavering. “I would not marry you if you were the last man on earth.”

“How dare you!” His hand rose, poised to strike.

Jane closed her eyes, bracing—yet the blow never came. She opened them to see Alistair behind the duke, his hand gripping the raised arm.

In a stern voice, Alistair said, “I suggest you leave, your grace. You are no longer welcome here.”

The duke wrenched his arm free. “You do not speak for Jane.”

“You are correct,” Alistair answered evenly. “She speaks for herself.”

Jane lifted her chin. “Leave. And never come back.”

The duke’s face mottled with rage. “You impertinent chit. You dare defy me?”

“Yes.”

With a final glare, he spun on his heel to face Alistair. “You have made a dangerous enemy, Alcott.”

“I expected as much,” Alistair retorted.

With a violent scoff, the duke stormed out, slamming the door behind him.

Jane’s knees trembled, but Alistair’s steady gaze anchored her. His eyes swept over her as though ensuring she was unharmed. “Are you all right?”

Jane drew in a breath, shaky at first, then steadier as she forced her shoulders back. “I am,” she said, though her heart still galloped within her chest. "And I am glad you came when you did."

Alistair's expression was grim, the muscle in his jaw tight. "You should not have been alone with that man."

"I was not," Jane replied quickly, gesturing towards the paneled walls. "My aunt has been observing from the servants' tunnel."

Alistair's frown deepened. "That would not have stopped him from striking you."

Before Jane could defend her aunt's caution, a panel in the wainscoting swung open with a soft groan of hinges, and Aunt Cosima stepped forth, a pistol gleaming in her hand.

"You are right, my lord," Aunt Cosima said calmly, as though brandishing a pistol in her own drawing room was the most natural thing in the world. "But in truth, you saved the duke from being shot."

Alistair's brows lifted high. "You would have shot a duke?"

Aunt Cosima's grip on the weapon was unflinching. "If he had laid a hand upon my niece, I would have done so without hesitation. Rank means very little when a man behaves like a brute. Besides," she added with a dry edge, "he intends to commit me to an asylum."

"I would have never let that happen," Jane stated.

Aunt Cosima turned her head, and her eyes softened as they met Jane's. "I know, my dear."

Alistair cleared his throat, his gaze moving between aunt and niece before settling on Aunt Cosima. "I was hoping to speak to Lady Jane… alone," he said. "That is, if it is agreeable to you."

Aunt Cosima lowered the pistol but did not yet relinquish it. "I have no objection, my lord. But I do not speak for Jane."

Alistair turned then, his green eyes fixing upon Jane, and in that moment, the gravity in his expression made her pulse quicken. "Are you agreeable?"

Jane pretended to be put out. "I suppose I can speak to you since you did just save me from the duke."

"I will always save you," Alistair said, his tone fierce with conviction.

The words struck Jane with more force than she had anticipated. They were not mere gallantry; he meant them.

Aunt Cosima spoke up. "Why don't you two take a turn in the gardens? Fresh air will do you both good. But rest assured, I shall be watching from the window."

Alistair stepped forward, extending his arm towards her. "Shall we, my lady?"

Her fingers hesitated for the briefest of moments before curling around his sleeve. "We shall."

Together they moved through the corridor and towards the rear of the townhouse in silence. A footman opened the back door, and they stepped onto the veranda. The cool morning air swept over her, carrying with it the mingled scents of roses, damp earth, and clipped herbs. It should have calmed her, but her pulse only quickened. She was acutely conscious of the warmth beneath her hand where it rested on Alistair's arm, of the strength she felt there, steady and unyielding.

Neither of them attempted conversation. Jane was grateful. Words would have betrayed her, for her heart was thundering —not with fear now, but with something altogether more dangerous. Affection. Admiration. Perhaps even the first stirrings of something she dared not name.

Her treacherous heart would not be silenced, whispering to her with every step that she felt far more for Alistair than mere friendship.

14

Alistair kept pace beside Jane, every step on the gravel path sounding heavier than the last. He had faced battlefields, ambushes, and the certainty of death without flinching, yet here—alone with her—he could scarcely summon the courage to speak. He did not want her to marry Lord Whitehill. The very notion set something sharp and hollow gnawing inside his chest. And yet... it was for the best. She would be safe, cherished, secure. Not his, but alive. Why did the thought of her belonging to another man feel like a blade twisting in his ribs?

Her voice cut through his torment, soft yet perceptive. "What troubles you?"

He startled slightly, then gave her the plain truth. "Everything. I was attacked again last night. In my own home."

Her breath caught. "I am sorry, Alistair. I am glad you are all right."

Jane's genuine concern warmed him, but it only strengthened his resolve. He could not keep her in the dark. She deserved the truth, even if it would drive her further from him. "The man who is trying to kill me is Jules Leclerc," he confessed, the name sour on his tongue. "A dangerous smuggler. He will not stop until I am dead."

She stopped short, turning to him with alarm. "What are you going to do?"

"I am going to stay and face him," he said, lifting a shoulder in a half-shrug that belied the storm inside him. "I will not run." His throat tightened, for this was the part he dreaded most. "But, Jane... I found something far worse last night."

"Which was?" she asked, her brows drawing together.

His mouth felt dry. "I believe you are his next target."

She paled. "Why—why do you believe such a thing?"

"I found your address on a note in my attacker's pocket," he admitted.

She shook her head in bewilderment. "But I have done nothing wrong."

"It doesn't matter," he said grimly. "You are associated with me. That is enough." He forced himself onward, though every word cost him. "There is a way to protect you. You could marry."

"And who do you suppose I should marry?" she asked, her words wary.

"Lord Whitehill." He pressed on before his resolve broke. "I spoke with him, and he is willing. His wife recently passed away during childbirth—"

But Jane didn't wait to hear him out. She turned sharply and strode back towards the townhouse.

"Jane! Wait!" he called, lengthening his stride.

"No," she threw back.

He hurried until he was before her, walking backward, desperation rising in him. "Just hear me out."

"Why should I? You ask me to sacrifice myself to a loveless arrangement. Are you mad?"

"Whitehill is honorable," he argued. "I served with him. He would keep you safe."

"I am safe here."

"No, you aren't," he insisted. "The man who attacked me last night was disguised as one of my own footmen. If my valet had not intervened, I would be dead."

She faltered, her chest heaving, and her eyes still blazing with anger. "I am sorry that happened, truly, but that is no reason for me to marry a stranger."

"He is a good man. He loved his wife. In time, you could—"

"Stop saying foolish things," she snapped, brushing past him.

His heart twisted. "Jane, I am trying to help you."

"Help?" she asked, letting out a dry laugh. "You want me to do precisely what I fled from before."

"Whitehill is nothing like the Duke of Brackenford," Alistair protested.

"I do not care!"

He caught her arm, gentling his hold, turning her towards him. "Jane, please. I cannot bear the thought of harm coming to you."

Something in her expression softened at his plea. Yet her answer remained firm. "I know you mean well. But I will not marry Lord Whitehill. My aunt will hire more guards."

"That is not enough!" The words tore from him. Before he could think better of it, he blurted, "Marry me, then."

She froze. "Pardon?"

"If we wed, I could keep you safe. I would send you to my country estate in Sussex, guarded day and night. You would be beyond his reach."

Her gaze searched his. "And you would not come with me?"

"No. You must be far from me. It is me who he wants. I could not endure the thought of you caught in his net."

Her eyes softened again, but this time with a sorrow that pierced him. "I will not marry you either, Alistair. But I do... appreciate the offer."

"Why not?" His voice cracked despite himself. "It is the perfect solution."

"For you, perhaps. Not for me." She drew herself up, her tone resolute. "I want to marry for love. Did you not tell me once that I deserved that?"

His heart clenched. "You do, but—"

"No," she said, speaking over him. "This is not safety. This is duty dressed up as kindness. Do you even want to marry me?"

He reached for her hand, desperate. "Yes," he burst out. "Because I want to keep you safe."

For an instant, something flickered in her eyes—disappointment, perhaps?—before it vanished behind resolve. "That is not enough reason to wed."

"We get along, don't we?" he tried.

She squeezed his hand, her gentleness undoing him further. "We do. You are a good man, Alistair. One of the best I know. But I will not chain myself—or you—to a marriage neither of us truly wants."

"How do you know what I want?"

A knowing smile curved her lips. "Because you speak only of duty, and not once from your heart."

He drew closer, unable to stop himself. "I am worried about you, Jane."

"I know," she responded. "And that is the only reason I am still standing here." Her hand tightened on his. "But you must care for yourself first."

"That is impossible," he asserted. "Knowing you are in danger because of me."

"I will be fine."

"And if you are not? Do you think I could live knowing I was the cause of your death? It would destroy me."

"Alistair..." She stepped back, but he closed the distance, lifting a hand to cup her cheek. His thumb grazed her skin. "Please, Jane... if not me, then consider Whitehill."

Tears gathered in her eyes, though she blinked them back. "No."

"Jane—"

Her voice broke, but her will did not. "You are asking me to throw away my future, and I will not do it."

"Would you truly be so miserable with me?" he asked, almost pleading.

Before she could answer, an unyielding voice cut between them.

"I do hope I am interrupting."

Alistair dropped his hand and turned to face Lady Cosima.

Her eyes narrowed, brows arched in sharp disapproval. "What is so urgent that you feel entitled to such familiarity with my niece?"

Jane turned her face away, brushing at the tear that betrayed her. And Alistair's heart sank like a stone. He had caused that pain. He was the reason for her tears.

"Go inside, Jane," Lady Cosima commanded. "It is time I spoke with Lord Alcott privately."

Jane obeyed without a word, slipping past them and vanishing into the house. She did not look back.

Alistair longed to call after her, to promise that he would make everything right—but he could not. He would not lie. He cared for her far too much to bind her in false assurances.

And so he stood, helpless, watching her retreat from him into the safety he could never truly give.

Lady Cosima's arms folded across her chest, her stern gaze pinning him where he stood. "Well, do you want to explain yourself, my lord?"

Alistair forced himself not to flinch beneath her scrutiny. He had stared down the barrels of muskets and the eyes of dying men, but somehow this woman's disapproval struck far closer to the mark. He could evade, as he had with others, but he owed her honesty—perhaps it was the only chance he had of proving his intentions towards Jane.

"I did things in the war I am not proud of," he admitted. "My actions have placed my life in danger, and—worse still—they have endangered Jane's. A dangerous man wants me dead, and I fear she may be his next target."

At once, some of the steel in Lady Cosima's expression eased, though her eyes remained alert. "Who is this man?"

"Jules Leclerc," Alistair replied.

Lady Cosima's lips parted in a startled breath. "I have heard that name. My husband feared him and his men."

He inclined his head grimly. "Then you know what we are up against."

Her arms lowered, and she straightened with a decisive nod. "I shall hire additional guards to keep Jane safe. No one will get to her."

Alistair shook his head, frustration tightening his chest. "Forgive me, but I doubt that will be enough. I was attacked in my own household by a man disguised as one of my footmen. If danger can slip through doors I considered secure, it can slip through yours as well."

Her eyes narrowed thoughtfully, then she countered, "Then we shall retire to my country estate, where every servant is loyal to me. It would be easier to perceive a threat in such a place."

The thought of Jane gone from London—gone from his reach—struck him like a blow. But isn't that what he wanted? He would miss her presence more than he dared admit, yet the logic was sound. The farther from him she remained, the safer she would be. He somehow managed a terse nod. "Very well."

Lady Cosima took a deliberate step nearer. There was no censure in her face now, only shrewd awareness. "You care for my niece." It was not a question.

His instinct was to guard himself, but in that moment he saw no reason to deny it. "I do."

"And yet," she pressed, her tone laced with challenge, "you would have her marry another?"

Surprise flickered through him. "You heard that?"

Her mouth curved in the faintest of smiles, though her eyes gave nothing away. "I daresay the gardens are not as private as one would think."

Heat crept up the back of his neck, and he lowered his head, unable to meet her gaze. "Lord Whitehill would have kept her safe."

"You would let her go so easily?" she asked, her voice quieter now, but with the weight of an accusation.

His eyes snapped back to hers. "Easily? No. But I would do anything to protect her. Even if it means I lose her."

Lady Cosima regarded him for a long, measured silence, as though weighing the full content of his soul. At last, she said, "That is admirable."

Alistair swallowed hard, fighting the ache in his chest. "It is my fault she is in this mess, and I owe her my life. I would do anything for her."

And heaven help him, he meant every word.

"I believe you," Lady Cosima said at last, her voice carrying the weight of finality. She took a step back. "We will depart at first light tomorrow."

"Thank you."

Lady Cosima held his gaze. "Take care of yourself, my lord." And with that, she walked away, leaving him alone in the gardens.

Jane did not quite know what to feel. Anger simmered within her, but beneath it lay hurt, betrayal, and—most bitter of all—sorrow. She had been foolish enough to let her heart turn towards Alistair, foolish enough to believe his attentions meant something beyond gratitude and protection. And yet, when he spoke of marriage, it was not of affection, not of love, not of any tenderness that might bind two souls together. No, his offer had been born of duty alone.

Duty.

How she despised that word.

Had it not already chained her life, bound her like a prisoner to the expectations of men? Her father had demanded she marry the duke for the family's advantage. Now Alistair, of all people, spoke of duty as though it were noble. Worse still, he had gone so far as to suggest she might wed Lord Whitehill—a man she scarcely knew. Yes, she had heard that his reputation was honorable, that his deeds were kindly spoken of in Society, but what of that? He was a stranger to her. How could Alistair even conceive of such an idea? The insult of it burned within her.

Her only wish was to be alone, to gather her scattered thoughts and piece together the tatters of her heart. Yet as she passed through the entry hall, a knock resounded upon the front door. The butler hastened to answer it, and when the door swung open, there—of all people—stood her brother.

Jane stiffened, barely suppressing a groan. What could Adam want now? His presence was never welcome, least of all when she was raw with emotion.

With a weary sigh, she forced herself to speak, though her voice was edged with sharpness she could not disguise. "What do you want?"

Adam's brow arched, his eyes narrowing upon her face. "You have been crying."

The words struck her with humiliation, though she raised her chin. "I have," she admitted. "But it matters not."

He stepped towards her. "It does matter. Did Aunt Cosima make you cry?"

"No."

"Then who?"

She shook her head, unwilling to lay her heart bare before him. "What do you want, Adam?" she repeated, her tone clipped. She had no strength for pleasantries.

He frowned, shifting uneasily. "I was hoping that we could talk."

"We are talking."

"Privately," he pressed.

Against her better judgment, she gestured towards the drawing room. "Very well. We can speak in there."

She entered first, crossing into the center of the room, her back straight and her gaze expectant. When Adam followed, she folded her arms, bracing herself.

"I... uh..." He faltered, an uncharacteristic hesitation. "I need your help."

Jane blinked in surprise. That was the last thing she had anticipated. "Is that so?"

"Yes. Our estate is in difficulty. With the duke's suit for breach of contract, we are in a grave situation—financially speaking. I, well... I was hoping you might prevail upon Aunt Cosima to give us money."

Jane's mouth parted in disbelief. "You are asking me for money?"

Adam shifted, clearly uncomfortable beneath her gaze. "I would ask Aunt Cosima directly, but she hates me."

"She does not hate you."

He gave a crooked smirk. "She hates me."

"She may not hold you in the highest regard, but that is with good reason," Jane retorted. "I can ask her, but I cannot promise what she will do."

His smirk faded into a scowl. "This is all your fault, you know. Had you only married the duke, none of this would have come to pass."

"I told you that I would not marry him."

"It was your duty."

She rolled her eyes heavenward. "And what of your duty, Adam? No one pressed you into chains for the family's sake. You never sacrificed as I was expected to."

Adam grew solemn, his expression hardening. "I intend to do my part. I will marry an heiress to keep our estate afloat. I know my duty, and I embrace it."

She found herself actually feeling sorry for her brother and found herself saying, "I am sorry."

"For what?"

"That you will never know love."

He gave a careless shrug. "I never said I would not. That is what a mistress is for, not a wife. Marriage is a business transaction, nothing more."

"I disagree."

Adam dismissed her with a wave. "Regardless, the duke is still willing to marry you, even after the spectacle you made yesterday."

"Spectacle?" she echoed in disbelief. "He tried to strike me! Only Lord Alcott's intervention spared me."

"Pity," Adam muttered, as though the duke's cruelty were inconsequential.

Her patience snapped. "It is time for you to leave."

"Not before you promise to ask Aunt Cosima for the funds," he pressed.

Before Jane could answer, a familiar voice cut through the air.

"What funds?"

Adam flinched, paling as Aunt Cosima swept into the room, her presence commanding as ever.

"Aunt Cosima," Adam said with forced cheer, "what a pleasure. You are looking well."

She leveled him with a pointed stare. "Spare me the flattery.

What do you want?"

Adam straightened. "We are in need of assistance. The duke's suit threatens to ruin us. I hoped you might be generous enough to help."

"And why, pray tell, should that be my concern?"

His jaw clenched. "If Jane had only married the duke, we would not be forced into this position."

Aunt Cosima's eyes grew sharp. "Did you or your father ever ask Jane what she wanted when you signed the contract?"

"No, but—"

"Then this is the consequence of your arrogance. The fault is yours, not hers."

Adam's eyes darkened. "It was an advantageous match. She was a fool not to accept it."

"And what did you stand to gain?"

He hesitated, then muttered, "Twenty thousand pounds."

Jane gasped, her hand flying to her mouth. "The duke was to pay you to marry me?"

"Yes, and we kept your dowry as well," Adam snapped. "Now do you see the position you have placed us in?"

Jane's stomach churned. All her life, she had been nothing but a transaction.

"Put your big-boy breeches on," Aunt Cosima said, "and accept that this is your doing."

Adam's face mottled with fury. "No! This is Jane's fault, not mine!"

Aunt Cosima looked unimpressed by his admission. "And that is precisely why I will not lift a finger to aid you. You blame everyone but yourself."

"You have the funds," Adam growled.

"I do," she replied. "But they are mine to command."

Adam took a step towards her, his voice full of condescension. "Do not think yourself above me. You had to marry a common merchant to gain your fortune."

"And I have never regretted that choice," Aunt Cosima replied.

"You are nothing but street rubbish—"

"Adam!" Jane interrupted. "You will not speak so to her."

But Aunt Cosima waved her off. "Do not trouble yourself, dear. His words cannot wound me."

"Even so, I will not endure him insulting you," Jane insisted, turning towards her brother. "Go, Adam. And do not return."

He stepped towards her, his breath sour with brandy. "You think because you are an heiress you are better than me."

"I have never thought that," she said firmly.

"The money you inherit is tainted," he hissed. "You could have been a duchess."

Jane's shoulders straightened. "Must we rehash this same tired argument again?"

Adam's glare burned into her. "This is not over."

"It is," Aunt Cosima declared. "We are leaving for my country estate soon enough."

"Good. London will be glad to be rid of you both," Adam sneered, his lip curling with disdain. "I don't even know why I bothered to come. I should have known you would not help us."

"Then you should have trusted your first instinct," Aunt Cosima retorted.

Adam gave a harsh scoff and spun on his heel. Moments later, the slam of the front door reverberated through the house, rattling the windows.

Aunt Cosima released a slow breath, then said with perfect composure, "Well, I must admit I shall not miss him when we are at the country estate."

"I am sorry for what he said to you."

Her aunt gave a small, dismissive smile. "His low opinion of me is nothing new, my dear. And it is no different from what most of the *ton* think of me."

"Well, he is wrong, as is anyone else who dares to think such a thing. You are one of the best people I know."

Aunt Cosima's eyes held a trace of weariness. "You are kind, Jane, but I know I can be rather… eccentric at times."

"So can everyone," Jane replied quickly, unwilling to hear her aunt belittle herself.

With graceful dignity, Aunt Cosima crossed the room and settled upon the settee, patting the cushion beside her. "Come. Sit with me. And tell me—why were you crying after speaking with Lord Alcott?"

Jane bit her lower lip as she blinked back the tears that had started to form. She had not wished to discuss this, least of all aloud.

As though sensing her hesitation, Aunt Cosima continued, "You should know, I overheard everything. And afterward, Lord Alcott and I had a very frank talk."

Jane's heart ached. "Then you know… that he suggested we marry, but only from duty. Nothing more."

"Is that why you are so very upset?"

"I do not know why I am upset," she attempted.

"I think you do," Cosima said, her voice carrying both sympathy and certainty. "I think a part of you would like to marry him. But not because of duty."

Jane turned her face away, for tears were welling faster than she could blink them back. "It does not matter what I want. I turned him down."

"As well you should have," Aunt Cosima agreed. "But, my dear, that did not answer my question."

Frustration bubbled up inside Jane. "Why must it matter? You have made it very clear that you do not approve of him."

Aunt Cosima rose and came to stand before her, her gaze piercing but not unkind. "You love him, do you not?"

The words stole the air from Jane's lungs. She could deny it no longer. She did love Alistair. With him, she felt understood in a way no one else had ever managed. He made her laugh, challenged her thoughts, and somehow, she liked herself more when he was near.

In a voice no stronger than a whisper, she confessed, "I do."

"I see. But you must remember—if you marry him, you forfeit your inheritance. Is that truly what you desire?"

Jane's tears spilled freely now. She swiped them away, shaking her head. "I have no intention of marrying Alistair. Not now. Not ever."

For a fleeting instant, it seemed as though her aunt looked disappointed, though she masked it quickly. "Good," she said briskly. "But I did promise him that I would keep you safe. Which is why we leave tomorrow, at first light, for my country estate."

Jane nodded, though her heart felt heavy as lead. "I think that is for the best."

"As do I." Cosima placed a gentle hand on Jane's sleeve, her touch reassuring. "You will love the estate. It sits beside woodlands, and in the evenings you may catch sight of deer grazing. It is a peaceful place."

Jane forced a smile to her lips, though it did not reach her heart. "It sounds lovely."

"Come then, we should begin packing."

Jane allowed herself to be guided from the drawing room. Yet with every step she took, her heart whispered its protest. For though the country promised peace and safety, she could not escape the truth—leaving London meant leaving Alistair. And in her soul, it felt very much like a mistake.

15

Alistair sat in the farthest corner of White's, half in shadow, a forgotten glass of brandy warming in his hand. The low murmur of voices and the occasional bursts of laughter around the gentlemen's club did little to brighten his mood. He ought to feel some measure of relief. After all, Jane was leaving London. She would soon be tucked away in her aunt's country estate—far from him, far from the dangers that followed in his wake. That had been his plan. His wish. His demand.

So why did his chest feel hollow? Why did dread coil in his gut like a living thing?

The memory of her face haunted him. The flash of hurt in her eyes when he had suggested marriage between them—an arrangement, nothing more—just so he could shield her. He knew it had been clumsy, perhaps even insensitive. Yet every word had been born of desperation. He wanted only her safety. And it was his fault she was in peril at all.

Blast it, he had the strongest urge to abandon this chair, this club, this cursed brandy, and ride after her—fall to his knees and beg her never to leave him. But that was madness. A man had no right to such a plea when he was nothing but danger to her. No—the wisest thing, the only thing, was to let her go.

A sudden movement drew him back to the present. Lord Rupert sank into the armchair opposite, his expression one of cheerful irreverence. “Good gads, Alcott, why do you look like death’s poor cousin?”

Alistair did not even look up. “What do you want?” he muttered, dragging the glass to his lips.

“Nothing, save the questionable pleasure of your company.”

He gave a short, derisive huff. “Unlikely.”

Rupert leaned back with a grin. “What happened to you? You used to be much more pleasant.”

Alistair’s gaze dropped to the amber liquid in his glass. The silence stretched until at last he said, flatly, “Go away.”

“I will. But first there is something I suspect you’ll want to hear.” Rupert leaned forward, his voice lowering. “I spoke again to the fellow who attacked me. It seems he wasn’t entirely truthful in his first confession.”

Alistair’s head came up, sharp. “How so?”

“Well, I made a visit to Newgate this morning and asked him—nicely, of course—to explain how I was meant to be his victim.”

Alistair’s brow arched with skepticism. “You? Nicely?” He knew well enough that Rupert had earned a reputation as one of the Army’s most effective interrogators.

Rupert gave him an injured look. “I didn’t kill him, if that’s your fear. I merely suggested he might part with a finger or two should his tongue remain idle.”

“And did he?”

A flash of mock indignation crossed Rupert’s face. “Of course not! I’m not a monster.” He paused. “Though I can’t say I left him entirely comfortable.”

Alistair’s frown deepened. “How in the blazes did you gain leave to interrogate a man inside Newgate?”

"Does it matter?"

He shrugged. "I suppose not."

Rupert straightened and drew a folded paper from his pocket. "Regardless, I discovered where he lodged. His rooms were a shambles, but I found this."

Alistair set down his brandy, suddenly intent. "What is it?"

"The layout of a country estate in Lavenham." Rupert spread the paper across the table. "Does this mean anything to you?"

Alistair leaned forward, snatching it before Rupert's hand had fully withdrawn. His blood went cold. "Lady Cosima's estate is in Lavenham."

Rupert let out a whistle. "Well, it is a good thing she is still in London, then."

Alistair's jaw clenched. "No. She and Lady Jane depart tomorrow at first light."

"Then we stop them."

Alistair surged to his feet, shoving the paper into his pocket. "My thoughts exactly." He strode out of White's with Rupert on his heels, his pulse thundering in his ears.

Once in his coach, he barked rapid directions at the driver before slamming the door. Rupert settled opposite as the vehicle lurched into the crowded streets. Alistair's knee bounced restlessly, his gaze fixed on the passing windows, his mind reeling. How had Jules's men obtained a layout of Lady Cosima's country estate? How had they known the ladies would seek safety in Lavenham?

Rupert's calm voice cut through his thoughts. "We will reach them in time."

"What if we don't?" Alistair's tone was harsh. "Jules always seems to be one step ahead."

"Even the cleverest adversary stumbles eventually."

"Is that supposed to comfort me?" Alistair muttered.

Rupert studied him with a strange intensity. "I've never seen you so restless. You were steadier on the Continent than you are now." He tilted his head. "Unless there is more at stake here?"

Alistair's eyes snapped to his. "Do not analyze me."

Rupert raised his hands in mock surrender. "As you wish. It is merely an observation."

Alistair turned away. The last thing he wanted was for anyone—least of all Rupert—to glimpse the truth of what Jane meant to him.

"Do you know why Lady Cosima is leaving London?" Rupert asked.

"I thought it was best if they got as far away from me as possible," Alistair replied.

Rupert looked amused. "Ah, that would have been a good plan had it been less obvious that is what you would have done."

Alistair looked heavenward. "I would prefer if we sat in silence."

"We could, but chatting with you is much more enjoyable. You are being a delight."

Knowing his friend was goading him, Alistair decided to change subjects. "I was attacked again. This time in my own home."

All humor left Rupert's expression. "When?"

"Last night in my bedchamber," he revealed. "Danvers shot him."

Rupert settled back into his seat. "How is your dear batman doing? I have missed him since the war."

"I do not think the feeling is mutual."

"I shot him by accident," Rupert defended. "How many times do I have to explain myself? He was sneaking around the tent and I was on duty. What choice did I have?"

Alistair chuckled. "He was lucky you are such a lousy shot."

Rupert looked insulted. "I have an excellent aim, but I

wasn't trying to kill him—merely wound him," he explained. "If he was the enemy, I needed him alive to interrogate him."

"Frankly, I am surprised you became a barrister. You always seemed to enjoy the immense pressure of war."

"No more than you," Rupert replied. "But being a barrister is far less exciting than being a soldier, but much more predictable. Safe."

"I suppose you have a point," Alistair said. "Although my life is hardly predictable now with Jules after me."

Lord Rupert's eyes grew determined. "We will find him and make him pay for what he has done."

"And if we don't?"

"Then we die trying."

Alistair had to admit that he didn't like that option, but he kept quiet. He may welcome death, but Jane did not deserve the same fate. She was an innocent in all of this.

When the coach halted at Lady Cosima's townhouse, Alistair strode up the steps and pounded at the door. Relief and dread warred in his chest as the butler appeared.

"I must speak with Lady Cosima," Alistair demanded.

The butler bowed slightly. "I regret to inform you, my lord, she has already departed for her estate."

The words struck him like a blow. "What? They were to leave tomorrow at dawn."

"The driver thought it best to make an early start, to avoid poor weather. They left no more than an hour ago."

Rupert touched his arm. "We can still catch them."

"Only if we ride hard," Alistair said grimly. He fixed the butler with a hard stare. "I need you to prepare two of your fastest horses. Now."

The man faltered. "My lord—"

Alistair cut him off. "Unless this sentence ends with you following my orders, we are going to have a problem," he growled. "Do we have a problem?"

"No, my lord," the butler responded. "I will see them brought around front at once."

Once the door shut behind them, Alistair turned sharply towards the street, scanning the branching roads as though sheer force of will might summon the ladies back into sight. "Which way do you suppose they went?"

Rupert joined him on the step. "I would assume whichever road offered the most respectable accommodations for two ladies traveling together."

Alistair gave a curt nod. "Then I know which road they took." His mind's eye could already trace the familiar coaching inns, the mile markers, and the dangerous stretches of woodland where an ambush would be easiest.

Rupert turned towards Alistair, his expression unusually solemn. "We will find them and bring them home."

The words rang hollow. Alistair's chest constricted. "This is all my fault," he admitted, his voice ragged.

"No," Rupert countered. "This is Jules's fault."

But Alistair dropped his head, the weight of his guilt bowing him. "How in the blazes am I to keep Lady Jane safe, when I cannot even manage to keep myself alive?" The memory of last night's attack in his bedchamber returned like a shadow, the taste of gunpowder and blood still vivid.

"You will find a way," Rupert said, unflinching. "Besides, I have contacts at the Home Office. We are not the only ones searching for Jules."

Finding himself curious, he asked, "How do you have contacts at the Home Office?"

Rupert's mouth curved with that infuriating half-smile. "It is one of the benefits of being a barrister."

Alistair studied him with narrowed eyes. His friend was keeping secrets—he was certain of it—but now was not the moment to pry. There was only one thought hammering in his mind, one name beating through his veins with every pulse. Jane. She was all that mattered. She always would be.

He tugged out his pocket watch and flipped it open. If they rode hard, they might still catch the ladies before darkness cloaked the roads.

Moments later, two horses were led round. Alistair swung into the saddle in one fluid motion, his grip hard on the reins. He barely registered the dark clouds roiling above or the sting of wind at his face. The danger to himself was inconsequential. All that mattered was that he reached Jane before Jules did.

He leaned low over the gelding's neck, spurring it forward. Rupert followed close behind as they plunged into the crowded streets.

He would reach her before Jules.

Or he would die in the attempt.

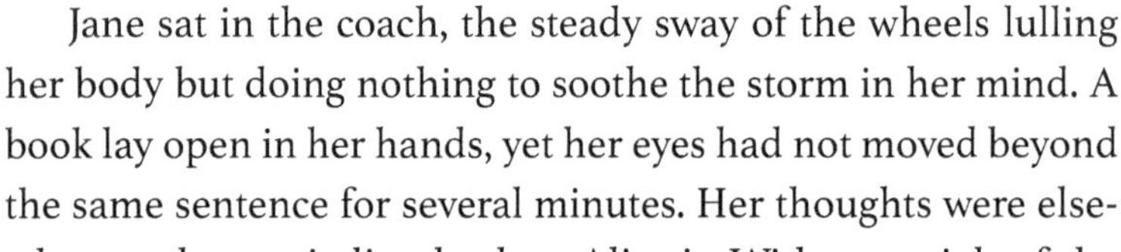

Jane sat in the coach, the steady sway of the wheels lulling her body but doing nothing to soothe the storm in her mind. A book lay open in her hands, yet her eyes had not moved beyond the same sentence for several minutes. Her thoughts were elsewhere—always circling back to Alistair. With every jolt of the coach, it seemed as though her heart cracked a little more.

It was absurd. He had asked her to leave, pleaded with her even, insisting she must be far away from him and the dangers that shadowed his life. That rejection alone ought to have been enough to still her feelings. However, that was not the wound that tormented her. No, it was his proposal. He had offered for her hand, not out of love, but out of duty.

And she, foolish creature that she was, had gone and fallen in love with him.

Drat and double drat.

Why must her heart betray her so? To love a man who prized obligation above passion was to court misery. And still, she could not stop loving him.

Her aunt's voice broke gently into her reverie. "It will be all right, my dear."

Jane snapped the book closed, admitting with a sigh, "I hope that is true. But a very dangerous man wants Alistair dead."

"There is nothing you can do about that," Aunt Cosima replied.

"I know," Jane said, her shoulders drooping. "I only wish there were some way I could help him."

"And how would you help him?" her aunt asked, arching one brow. "With your secret ninja skills?"

Despite the heaviness of her heart, a laugh slipped out of Jane. "I have no such skills, and you know it."

"Pity. They would be most useful at times like these."

Setting her book aside, Jane reached for her aunt's hand. "Thank you. For everything you have done for me."

Aunt Cosima waved her hand in airy dismissal. "Oh, pish-posh, I require no thanks."

"But I owe you everything," Jane pressed. "You have let me be myself. You have not turned your back on me, not once."

"And I never shall," her aunt said simply.

Jane's heart warmed, and she smiled faintly. "For that, I am most grateful..." Her words trailed off as the coach gave a violent lurch and came to an abrupt halt.

Aunt Cosima peered out the window. "Now, why on earth have we stopped?"

Jane's chest tightened. "Whatever the reason, it cannot be good. We are in the middle of nowhere."

The coach door flew open, and Jane's breath caught. Her brother stood there.

"Adam?" she whispered in disbelief. "What are you doing here?"

His hand shot out, clamping on to her arm. "What I should have done weeks ago," he snarled, yanking her from the safety of the coach.

Aunt Cosima scrambled out after them, her voice sharp. "Unhand her this instant, young man!"

"I don't think so, old woman," Adam spat. "Jane is coming with me. She is going to marry the duke, just as she was meant to."

"Absolutely not!" Jane cried, struggling against his iron grip. "I will not marry him!"

Adam's fingers dug painfully into her arm. His smile was cruel. "How very sweet that you think you have a choice."

From her reticule, Aunt Cosima produced a small muff pistol, her eyes blazing. "Release her, or I swear I will shoot you."

Adam gave a derisive laugh, gesturing behind him. Two men stood there with their pistols raised. "Look about you. You are outnumbered and outgunned. One twitch of your finger, and you and Jane both die."

"I could still shoot you first," Aunt Cosima snapped.

"You could," Adam agreed, "but then she would pay the price."

Jane's heart pounded. She saw the fire in her aunt's eyes, the sheer determination, and she knew something reckless would happen if she did not intervene. "It is all right, Aunt," she said quickly, forcing calm into her voice though her stomach was knotted with dread. "I will be fine." The words tasted like lies.

Aunt Cosima hesitated, torn, then slowly lowered the pistol. "I will fetch help."

"Try if you must," Adam sneered, "but it will be too late. By the time you return, Jane will be the duke's wife."

As he began to drag her away, the sharp click of a cocked pistol cracked through the air.

Adam froze. "Do not do anything foolish, you piece of rubbish."

"I won't allow you to harm Jane," Aunt Cosima vowed.

Jane turned her head, despite his brutal grip on her arm. "Please, put it down. I could not bear it if anything happened to you."

"But, Jane, I promised you," her aunt said, her voice breaking. "I swore no one would hurt you again."

Jane forced a weak smile, desperate to ease her. "Do not worry. Remember—I have secret ninja skills."

It was enough. Aunt Cosima's hand faltered, and she lowered the pistol. "I will find a way to help you, my darling girl."

"I know you will," Jane whispered.

Adam jerked her towards another coach, each step filling her veins with dread. He shoved her inside, forcing her down onto the bench, then sat opposite, smugness radiating from every movement.

"You should be happy," he said, his lips curling. "You are about to marry a duke."

"I will not marry him," Jane declared.

The back of his hand struck her cheek, sharp and stinging. "Oh, but you will. It amuses me that you still think you have any choice."

"I can still say no," she muttered, her cheek burning.

"Perhaps in London," Adam said coldly. "But not where we are going. In Gretna Green, an anvil priest cares only for his fee."

Jane's heart plummeted. Gretna Green—the anvil priests would wed any couple that paid, consent or no.

Adam leaned back as the coach rattled onward, utterly

satisfied. "How fortunate you were going to the country. It was near impossible to abduct you from Aunt Cosima's townhouse."

Her voice trembled. "Does Father know?"

Adam's expression hardened. "He does. Though it took some persuading. He still hoped we could talk some sense into you. But this—this is quicker, cleaner."

"And I am the sacrifice," Jane said bitterly.

"You call it sacrifice, I call it salvation," Adam retorted. "Your marriage to the duke will solve all our problems, though you are too selfish to see it."

"Selfish?" Jane's voice rose. "You mean it will line your pockets."

Adam gave a careless shrug. "I never claimed it was fair. But truly, why protest? You will be a duchess."

"I do not want to be a duchess."

"Would you rather be a viscountess?" he mocked. "I have seen the way you look at Alcott. It is disgusting."

Her throat tightened. "I do not want to be either."

"Oh, are there cracks in the façade of your happiness together?" he taunted. "What has he done to earn your scorn?"

"Nothing."

"Something, surely," Adam pressed. "Did he take liberties with you?"

Jane's lips thinned. "Alistair is a good and honorable man. He would never dishonor me in such a fashion."

"Then what is it?"

Jane's heart gave a painful throb, but she forced the words out. "If you must know, he offered for me."

Adam barked a laugh. "Naturally. He did not want you when you were penniless, but now that you are an heiress—of course he does."

"That is not true!" Jane cried. "He is not like that."

"Regardless," Adam said with chilling indifference, "once

you wed the duke, he will pack our dear Aunt Cosima off to an asylum and petition for your inheritance."

"Aunt Cosima is not mad."

He gave a dismissive wave. "I could not care less."

Her eyes widened. "You would allow her to be discarded? Forgotten? Thrown away?"

With a glance out the window, Adam's face was as hard as stone. "There is no love lost between your precious aunt and me."

"She is still your family," Jane whispered, horrified.

His mouth twisted. "Cosima may share our blood, but she is no family of mine."

Jane drew in a sharp breath, the enormity of his cruelty pressing upon her. "You are a monster."

"You can call me what you want, but it is the truth," Adam said. "I just wish I had thought of it before."

"I won't let you do it."

Adam huffed. "And what are you going to do to stop me? You are just a worthless female. You have no real value."

Jane's gaze flicked towards the coach door, her heart thudding so violently that she thought Adam must surely hear it. Could she jump? Could she fling herself out into the open road, and take her chances with the hard earth beneath the wheels? The thought was madness, and yet... freedom, however fleeting, was better than the prison awaiting her.

Adam's sharp eyes followed the direction of her glance. "Do not be foolish," he snapped. "If you survive the fall, you will only be crushed beneath the coach wheels."

"It would still be more preferable," Jane stated, her voice trembling with conviction, "than marrying the duke."

Adam let out a harsh laugh. "Good heavens, do you even hear the words spilling from your lips? You are about to be a duchess! The old curmudgeon will not live forever, and when he dies, you will inherit title, wealth, and consequence."

"That is assuming I live long enough to enjoy it," she muttered, almost to herself.

Her brother leaned forward, his face close enough that she could smell the bitter tang of brandy upon his breath. "All you must do is provide a son. That is your one duty. Do that, and you will be safe."

"And if I bear a daughter?" she asked, already suspecting the answer.

His lips curved into a chilling smile. "Then it is your funeral, not mine."

Jane stared at him, stunned by the casual cruelty in his words. Had there ever been a time he had truly cared for her? If there had, she could not recall it. All her life he had looked upon her with contempt, treating her as a burden, an inconvenience. She had been an afterthought to him, always.

Adam's eyes flicked up and met hers. He scowled. "Do not look at me that way."

Her brows knitted. "And how, pray tell, am I looking at you?"

"As though you are better than me," he growled. "But you are wrong. I know my duty. You, with your fantastical notions, your silly ideas of what life should be—you are nothing but a dreamer."

Jane clasped her hands tightly in her lap. "Do not make me do this," she pleaded, her voice breaking despite her effort to sound strong.

"The deal is done," he said flatly, as though sealing her fate.

Her eyes stung with tears she refused to shed. "Then undo it," she whispered desperately. "Please, Adam. I beg you."

His gaze hardened. "And why would I do that?" His tone was quiet now, deadly. "If it is ever a choice between you or me, I will always choose myself."

In that moment, Jane understood—whatever bond of

family she had clung to, whatever hope she had harbored that Adam might have some small measure of brotherly feeling left for her—it was gone. Perhaps it had never existed at all.

16

Alistair leaned low over the neck of his horse, urging the animal into a desperate pace. The wind cut against his face, the pounding of hooves a thunderous echo in his ears. They had been riding for hours with no sign of Lady Cosima's coach, and the gnawing dread in his chest grew sharper with every passing mile. He cast a glance at Lord Rupert, noting the grim determination etched across his features. Neither of them would yield, not while Jane's safety hung in the balance.

Please let me not be too late.

That thought burned through him, spurring him to dig his heels harder, even as he felt the strain in his horse beneath him. His own muscles ached, his body screaming for rest, but his heart knew no such weakness. If Jane had been taken—if she had been harmed—he would never forgive himself.

At last, rounding a bend in the road, he spotted a coach standing still in the lane. His heart lurched as his eyes fell upon a slight, familiar figure—Lady Cosima. Relief and dread tangled within him. He reined in hard, the horse skidding to a halt.

"Where is Lady Jane?" he called out.

A look of relief softened Lady Cosima's anxious features. "Adam took her. You must get her back."

Her brother. Of course. Alistair's jaw tightened, rage sparking through his veins. "For what purpose?"

"He means to force her to marry the duke."

The words struck like a blade. That blasted duke again. He turned his gaze back down the road, fury rising in his chest. "How long ago?"

"Not long," Lady Cosima said quickly. "If you ride hard, you can still overtake them."

Rupert shifted beside him. "I am not certain our horses can endure much more. We have driven them near to exhaustion."

"They will rest when Jane is safe," Alistair snapped, already spurring his mount forward. His horse stumbled slightly before catching rhythm again. He muttered a brief apology under his breath, but there was no other choice.

Behind him, Lady Cosima's urgent cry rang out. "Go, my lord—please!"

He did not need to be told twice. He and Rupert pressed on, the pounding of hooves carrying them across the country road. And then—they saw it. A black coach, rattling at breakneck speed.

Rupert pulled his pistol and urged his horse close to the driver. The driver's alarmed shout split the air—"Highwaymen!"—and the coach lurched to a slower pace before halting altogether.

Turning his attention to the two guards on the back of the coach, Alistair ordered, "Drop your pistols."

The men quickly obliged, and Alistair dismounted his horse to collect their pistols, tucking them into his waistband.

The door creaked open, and Lord Barkley's smug face appeared. "What is the meaning of this?"

Alistair's blood boiled. He leveled his pistol at the man. "Unhand your sister!"

Barkley only laughed, infuriatingly calm. "I've no intention of releasing her. You'll have to shoot me first."

"I can arrange that," Alistair said, cocking the hammer back.

"Alistair!" Jane's voice cried, desperate yet unbroken. His heart squeezed painfully at the sound. She appeared in the doorway, struggling to get free. Barkley yanked her back by the arm.

"If you fire, you risk hitting Jane," Barkley taunted.

Alistair narrowed his eyes, his voice a growl. "Are you such a coward that you must hide behind your sister?"

Barkley sneered. "Call it what you like, but we are at an impasse." His tone shifted, sly and vile. "Let me take Jane to the duke, and I'll cut you in. Five thousand pounds for your troubles."

"Am I to assume the duke is paying for her hand?"

"Genius, is it not? The duke gets his duchess. We get paid and we get to keep Jane's dowry. A win-win." Barkley's smirk was unrepentant, as though he had made a brilliant bargain.

"You sold your own sister," Alistair said, disgust coating each syllable. "As though she were cattle."

Barkley shrugged indifferently. "What else is she good for?"

Before Alistair could speak, Rupert muttered, "Just shoot him."

But Barkley shoved Jane forward like a shield. "Go on, then. If you shoot me, you'll strike her first."

Rupert steadied his aim on his other arm. "I can still put a ball in him."

"No," Alistair said. His eyes never left Jane. *I will not risk her.*

In the next breath, Jane acted. With sudden fierceness, she drove her elbow into Barkley's gut and flung herself out of the coach. Alistair surged forward even as Rupert fired. Barkley screamed as the ball tore through his shoulder, blood blooming across his shirt.

"You shot me!" Barkley cried.

"You'll live," Rupert replied without a flicker of sympathy.

With his pistol still raised, Alistair hurried over to Jane. His eyes scoured her for injury. "Are you hurt?"

She shook her head, though her trembling voice betrayed her fear. "No—I'm fine."

Every instinct in him screamed to pull her into his arms, to hold her and never let go, but there was still danger. He turned his pistol back on Barkley. "If you so much as look at your sister again, I will kill you."

"What am I to tell the duke?" Barkley gasped, clutching his bleeding shoulder.

Alistair's lip curled. "Tell him you grew a conscience."

"Jane," Barkley pleaded, desperation breaking through. "Think of what you're refusing—power, wealth, a duchess's crown!"

Jane's chin lifted. "I don't want it. I never did. And I never want to see you again."

Her brother's face twisted in rage. "If you walk away, Father and I are ruined. Is that truly what you want for us?"

She met his gaze without flinching. "Goodbye, Adam."

Barkley shifted as though to follow, but Alistair's pistol snapped higher. "Stay where you are. Another step, and I'll end you. I am not so merciful as Rupert."

"Then go!" Barkley spat. "You are both dead to me!"

Alistair ignored him. He extended his hand to Jane, his voice gentler now. "We'll have to ride together until we reach Lady Cosima's coach."

"I have no objections," she responded.

He lifted her into the saddle before mounting behind her. The moment she leaned back against him, Alistair's arms tightened instinctively. She fit there—as though she had always belonged.

They rode through the countryside until Lady Cosima's coach came into view. The older woman gasped, relief flooding her face.

"Jane!" she cried, rushing forward as soon as Alistair dismounted and helped Jane down. The two women embraced tightly, and Lady Cosima clung to her niece as though she would never let go again.

Tears glimmered in Lady Cosima's eyes as she looked at Alistair. "Thank you, my lord. Thank you."

He inclined his head, swallowing down the storm of emotions still raging inside him. "It was my honor."

Rupert dismounted with a wry grin. "I have been waiting for the chance to shoot Barkley for quite some time. Today, fortune smiled on me."

"I wish I'd had the opportunity as well," Alistair muttered under his breath.

"The day is still young," Rupert quipped.

Lady Cosima, still holding Jane close, finally drew back and composed herself. "We shall be on our way to my country estate."

Alistair stiffened. *Not if I can help it.* He reached into his coat and withdrew the folded sheet Rupert had passed him earlier. "About that—I do not believe it is safe for you to return there." He extended the paper towards her. "This was taken from one of our attackers' lodgings. Is this the layout of your estate?"

Lady Cosima accepted the paper and unfolded it. The blood drained from her face. "It is." Her wide eyes lifted to his. "Where did you get this?"

"Rupert found it," Alistair explained grimly. "If they have your plans in hand, then your estate is no refuge. I think the safest place for you—for all of you—is my townhouse in London."

"Absolutely not!" Lady Cosima exclaimed.

Rupert bobbed his head in agreement with Alistair. "I must agree with Lord Alcott, my lady. He is one of the finest soldiers I have ever known. He will keep you safe, and if it eases your mind, I shall remain there as well until this danger has passed."

Lady Cosima frowned, clearly torn. "I do not know. If word got out... Jane could be ruined."

"No one will know," Alistair said firmly. He leaned forward, meeting her gaze with the unflinching steadiness that had carried him through battlefields. "My household is loyal. I shall make it clear that if anyone so much as breathes a word of your presence, they will be dismissed without reference. Discretion will be absolute."

Lady Cosima's sharp eyes narrowed, the lines of her mouth pursing in doubt. "Did you not almost die at the hands of one of your servants?"

Alistair stiffened, but before he could reply, Rupert gave a dry laugh, as though the matter were far less grave than it was. "He was a recent hire," he interjected.

Looking unimpressed, Lady Cosima asked, "Is it truly a time for jokes, young man?" she asked, turning to her niece. "What do you think, Jane?"

Jane pressed her lips together, considering, then said, "I think we should accept Lord Alcott's offer. I would feel much safer knowing he was there to protect us, especially after he just saved my life."

Her words struck Alistair in a place he had not realized was vulnerable. That she *trusted him*—not merely tolerated his company, but actively wanted it—meant more than he could say.

"And me," Rupert added with mock injury, a smile tugging at his lips. "Did you forget that I saved you as well?"

Jane's shoulders relaxed as she allowed herself a small smile. "I did not, my lord. Thank you."

The levity lifted some of the tension from the air, and Alistair seized upon it. Clasping his hands together, he said, "Then it is settled. We shall return to my townhouse until such time as it is safe for you to depart elsewhere."

Lady Cosima sighed. "Very well. But let it be known I go under protest."

"Duly noted," Alistair replied. "Might we ride in the coach with you? Our horses have been pressed near their limits."

She sniffed, though her eyes betrayed a flicker of gratitude. "Yes—but again, under protest. And only because you saved my niece's life this day."

Once their horses were secured, Alistair and Rupert climbed into the coach. Alistair settled himself across from Jane and Lady Cosima. The rhythm of the wheels on the road lulled them into silence, and for a time he was content simply to watch Jane.

At last, Jane broke the quiet. "Do you think Charlotte will object to us staying in your townhouse?"

"No," Alistair replied. "I think she will relish the company."

Jane's eyes searched his. "And what will you tell her?"

"The truth," Alistair said after a pause. "It is the only proper course left to us."

"I agree, wholeheartedly," Jane replied with a smile that he suspected was just for him.

That smile pierced through him, filling his chest with an ache that was both sweet and terrifying. How could she smile like that, after what she had endured today? How could she still shine with such resilience and warmth?

Just when he had believed his life would be duty, shadows, and the lingering weight of the war, along came Jane.

And now, with the world crumbling around them, he picked *this* moment to fall in love. It was madness.

Jane sat in a bedchamber at Alistair's townhouse, the hush of the evening pressing gently against the long windows veiled with soft blue drapes. The chamber itself was elegant—tasteful, even soothing—with a grand bed dressed in silken sheets. Yet she could not bring herself to take comfort in such luxury. Her thoughts were not on the furnishings but upon her family, particularly her brother.

Adam had abducted her and tried to barter her into marriage with the duke. Even now, she could scarcely fathom the treachery of it. She had long known there was no love lost between them, but somewhere, buried deep within her heart, she had clung to the foolish hope that beneath his harshness there lingered some faint spark of brotherly concern. That fragile hope was over now. Adam had shown his true nature, and in so doing, he had lost whatever claim he might have once had on her affections.

She straightened her shoulders. He had played his hand and lost. Now she must think no more of him. It was time to move forward.

A knock at the door startled her from her reflections.

"Enter," Jane called out.

The door opened to reveal Charlotte, radiant in a pale yellow gown that complemented her fair complexion.

"I came to see how you are settling in," Charlotte said with a smile.

Jane rose from the settee and gestured with a sweep of her hand towards the elegant surroundings. "Everything is so beautiful."

Charlotte's smile widened, her expression tinged with pride. "I designed this room myself. I thought it would be enjoyable to change things up."

"Bravo," Jane said. "You truly outdid yourself."

Charlotte stepped farther in and lowered her voice. "Alistair told me about what happened. I am truly sorry."

Jane forced her lips into a small smile, though her heart still ached from the memory. "It is all right. After all, one does not choose one's family, does one?" She tried to keep her tone light, as though her brother's betrayal were but a trifling matter.

Charlotte's expression softened. "Still, one hardly expects them to resort to such nefarious intentions."

"That is true," Jane admitted, though the words tasted bitter. She drew in a breath. "I am grateful to you for allowing us to stay here."

"I am delighted," Charlotte replied. "We have not had company in ages, and it will help ease some of my boredom."

"You are most kind."

Charlotte sat upon the edge of the bed. "Besides," she said with a conspiratorial smile, "even if I objected, I doubt Alistair would listen. He is rather enamored with you."

Heat rose at once to Jane's cheeks. She busied herself smoothing her gown, unwilling to meet Charlotte's knowing eyes. "I only hope no one discovers we are here," she said quickly, eager to divert the conversation.

"Do not fret," Charlotte reassured her. "Our servants know how to be discreet. Well, except for the footman who tried to kill Alistair—but he was newly hired."

Jane hesitated, then decided boldness was better than dissembling. "And what of Mr. Fairchild? Will he report on us being here?"

Charlotte stiffened, just a fraction, but Jane saw it, nonetheless. "I cannot see how he would know."

"I know about your secret," Jane admitted. "I once searched my uncle's study and found an article you wrote. It was not difficult to deduce the truth. Rest assured that your secret is safe with me."

"Will you tell Alistair?" Charlotte asked.

Jane shook her head. "No. It is not my secret to share. But I confess I envy you. I wish I had the courage to do what you have done."

"Write an article?" Charlotte blinked. "It is hardly a feat of strength."

"Not the writing," Jane clarified. "The boldness to act. To risk disapproval. I have lived in dread of offending my family my entire life."

Charlotte smirked faintly. "How ironic. You spent all those years yearning for their approval, and now you want nothing to do with them."

Jane lowered her gaze, the truth of it cutting deep. "My father only seemed to notice me when I obeyed his every command."

"My father never noticed me at all," Charlotte replied. "No matter what I did, it earned me nothing. So I ceased trying. I chose to live for myself instead."

"That is admirable."

Charlotte gave a wistful sigh. "Perhaps. But I would rather have had a father who doted on me, even excessively. Instead, I was merely an afterthought. My very existence reminded him of what he had lost—his wife. I was left in her stead, and he resented me for it."

Jane's chest ached with sympathy. "That was not your fault."

"I know," Charlotte said, though her voice wavered. "At least, part of me knows. But another part cannot help feeling... unlovable."

Jane crossed to the bed and sat beside her, reaching out to clasp her hand. "Oh, Charlotte. That is not true. Everyone deserves to be loved."

Charlotte gave a small shrug. "Well, my brother loves me. Perhaps that is enough."

"No," Jane insisted. "You are young, with a whole future before you. Why, you are the diamond of the Season."

Charlotte's gaze fell. "Perhaps. But I was eclipsed by the heiress of the Season."

Jane squeezed her hand. "Do not belittle yourself. You earned your title. My inheritance was mere circumstance, but your crown was won."

"Forgive me. I should not complain."

"You are not complaining," Jane said firmly. "And if you were, I would welcome it. Everyone needs to unburden themselves from time to time. It reminds us that we are human."

"Thank you. When I confide in Alistair, he always tries to solve my troubles. Sometimes I just want someone to listen."

Jane released her hand with a small smile. "That is what Alistair does. He is always seeking to mend what is broken."

"He is a good brother, especially since returning from the war. Before, he was miserable."

"I know he struggled with his father," Jane murmured.

"Yes. Father expected too much of Alistair and too little of me," Charlotte said dryly. "I am surprised he even remembered my name, considering he never once celebrated my birthday."

Jane's eyes widened. "Not once?"

"Why should he celebrate the child who had taken everything from him?" Charlotte asked. "Still, my governess would find ways to make it special, and that was enough, at least for a little while."

Jane felt a lump form in her throat. How different their lives were, and yet how alike the wounds left by neglect and cruelty.

A mischievous smile curved Charlotte's lips. "The worst part is that I was not easy on my governesses."

"Governesses? As in more than one?"

Charlotte widened her eyes in mock innocence. "I cannot help it if they fled after only a few months. Hardly my fault if they lacked stamina."

Jane laughed, the sound breaking free before she could stop it. "You are awful."

Charlotte gave a delicate shrug. "Perhaps. But if I am to confess the truth, I think a part of me misbehaved in hopes that Father would take notice of me. That he might scold me, or at least acknowledge me. But it did not work. He never cared enough to intervene."

The faint ache in Charlotte's voice tugged at Jane's heart. She reached out, resting her hand lightly on Charlotte's sleeve. "Well, you do not need to do that anymore. Just being you is more than enough."

Before Charlotte could answer, the dinner bell rang in the distance, its faint chime carrying through the walls.

Charlotte rose gracefully from the bed. "Shall we walk down to the dining room?"

Jane smiled as she stood. "I would greatly appreciate it, considering I have not the slightest notion where it is."

"That is precisely why I am here."

They stepped into the corridor together and the sconces lining the walls cast a warm golden glow, their flames flickering as though in greeting. Jane breathed in the faint scent of beeswax polish and lavender—details that reminded her how different this house was from the one she had grown up in. Here, the air felt tended, welcoming.

They walked in companionable silence for a time, but Jane's curiosity soon overcame her. In a lowered voice, she asked, "I find myself wondering—how is it that Mr. Fairchild seems to know all the latest gossip before anyone else?"

Charlotte's lips twitched knowingly. "That is simple. I pay my servants generously to keep me informed. One would be amazed at what they overhear in shops, at markets, even when we are waiting in line to purchase ribbons. And it is not just one servant—I have cultivated a network. They do my bidding without even realizing how useful they are to me."

Jane raised her brows, impressed. "That is ingenious."

"Indeed," Charlotte agreed. "And if that fails, there is always the simple art of listening while others grow indiscreet. People will spill their deepest secrets to anyone they think is inebriated. I have spent many balls with a glass of champagne in my hand, feigning tipsiness." She leaned in closer. "Quite frankly, I cannot abide the taste of the stuff, but you must never breathe a word of that to my brother."

"My lips are sealed."

Charlotte gave her arm a gentle squeeze before looping hers through it. "I knew I liked you for a reason."

They reached the top of the stairs, and Jane's gaze was immediately drawn downward. Alistair stood in the entry hall below, tall and steady, his broad shoulders unmistakable even in the dim light. Aunt Cosima was beside him, animatedly speaking, though Jane hardly registered her words.

As if sensing Jane's eyes upon him, Alistair looked up and smiled. She felt her lips mirror his without conscious thought.

He stepped forward, waiting at the base of the staircase. "Lady Jane," he greeted.

Charlotte, still at her side, lifted her chin. "And Charlotte. Don't forget that I am here as well."

Alistair chuckled. "And Charlotte," he echoed good-naturedly.

Jane's heart gave the faintest flutter at the sound of his laughter, and she found herself grateful for Charlotte's steadying presence at her side, lest she betray herself by lingering too long on the sight of him waiting for her.

Lord Rupert stepped out of the drawing room, his hand resting lightly on his stomach. "I will admit that I am rather starving."

"That is good," Alistair said, "because our cook has prepared a ragout of beef and custard pudding for dessert."

Jane's breath caught. "Those are my favorites!"

When her gaze flew to Alistair, she found his eyes already on her, sparkling with quiet amusement.

"I know," he said, his voice lower now, as though meant for her alone. "I asked your aunt what dishes you prefer."

Warmth spread through Jane's chest. The simple thoughtfulness of the gesture—so unexpected—stirred something tender within her. "That was most considerate of you," she murmured.

His expression grew earnest, the playful glimmer tempered by something deeper. "I want you to feel welcome here, Jane." He cleared his throat, as if realizing the intensity of what he had said. "At least… for the time being."

"I believe I shall—provided you continue serving my favorite dishes," she replied.

At that, Charlotte leaned in, nudging Jane's shoulder with her own. "Ask for a pineapple, please."

Jane turned, brows arched in confusion. "Why a pineapple?"

"Because I adore pineapple tarts," Charlotte replied, her lips forming an exaggerated pout. "But Alistair insists they are an unnecessary expense."

Jane bit back a laugh, then tilted her head towards Alistair with mock solemnity. "Well then, may I have a pineapple?"

Alistair bowed with a hand to his chest. "For you, my lady —anything."

Charlotte gave a dramatic sigh. "I feel betrayed, Brother. You deny me for years, yet you yield to her with a single request."

"If you did more than sit about scribbling all day, Charlotte, I might be persuaded to purchase you a pineapple," Alistair teased.

Jane's smile lingered, though she tried to temper it. She

could not quite recall when last she had felt so at ease in a household not her own—when last she had been teased, indulged, and... seen. And though she told herself it was all in jest, she could not shake the pleasant flutter in her heart at Alistair's words: *for you, my lady, anything.*

17

Alistair sat hunched in his study, the glow of the hearth the only light in the room. He stared into the flames, trying in vain to quiet the storm in his mind. Jane's face lingered there, her smile, her stubborn chin, and the haunted glint in her eyes when she thought no one noticed. Every possible danger she might face uncoiled before him in a relentless parade—kidnapping, betrayal, Jules's vengeance. He had faced many terrible obstacles in his life, yet nothing unsettled him so deeply as the thought of harm coming to her.

The door creaked. He straightened and saw Lady Cosima glide in, wrapped in a white dressing gown. She carried herself with the same regal poise she always possessed, though the faint lines about her eyes were softened in the firelight.

"I see that my instincts were correct," she said. "I knew you would be awake."

He managed a faint smile. "I couldn't sleep."

"Nor could I," she replied. "I have never slept well in a strange house. It has been that way since I was a girl."

"I am sorry for that."

She waved a hand. "Not your fault, my lord."

"But it is my fault you are here," Alistair said. "You and Jane were dragged into this danger because of me."

Her sharp eyes turned to the drink cart. She lifted a decanter with a questioning arch of her brow.

"Please," he granted.

She poured a measure of brandy, then crossed the carpet to sink into the chair opposite him. "Tell me," she started, "are you any closer to finding Jules Leclerc?"

Alistair let out a breath. "No, we are no closer. He is a shadow. Always just beyond reach."

"That is disappointing." She sipped her drink. "I would like, eventually, to go home."

"I can imagine."

Her gaze flicked upward. "I noticed the guards you placed outside our chambers tonight."

He inclined his head. "I will do everything in my power to keep you both safe."

"I know you will." She leaned back, brandy glass balanced in her fingers. "But I cannot help blaming myself. I promised Jane's mother I would look after her, but her father kept her far from me. I did not even know she was engaged until I read it in the newssheets."

"You are more than making up for lost time now," Alistair said.

"Am I?" she asked. "The poor child was raised by two brutes. I fear she lost her voice somewhere along the way."

Alistair could not help a smile tugging at his lips. He remembered Jane's sharp retorts, and her spirited defiance. "No, I assure you, she has her voice. She does not hesitate to use it on me when the situation warrants it."

That coaxed a laugh from Lady Cosima. "Good. But you should have seen her as a child. She was so bold, so fearless. My little trickster. It all changed after her mother died. She became more withdrawn, and I fear it would break her mother's heart."

"Be patient," Alistair urged. "She is still there, beneath the quiet. If you listen closely, you will hear her."

Lady Cosima shook her head. "I only want her to be happy."

"As do I," Alistair said, and the truth of it came out more fiercely than he intended.

Her eyes narrowed in keen appraisal. "That is what we have in common."

For a long moment, the fire crackled between them. At last, Alistair reached for the glass at his elbow, the weight of his decision heavy in his chest. "When this is over," he said slowly, "I intend to court Jane properly."

Lady Cosima set down her glass, her expression unreadable. "You should know that I must approve her husband before she can inherit."

He lifted his drink, the corner of his mouth curving wryly. "With respect, Madam, I do not give a whit whether you approve of me. All I care about is whether Jane does."

Her gaze pierced him, searching. "You do realize how wealthy I am, don't you?"

"I have more than enough to provide for her. She will never want for anything," he replied firmly.

"And safety? What of that?"

The word struck him like a blow. He winced. "I would not dream of pursuing her while danger lingers. Not until this threat is ended."

"Good," she said briskly, standing and smoothing her wrapper. "But that does not mean I like you, Lord Alcott."

He rose as well. "Perhaps not. But I am grateful for what you have done for Jane."

She inclined her head, then swept out.

Before he could sink back into his chair, Rupert entered,

closing the door behind him. His expression was grim, but his eyes were alight with purpose.

"I come bearing news."

Alistair straightened at once. "What news?"

"Someone spotted Jules leaving a warehouse near the docks. He entered a townhouse not far from here."

Alistair shot to his feet. "Then what are we waiting for?"

Rupert lifted a steadying hand. "We cannot simply go half-cocked, storming the structure. We don't know what lies inside."

"So we let him slip through our fingers again?" Alistair demanded.

"I never said that," Rupert countered calmly. "I've sent word to Warwicke, asking him to bring Bow Street Runners. They'll be here soon."

"That could take hours," Alistair snapped.

"Do not fret. I've already placed someone to watch the townhouse. Jules will not leave unnoticed."

Alistair eyed his friend curiously. "Pray tell, how exactly did you receive this word?"

"A messenger," Rupert replied.

"And how did they know you were here? We told no one."

A smirk played about Rupert's lips. "I wouldn't worry about it."

"You say that often," Alistair muttered. "What are you hiding?"

"Nothing. Can't a barrister have his secrets?"

Alistair studied him. "Most barristers are dull creatures, but you are not. Why is that?"

Rupert tugged on his lapels with mock pride. "Thank you. I shall take that as a compliment." He grew sober. "But when we move on this townhouse, I need to know you are prepared for anything."

Alistair's brow furrowed. "I was a soldier. Same as you."

"Yes, but war has a way of changing men," Rupert said, his gaze sharpening. "You seem less angry at the world than when last we fought side by side. I wonder what—or should I say, *who* —altered your outlook."

"What did I say about analyzing me?"

Rupert only lifted his palms. "Merely an observation, my friend."

Turning to the mantel, Alistair braced his hands upon it. The fire warmed his face, though his thoughts ran cold and clear. "I fought against this life—against becoming what my father wanted. I longed for my own path." His voice dropped. "But now I see this is who I am. Not merely a lord. Not an estate owner. But a man with purpose."

Rupert's voice was quiet. "And what purpose is that?"

Alistair's jaw set. "Through Parliament, I can enact true change. I can be a voice for those who have none. That is where my duty lies."

"Ah, a noble crusader."

"Call it what you like," Alistair said. "But there is more to this title than balancing ledgers and attending balls. Much more."

Rupert gave a dry chuckle. "I will have to take your word for it, considering I am but a mere third son of a marquess."

Alistair turned his head towards him. "Some might call you fortunate that you were spared such grave responsibility."

Rupert huffed, and in the set of his shoulders there was something almost weary. "I still have burdens, just as everyone does."

There was a ring of honesty in his voice that made Alistair pause. He was tempted to press the matter, to discover what weighed so heavily on his friend, but before he could frame the question, the door opened.

Warwicke strode into the room and announced, "I was able

to round up five Bow Street Runners. They are waiting in the alley by the townhouse."

Alistair surged to his feet, his heart quickening. "Then let us go."

Rupert gestured with a faint smile, though his eyes were sharp. "You lead the way."

The three of them swept from the study, boots echoing on the marble floor as they moved swiftly through the entry hall. Alistair's mind was already racing ahead—what they might find, what dangers might lie within that townhouse, and most of all, whether Jules was finally within his grasp.

But a soft voice pierced his focus.

"Alistair?"

He froze, turning towards the grand staircase. At the top stood Jane, wrapped in a white gown, her blonde hair plaited in a long braid that tumbled over her shoulder.

His chest tightened. "Jane."

She descended one step, worry etched in every line of her face. "Where are you going at this late hour?"

He was moving before he knew it, striding up the stairs. He stopped beside her and was close enough to catch the faint trace of lavender clinging to her wrapper.

"You shouldn't be out here," he said. "Go back to your room where it is safe."

"That did not answer my question," she countered.

His hand found her sleeve, his thumb brushing the soft fabric. "There has been a sighting of Jules Leclerc. We are going to investigate, to see if this can at last be ended."

She searched his eyes. "Is it safe?"

Alistair hesitated a moment, then forced conviction into his tone. "Safe enough." He prayed he was not lying to her.

Her brows drew together. "That sounds rather vague."

From the entry hall, Rupert called out, "I promise, my lady, I will bring Alistair back in one piece."

Something in Rupert's tone seemed to reassure her, if only a little. Jane exhaled slowly and said, "As long as he is alive."

Alistair's heart clenched at her words. Without thinking, he leaned closer and pressed his lips to her cheek, lingering just long enough to feel the warmth of her skin. "Lock your door when I am gone. And if you need anything—anything at all—call upon the guard stationed outside."

"Yes, Alistair."

He studied her then, truly studied her, committing each line and curve of her face to memory. Her wide eyes, the stubborn tilt of her chin, even the faint shadows beneath her lashes. Just in case. Just in case this was the last time.

"Goodbye, Jane," he said.

She managed a half-smile, but he could see the worry beneath it, plain as day. Botheration. He wanted nothing more than to take her in his arms and swear he would return. But there was no time, and promises might be lies in the making.

With one last look, he tore himself away and descended the stairs, every step weighted with the knowledge of what lay ahead and what he was leaving behind.

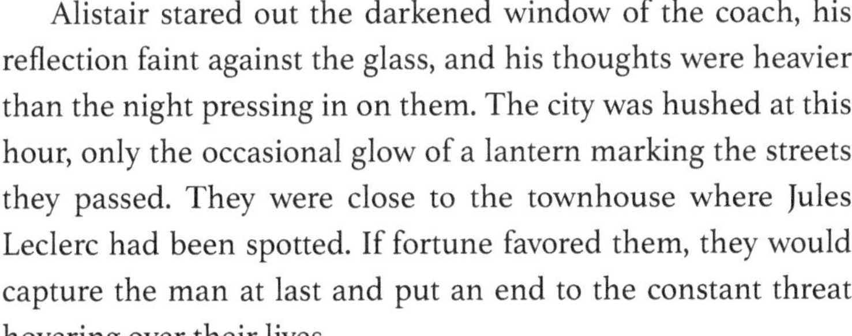

Alistair stared out the darkened window of the coach, his reflection faint against the glass, and his thoughts were heavier than the night pressing in on them. The city was hushed at this hour, only the occasional glow of a lantern marking the streets they passed. They were close to the townhouse where Jules Leclerc had been spotted. If fortune favored them, they would capture the man at last and put an end to the constant threat hovering over their lives.

The coach rocked suddenly as Rupert rapped the roof with his gloved hand. The driver drew the horses to a halt. Rupert leaned forward and directed, "This is where we get out. We don't want Jules to see us coming."

"Follow me," Warwicke ordered, exiting the coach. "The Bow Street Runners are waiting."

Alistair adjusted his grip on the pistol at his side before stepping down onto the cobblestones. The night air carried a sharp chill, mingled with the faint stench of excrement.

Warwicke turned abruptly into an alleyway, the shadows swallowing him. Alistair followed, his pulse quickening. In the narrow passage, five Bow Street Runners stood waiting, their red waistcoats dark against the gloom, pistols glinting in the thin light. They looked like hard, ready men, but even so, Alistair knew Jules would not be easy prey.

"Is everyone ready?" Warwicke asked, his voice carrying a controlled tension. "We don't know what awaits inside, nor how many guards Jules has at his disposal."

The men nodded, faces grim.

Warwicke lifted his pistol. "Shall we?" His tone was deceptively light, but Alistair caught the flint of apprehension beneath it.

They advanced towards the white brick townhouse. Its three levels rose stark against the dark sky, iron railings black and cold at its front. No candlelight glimmered in the windows.

Three Bow Street Runners slipped off towards the rear while Rupert approached the front door. He reached out, fingers steady, and turned the handle. The latch yielded without resistance.

A warning prickle shot down Alistair's spine. Unlocked. Too easy. Rupert must have felt it too because he cocked his pistol before stepping inside.

Room by room they searched. Each chamber lay barren, hollow with silence, as though recently vacated. Their footsteps rang too loud, the groan of the stairs too ominous. Alistair's unease deepened. Had they been expected? Had Jules been warned?

At the end of the upper corridor, the faint flicker of light spilled from beneath a door. Rupert lifted a hand, signaling caution, before reaching for the latch. The door creaked open.

A man sat with his back to them, a lone candle clutched in his hand, its flame wavering against the gloom.

"Hands up!" Warwicke barked, his pistol leveled.

The figure did not move.

They closed in, circling—and that was when Alistair's stomach plunged. At the man's feet lay a makeshift bomb.

"Bomb!" Alistair shouted, his voice sharp with urgency.

As if his words had been a cue, the man bent low and touched the flame to the fuse.

"Run!" Rupert cried.

The world erupted. Fire and smoke burst behind them, the explosion hurling Alistair forward like a doll. His ears rang with a piercing shriek, dust choking his lungs as he hit the ground hard. Pain ricocheted through his body, but when he blinked through the haze, he realized with a sick lurch—it had been a trap. Jules Leclerc had lured them here deliberately.

"Alcott!" Warwicke's voice broke through the ringing.

He forced his eyes open. Warwicke loomed above him, reaching down. "Are you hurt?"

Alistair grasped his arm and hauled himself upright, swaying. "I don't think so." His heart jolted. "Where is Rupert?"

He turned and spotted Rupert sprawled in the corridor. Dread clawed at him as he stumbled to his friend's side. He dropped to his knees. "Rupert! Can you hear me?"

A faint wince, then a rasped reply. "Yes. But could you speak softer, please?"

Relief swept through him. "We need to get out of here. Can you stand?"

"I can," Rupert muttered, levering himself up. "But I'd rather not. We were played, Alistair."

Warwicke appeared, his face hard. "Someone tipped him off."

"But who?" Alistair demanded. The thought gnawed at him —betrayal within their circle.

Rupert staggered, pressing a hand to his side. "Let's pray that was the only—"

Another explosion thundered from below. The floor beneath them shuddered. Smoke billowed up the stairwell.

"Thomas! Mark!" Warwicke shouted, sprinting down the corridor. Alistair followed, his lungs burning with dust.

The study lay in ruin, its ceiling collapsed inward, timbers splintered and aflame. Smoke clawed at their throats.

"No one could have survived that," Alistair said, resting a hand on Warwicke's shoulder.

"I hope you're wrong," Warwicke murmured, anguish etched in his features.

Rupert caught up to them. "Who was caught?"

"Three men. The ones who went around back," Warwicke said tightly.

A tall Bow Street Runner rushed forward, desperation raw in his voice. "My men!" He tried to heave a heavy joist from the wreckage.

"It's no use, John," Warwicke said, his tone heavy. "They're gone."

John's jaw hardened. "Then Jules will pay for this."

"Yes," Warwicke agreed. "He will."

Alistair's mind raced. Something struck him cold. "What if this was all a ruse? A distraction to draw us away from my townhouse?"

Rupert turned, frowning. "To what purpose?"

Alistair's heart seized. "To leave Jane unprotected."

Rupert countered quickly, though his words rang hollow.

"She has a guard at her door, as does Lady Cosima. They are safe."

"Are they?" Alistair shot back. Already he was striding towards the main door. He could not shake the dread curling through his gut. He would not rest until he saw Jane with his own eyes.

Warwicke called after them. "I will remain and speak to the constable. He will want answers."

Alistair barely heard him. He burst into the night air, Rupert limping close behind. Together they climbed into the waiting coach.

Alistair rapped sharply on the roof. "Drive!"

The coach rattled as it surged forward, wheels clattering against the uneven stones. Alistair braced himself against the seat, every muscle taut, his pulse hammering as if it sought to break free from his chest. For the first time in his life, he knew true fear—not for his own safety, but for Jane's. The mere thought of her vulnerable while he was miles away clawed at him with merciless force.

Across from him, Rupert managed a pained smile, though his tone was calm as ever. "It will be all right."

Alistair was unable to share his friend's confidence. "How did Jules know we were watching him?" His voice was harsher than he intended, but the question burned. Someone had betrayed them.

Rupert leaned back into the shadows of the coach. "I don't know."

Alistair's fists clenched, his knuckles white. He forced his gaze out into the black of night, as though the answer might lie in the shifting streets they left behind. He only hoped they weren't already too late.

"You need to calm yourself," Rupert said after a long silence. "You are letting your emotions dictate your actions. That can get you killed."

Alistair snapped his head back towards Rupert. "I just almost got blown apart by a bomb. I think I have a right to be emotional."

Rupert only shook his head, maddeningly unruffled. "No. You are alive, and you need to focus on staying alive. If not for your own sake, then for Jane's."

The reminder struck deep. His breath stilled, sobered by the truth of it. "You're right. I am no use to Jane if I am dead." He hesitated, the darker thought creeping in. "Do you think someone in my household tipped off Jules?"

Rupert's gaze sharpened. "I don't know. But very few knew what we were doing tonight."

"If I discover one of my servants betrayed me, I'll see they suffer for it."

A faint smirk tugged at Rupert's lips. "That's the spirit."

Alistair glared. "I don't know how you can make light of this."

"We are alive, are we not?"

"Barely," Alistair muttered.

"True enough." Rupert's expression grew more serious. "What troubles me is Jules's boldness. He no longer stains his own hands. He manipulates others, makes them the pawns of his schemes."

Alistair leaned back against the worn seat, exhaustion creeping in around the edges of his fury. His mind replayed the image of the candle, the fuse, the deliberate timing. "The man could have set off the bomb the moment we entered that room. But he waited. Why?"

Rupert shrugged. "To cause the most damage?"

"If that were his aim, why not use a shorter fuse?" Alistair pressed. "He could have ensured our deaths. Instead, he let us escape."

A pause. Rupert's smirk faded. "I don't know."

Alistair raked a hand through his disheveled hair, the smell of smoke still clinging to him. "What if Jules is toying with us? Keeping us alive until the moment suits his purpose."

"Which is?" Rupert asked.

Alistair's hands dropped heavily to his knees. He shook his head. "I wish I knew." The uncertainty gnawed at him more than the blast ever could.

Suddenly, the coach lurched to a jarring halt. Shouts came from the driver above.

Alistair's stomach sank. "This cannot be good."

He shoved the door open and leapt down onto the street, pistol already in hand. Ahead, the flicker of lanternlight revealed a scene that set his teeth on edge: an overturned coach sprawled across the road, its wheels still turning slowly, as though recently toppled.

Another trap. He could feel it in his bones.

Alistair broke into a run, his boots striking hard against the cobblestones as he cut through the darkened street. The night air bit at his lungs, sharp and cold, but he pushed on. Pain lanced through his ribs with every breath, each inhale like a knife digging deeper, yet he refused to yield to it. His body screamed for him to slow, but his mind drove him forward with ruthless insistence.

He thought of Jane.

And that was enough of a reason to keep moving.

18

Jane lay in bed, her eyes tracing the carved edges of the canopy above her. The silken drapes stirred gently with the night breeze that slipped through the open window, carrying with it the faint scent of the gardens' roses.

She was exhausted but her mind refused to quiet. Each time she closed her eyes, her thoughts turned to Alistair. What if something happened to him tonight? The very notion hollowed her chest. She loved him—she knew it now with certainty as unshakable as the stars beyond her window. She had never loved another, nor would she. The endless search of her heart ended with him. With him, she could breathe, she could be wholly herself. He understood her in ways no one else ever had.

A faint scrape—a noise outside the window—pulled her abruptly from her reverie.

Jane sat up sharply, her heart pounding in her ears. Her eyes darted to the window just as a shadowed figure hoisted himself over the sill and into her chamber.

She opened her mouth to scream, but the man leveled a pistol at her and pressed a finger to his lips.

Terror clawed at her throat. He was short, with wild, dark hair and a bulbous red nose that stood out in the moonlight. His clothes were rumpled, his eyes mean and unfeeling.

"Hello, love," he rasped, his voice thick with menace. "We are going to have ourselves a little chat."

Dread knotted her stomach, but she forced her voice steady. "About what?"

"I am to ask you a very important question," he said, dragging a chair to her bedside, the pistol never wavering. He sat heavily, his smirk cruel. "And your answer will seal your fate. Tell me, do you love Lord Alcott?"

Her lips parted, but she hesitated. To confess her heart's truth to this stranger felt like betrayal—like giving him something precious he had no right to know.

The man's smirk deepened. "That is all I need to know." He cocked the pistol. "A pity, really. You're a pretty enough thing."

Jane swallowed hard, summoning what courage she could. "If you shoot me, the guard outside my door will hear you."

His eyes glinted with amusement. "Ah, but I am not worried about that."

"Why?"

"Because someone saw to him," he said smugly. "So it's just you and me, my lady."

Her stomach turned. Who could have betrayed them? Summoning defiance, she lifted her chin. "You are lying."

"Go and see," he taunted. "But run, scream, or make a sound and I'll put a bullet in your back."

Her legs shook as she slid from the bed, each step towards the door heavy with dread. She cracked it open, and her worst fear was confirmed. The guard's post was empty.

Her pulse thundered. Who had tempted him away?

The intruder chuckled behind her. "You must be wondering who betrayed you. Tempting to know, isn't it? But not my secret to tell."

"Lord Alcott says his men are loyal," she said, clinging to conviction.

"Oh, they are," the man allowed. "But even the loyal can be persuaded with a few well-placed gold coins." He gestured lazily to the bed. "Sit."

She obeyed, perching on the edge of the mattress, every muscle taut with fear. "Did Jules Leclerc send you?" she demanded.

"Since you are about to die, I see no harm in telling you," he said. "Yes. Lord Alcott earned himself a powerful enemy when he killed Jules's father."

"His father deserved his fate."

The man shrugged. "Perhaps. But I was paid well to kill you. And I intend to do so. Your precious lord, meanwhile, is being lured to his own grave. If fortune favors me, he is already dead. If not, he'll return home to find you are."

"What do you mean dead?"

"Jules sent him to an abandoned townhouse... to watch him blow sky-high." He grinned. "Whether your viscount lives or dies, it makes no difference. Jules wins. Just as he always does."

"He is a monster," Jane whispered.

The man's eyes glittered. "He is a visionary." He reached for a pillow, pressing it against the pistol. "This will do nicely to muffle the shot."

Her breath hitched as he raised the weapon. She closed her eyes, bracing for the end. Instead, a guttural grunt split the silence.

Her eyes flew open. The man staggered, a knife protruding from his chest. He collapsed heavily onto the carpet, lifeless.

Jane gasped, her hands flying to her mouth. Slowly, she turned towards the window. A young woman stood framed in moonlight, her dark hair pulled back at the nape of her neck, and her posture poised.

"Who... who are you?" Jane stammered.

The stranger smiled faintly. "Someone who thought you might need help," she said, her words softened by a lilting French accent.

Jane rose unsteadily. "Wait! I do not even know your name."

"Rosalie," the woman replied before disappearing out the window. Jane hurried to the sill just in time to see her vanish into the shadows of the trees.

The door burst open behind her.

"Jane!" Alistair exclaimed. He strode in, Lord Rupert close on his heels. Alistair froze at the sight of the corpse, then whipped towards her, eyes blazing with questions.

She shook her head quickly. "I didn't do it. A woman—she saved me. She said her name was Rosalie."

Rupert's brows shot up. "Rosalie? She killed him?"

Jane nodded, tears threatening to spill. "He was about to shoot me. If not for her, I would be dead."

In an instant, Alistair crossed the room and gathered her into his arms. She sank against him, trembling, relief and fear spilling over in sobs.

"It's over," he murmured against her hair. "You are safe now."

But Jane knew better. Jules would never stop—not while either of them still lived.

When she finally pulled back, her voice was raw. "How did you escape the bomb?"

Alistair managed a grim smile. "It was nothing I could not handle. My greater concern is you."

Her aunt's voice pierced the moment. "Unhand my niece, my lord."

Alistair only eased his hold, staying close, for which Jane was most grateful.

Cosima's gaze fell to the body on the ground, then back to Alistair. "Did you do this?"

"No," Alistair replied. "I was not granted that pleasure."

Her eyes widened. "Then Jane—?"

"No," Jane broke in. "A woman came through the window and killed him with a dagger. She saved me."

Her aunt's expression hardened. "Who was she?"

Rupert answered, "Someone who would not want recognition, my lady."

Alistair's eyes narrowed. "If it was the same Rosalie, then she is the one whose life we spared after we killed her father."

Cosima's eyes sharpened. "Then why is she here?"

Alistair exhaled. "She said she came to warn us. I never imagined she would do… this. Truthfully, I did not think her capable of it."

Jane turned her head towards the door, her pulse still unsteady. "My attacker said that someone betrayed us by luring the guard away."

"Did he say who it was?" Alistair asked.

"No," Jane replied. "Only that he bribed him with a few gold coins." The simplicity of it made her stomach turn. Her life had nearly ended for so little.

Aunt Cosima stepped closer and held her arm out towards her. "You will sleep with me tonight, dearest. And I expect to hear no arguments from you."

"You won't hear any. But I do not know how I am expected to sleep after all of this," Jane said.

Before her aunt could reply, Alistair placed his hand lightly on her sleeve, the warmth of his touch seeping through the thin fabric. "I will sit outside your door to ensure you are safe."

"You don't have to do that," she whispered, though her protest felt weak, halfhearted. She wanted him close; needed him close.

His eyes held hers with unyielding resolve. "I do. And quite frankly, it is the only thing I can think of doing now."

Jane let her breath ease out slowly, hoping her eyes conveyed the gratitude she could not bring herself to voice.

"Then I will admit that I would feel safer knowing you are there."

Something softened in his gaze at her words, and for a heartbeat the world narrowed to just the two of them, the silence between them brimming with unspoken things.

"Then it is settled," he said.

They lingered there, their eyes holding longer than propriety allowed, until Aunt Cosima, with impeccable timing, looped her arm through Jane's. "Goodnight, my lords," she said firmly, her tone brooking no argument.

As Jane allowed her aunt to guide her from the room, she cast one last glance at Alistair. The memory of his kiss upon her cheek earlier that evening burned in her thoughts. How desperately she wished he had repeated it now, when her heart so needed reassurance. But instead, she carried the memory of that fleeting touch with her into the night, guarding it as though it were a secret treasure.

Once they reached her aunt's bedchamber, Jane went straight to the window without a word. Her fingers fumbled against the latch in her haste, but at last it clicked shut with a decisive snap. She pulled the curtains tightly across, as though flimsy fabric might shield her from shadowed intruders.

Aunt Cosima watched her with patient eyes. "How are you faring, my dear?"

The question broke Jane's composure. She wrapped her arms around herself. "Someone almost killed me," she whispered. "I do not even know how to feel."

"It is quite all right to have your emotions in conflict."

"I think the one I feel the most is anger. I am angry that someone I do not even know thought my life was worth nothing, so he sent another to end it." Her voice thickened with the weight of her fury.

Cosima's gaze was steady, wise. "It is natural to feel that way.

But you mustn't let anger consume you, Jane. Anger will only chain you to the man who seeks to harm you."

Jane turned her face aside, frustration prickling. "That is easy for you to say," she muttered. "You were not the one staring down the barrel of a pistol, waiting for death."

Cosima cupped her cheek, her thumb brushing away the tear Jane had not realized had fallen. "Come to bed, Child. Rest. The night makes all fears sharper, but daylight brings a different perspective."

Jane exhaled shakily, reluctant but weary. Crossing to the bed, she hesitated. With a pounding heart, she bent down to glance beneath the frame, half-expecting to find another shadow lurking there.

But the space was empty.

She drew in a breath that shook more than she wished it would, then climbed into bed. The mattress dipped beneath her, and she pulled the covers up to her chin, cocooning herself as though the blankets might shield her from her memories.

Still, she could not silence the thought that somewhere out there in the dark, Jules Leclerc was waiting, plotting his next move.

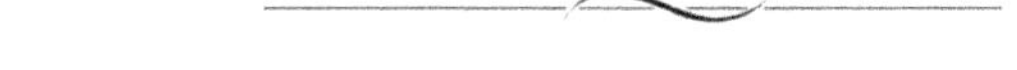

Alistair startled awake, his back stiff from sleeping upright in the chair outside Lady Cosima's bedchamber. He blinked several times until his sister's face came into focus—Charlotte stood over him, arms crossed, her brow knit with disapproval.

"Why are you sitting outside of Lady Cosima's bedchamber?" she asked, her tone sharp with suspicion.

He rubbed the weariness from his eyes, forcing his voice into calmness. "I am ensuring they are safe."

"But you were sleeping," she pointed out.

Alistair straightened in the chair. "I only just drifted off. Do not lecture me, Charlotte."

Her gaze narrowed. "What happened to the guard that was stationed here?"

"I sent him away."

"Why?"

Alistair stood, stretching out the stiffness in his shoulders. "Why must you interrogate me so early in the morning?"

"Because I find it strange, that is all," Charlotte said, folding her arms tighter across her chest. "You have never liked Lady Cosima, and now here you are, playing the gallant knight outside her door?"

His jaw tightened. "I do like Lady Cosima," he corrected. "She, however, does not care for me."

"Ah," Charlotte smirked. "That sounds far more plausible."

Suppressing the urge to roll his eyes, he pulled out his pocket watch. "And why aren't you at breakfast?"

"I could ask you the same thing."

Before either could continue, the door opened. Lady Cosima and Jane stepped into the corridor. His gaze instantly sought Jane's, and the moment their eyes met, his heart gave a traitorous lurch.

"Good morning," he said, softening his tone for her alone.

Her lips curved in the faintest smile, her cheeks blooming pink. "Good morning."

Lady Cosima briskly waved a hand. "We should go down to breakfast. I am famished," she declared, casting Alistair a glance. "Will you be joining us, my lord?"

"I will," he replied at once.

"Very good." She swept forward down the hall.

Alistair fell into step beside Jane and Charlotte.

His sister, never one to hold her tongue, turned knowing eyes on Jane. "Did you sleep with your aunt last night?"

Jane nodded. "I did."

"Was something wrong with your bedchamber?"

Jane bit her lip, and Alistair felt his chest tighten. He wanted to spare her the words, but she spoke them herself. "Someone climbed through my window last night and tried to kill me."

Charlotte stopped abruptly, her voice rising. "What? And I slept through such a commotion?"

"You are a dead sleeper, Sister," Alistair said dryly, attempting to minimize the danger.

"Not that dead," Charlotte huffed. "Surely the guard outside your chamber came to your rescue?"

Jane shook her head. "He left his post."

Charlotte's eyes flashed with confusion. "Why would he abandon it?"

"I don't rightly know," Jane murmured. "But fortunately, I was saved—"

Alistair cut in. "By me. I saved her."

Jane glanced at him curiously, but she did not contradict his words. Relief flickered through him because the truth was far more complicated, and he could not even explain it to himself.

"Well, I hope that guard was dismissed from his position for abandoning Jane," Charlotte stated.

"He would have been," Alistair said grimly. "But he has gone missing."

Charlotte's brow creased. "Missing? How can a servant simply vanish?"

Alistair's shoulders tensed. "We will find him. But we suspect he was the one who left Jane's window open and betrayed us."

"The servants always see more than they admit. Have you spoken to them yet?" Charlotte asked.

"I have not," Alistair admitted.

They reached the dining room and he pulled out chairs for the ladies. Then he sat at the head of the table. He had only just lifted his fork when Malone appeared in the doorway.

"A word, my lord."

Alistair arched a brow. "What is it?"

"Privately, if you don't mind."

The butler never asked for such things. Alistair set down his utensils and rose. "Very well. Continue without me," he told the others.

Once in the corridor, Alistair lowered his voice. "What has happened?"

The butler's mouth pulled into a tight line. "We located the guard who was assigned to Lady Jane."

Alistair grew impatient. "Well, where is he?"

The pause was too long. "He was found amongst the ice, my lord."

"Pardon?"

"His body was shoved into the ice storage. The delivery this morning revealed him."

Alistair resisted the urge to slam his fist against the wall. Another body. Another betrayal. "Have you sent for the constable?"

"Not yet. We wished to inform you first."

Charlotte suddenly appeared in the corridor, quick as ever to insert herself. "Who was the last person seen with the deceased?"

The butler looked apologetic. "I do not know, my lady. But I can ask."

Charlotte waved a hand. "I shall see to it." And off she swept towards the servants' staircase.

Alistair exhaled sharply. "Wake Lord Rupert and tell him the guard is dead. Inform me the moment the constable arrives."

"Yes, my lord."

When Alistair reentered the dining room, he nearly

collided with Lady Cosima. She staggered, and he instinctively steadied her.

"Were you eavesdropping?" he asked, though he already knew the answer.

She lifted her chin, entirely unrepentant. "How else am I to learn what goes on under your roof?"

"I could always tell you," he drawled, though he doubted she'd believe him.

"Well, now Jane and I are aware of the situation," she said. "That saves us all time."

Back at the table, Jane's voice trembled. "Does this mean the guard wasn't the traitor?"

"Not necessarily," Alistair answered. "He could have been silenced by his allies. It is too early to know."

Lady Cosima sniffed. "I don't like this. Too many have died in your household already. Do you know how many people have died in mine? None."

Alistair ground his teeth. "This is not a common occurrence."

"Where did Charlotte go?" Jane asked.

"To question the servants," he replied. "She hopes someone saw the guard before he disappeared."

Jane's brow furrowed. "And if no one did?"

"Then we piece together what we can and follow it back to Jules." He tried to sound more confident than he felt.

Jane toyed with her chocolate cup, her voice quiet. "Do you believe the guard was working with someone here... in your household?"

The thought made his stomach turn. "Anything is possible."

Before he could say more, Charlotte swept back in, triumph in her stride. "I spoke to Sally, who spoke to Deborah, who then spoke to Bridget—"

Alistair cut her off with a sigh. "Charlotte, the point?"

Her expression grew solemn. "The last person seen with Luke—the guard who was killed—was Marie."

Jane gasped. "Marie? My maid?"

"Yes. Bridget saw them kissing by the ice storage."

Jane's voice shook. "Marie would never... no. That is impossible."

Alistair pushed his napkin aside and rose. His instincts were screaming now. "We shall find out at once."

Jane stood, too, her eyes full of worry. "I know Marie. She wouldn't kill anyone."

"Perhaps," Alistair said. "But she may very well be the last person who saw him alive. And I will have answers."

"May I come?" Jane asked.

He hesitated. "Yes. But you must allow me to ask the questions."

"I can do that."

He gestured towards the door. "Shall we?"

Together they climbed to Jane's chamber, where they found Marie stripping the bed. She startled at their arrival, her arms full of linens.

"My lady, I didn't think you would return to this chamber," she stammered.

"No, you were right," Jane said, her eyes darting to the blood spot that still resided on the carpet even though the body of her attacker was gone.

Alistair stepped closer, his gaze narrowing on the scratches marring Marie's face. "Where did you get those?"

Marie gave a strained smile. "I must have scratched myself in my sleep."

His eyes dropped to her hands—blood under the nails. He caught her wrists before she could hide them in the laundry. "And this?"

Her lips pressed together. "From scratching myself."

"Convenient," Alistair muttered, before rolling back her

sleeve. A large bruise marred her arm. "And how did you come by this?"

"I fell," she blurted, yanking free. "On my morning walk."

"You fell," Alistair repeated in disbelief.

"Yes. And I do not appreciate this interrogation. I have done nothing wrong," Marie said, taking a step back.

"Other than kissing Luke," Alistair countered sharply. "The man who was killed last night."

Marie's eyes widened in shock. "Luke is dead? How?"

"I was hoping you could tell me," Alistair said.

Looking unconcerned, Marie asked, "How would I know? My only crime was being too familiar with him last night. Nothing more."

At that moment, Rupert appeared in the doorway. He leaned a shoulder against the jamb, utterly casual, though his eyes told another story.

"I suspected it might be you," Rupert said, his eyes fixed on Marie. "When I learned the guard had died, it seemed altogether too convenient that you had unlimited access to your mistress and her bedchamber. So I took it upon myself to search your belongings."

Marie's eyes blazed with fury. "You had no right," she spat, clutching the bundle of sheets to her chest as if it might shield her.

Rupert's mouth curved in a humorless smile. "If I was wrong, I would have apologized. But as it happens…" His tone darkened. "I found a stocking filled with gold coins."

A prickle of foreboding skittered down Alistair's spine. He knew where this was going before Rupert spoke the words.

"And didn't Jane's attacker say the one who betrayed us was paid in gold coins?" Rupert finished.

Marie's mouth dropped open, her face growing increasingly pale. "I have been saving my pennies, my lord. That is my savings."

"That," Rupert started, "is more money than you would make in a lifetime of servitude. Far more likely, you opened the window in Jane's chamber, lured the guard away with promises of indiscretion, and killed him."

Marie's hands trembled, and her voice cracked with outrage. "That is absurd! Pure speculation!"

Rupert pushed off the doorframe, standing straighter now. "You are a terrible liar. Your legs are shaking. Your voice is unsteady. Your breathing shallow. Even if we were stupid enough to believe you, there is one thing you cannot explain."

"And what is that?" Marie asked, her voice faltering.

Rupert's lips twitched, but there was no amusement in the gesture. "The knife you used to kill Luke. It was shoved into the straw of your mattress. You didn't even bother to wash the blood off."

Marie swayed where she stood, the sheets slipping from her hands. "That knife... it is... uh..." Her frantic eyes swung to Jane. "You believe me, my lady? Don't you?"

Jane's face crumpled with sorrow. "No. I don't."

Marie's shoulders collapsed. Her lips trembled as she whispered, "I had no choice. I was threatened. It was either him or me."

Alistair stepped forward, his voice a low growl. "Spare me your reasonings. You endangered Jane."

Rupert didn't even look away from the maid. His eyes were flat, unreadable. "Give me five minutes with Marie," he said, his tone deceptively mild. "Alone."

Alistair gave a slow nod. "Do what you must."

"I always do," Rupert replied, his words carrying a weight Alistair had learned never to question.

Placing a steadying arm at Jane's back, Alistair guided her towards the door.

"Why are you leaving Lord Rupert alone with Marie?" she asked.

Once they were in the corridor, Alistair closed the door firmly behind them. “Rupert is very good at gathering information.”

Jane’s wide eyes flicked to the door. “But… how does he do that?”

Alistair held her gaze, wishing he could give her comfort. Instead, he offered only the truth he could afford. “It is best that you don’t know.”

And he hoped she never would.

19

Jane felt utterly helpless as she stood outside her own bedchamber door. Her palms itched with the need to push it open, yet all she could do was stand there. The low murmur of Lord Rupert's voice reached her, but the words blurred together, muffled beyond her understanding. The uncertainty gnawed at her. What was happening to Marie?

"I should go in there," Jane stated, the urgency spilling out before she could stop herself.

Alistair's steady hand brushed her sleeve as he shook his head. "Let Rupert do what he does best."

Her brow furrowed. "And what, pray tell, is that?"

"He has a particular set of skills for... acquiring information," Alistair replied carefully.

She blinked, incredulous. "You mean torture?"

"If the situation warrants it." His voice held a grim weight, the kind of tone that made her stomach twist.

"And you just stand by and let it happen?" she asked.

Alistair exhaled slowly. "I know it sounds awful, but if your maid knows anything about Jules, we must hear it."

"But what if she doesn't?"

"Regardless, she did murder a man," Alistair reminded her. "She is not an innocent in all of this."

Before Jane could form a reply, a scream tore through the door, high and piercing. Jane's blood froze. Her hand shot to the latch, her whole body leaning forward to rush in, but Alistair stepped swiftly between her and the door, his chest blocking her path.

"It will be all right, Jane," he murmured.

Her heart thudded. "How?" she asked, her voice cracking. "Lord Rupert is hurting her."

Alistair had no answer, only silence that deepened the ache inside her.

Moments later, the door opened. Lord Rupert emerged, composed, his expression guarded. "Marie doesn't know Jules's whereabouts," he reported, "but she can summon someone who does."

Jane's gaze darted past him. Marie sat slumped on the edge of the bed, clutching her arm to her chest, her face pale and wet with tears. Jane's heart squeezed with pity and unease.

"How?" Alistair asked flatly.

"She will hang a sheet from the clothing line," Rupert explained. "A particular signal, requesting Jules's messenger."

Alistair frowned. "And how can we be certain she won't betray us?"

"Trust me," Lord Rupert said, his voice devoid of warmth. "She fears me more than Jules just now."

Jane shivered at his words, torn between relief and horror. Lord Rupert had revealed a side of himself she had not fully seen before—controlled, dangerous, and wholly unyielding. Yet strangely, she did not fear him.

"Come along," Rupert ordered, motioning sharply to Marie. "Put the sheet up. We will wait for the man to show."

Marie staggered to her feet, tears streaking her face. "And if he does not come?"

"Let's hope that doesn't happen... for your sake," Rupert retorted.

Jane swallowed hard. She wanted to tell Rupert he was being cruel, but the weight of Alistair's earlier words pressed against her. Marie was not innocent. She had lured Luke to his death and had profited from it.

"Will Jules come himself?" Alistair asked.

Marie shook her head. "Never. He sends others. I only met him once."

Compassion stirred in Jane despite herself. "Why did you betray us, Marie?" she asked, more out of curiosity than anything else.

Marie's shoulders sagged, her voice breaking. "He threatened my family. Said he would kill them if I refused."

"And he told you to kill the guard?"

The maid's gaze fell to the floor. "He told me to do whatever it took to keep the man from returning to his post. I had no choice."

Alistair's hand brushed gently against the small of Jane's back. "Everyone has a choice," he said firmly. "You could have come to me."

Marie's chin lifted, her eyes glistening. "And what of my family? You could not protect them."

"I would have tried," Alistair responded.

"You do not understand," Marie whispered. "Jules has spies everywhere. His reach is too strong."

Rupert scoffed. "Jules Leclerc is only a man. You give him far too much power by immortalizing him."

Marie's lips trembled. "Or perhaps you underestimate him."

Before Jane could dwell further, the butler approached them with his calm, measured voice. "The constable is here, my lords."

Alistair inclined his head. "Tell him we will attend him shortly."

Seizing Marie's arm, Rupert ordered, "Let us go. And if you even attempt to flee, I shall shoot you where you stand."

Marie flinched. "You promised leniency if I helped. Do you mean it?"

"I gave you my word," Rupert replied. "But I cannot speak for the magistrate."

"I understand," Marie said, sounding weary and broken.

Jane followed Alistair as Rupert dragged Marie outside to the courtyard. Her chest tightened as she watched Marie stumble to the basket of laundry, her hands trembling as she pinned a white sheet to the line. The cloth fluttered faintly in the breeze, an innocent-looking flag that might summon a monster.

"Now we wait," Marie informed them.

"How long do you typically wait?" Rupert asked.

"He will come at dusk," she answered.

"You did your part," Rupert said. "But you still must face justice."

Marie bowed her head. "I understand."

As Rupert led her away to the constable, Jane's heart squeezed painfully. "I feel badly for her," she admitted in a hushed voice to Alistair.

His expression was somber, yielding no sort of sympathy for Marie's plight. "She chose to kill Luke."

"True, but Jules threatened her family. I cannot fault her for wanting to protect them."

Alistair's hand found hers briefly. "You have a merciful heart, Jane. But actions bear consequences."

She grew quiet. "Do you think she will be hung?"

"I will speak in her favor," he said. "But the decision rests with the magistrate."

Jane nodded, though her heart was heavy.

Before she could speak again, a voice rang out from across the courtyard.

"There you are," a man called.

Jane turned sharply. Lord Luca approached, a worn satchel slung across his shoulder, his expression unusually earnest.

"What do you want?" Alistair asked warily.

Unperturbed, Lord Luca lowered his voice as he drew near. "I overheard a most interesting conversation at The Tipsy Badger tavern. It was about Jules Leclerc." His eyes flicked between them. "And, Alcott, your name was mentioned more than once."

Alistair's shoulders stiffened. "What did you hear?"

Lord Luca's expression was grave. "You have made a powerful enemy out of Jules, and he intends to see you dead."

Alistair looked unimpressed by Lord Luca's declaration. "I know all of this," he replied with unnerving composure.

But Luca pressed on. "Yes, but I followed one of the men I overheard discussing you. He led me to a townhouse in Mayfair, well-guarded, men patrolling the gardens as if they were soldiers on a battlefield. I believe Jules Leclerc resides there."

Alistair's eyes sharpened. "How can you be so sure?"

"Why else would there be armed guards in the gardens of a London townhouse?" Lord Luca asked.

"Did anyone see you?" Alistair asked.

"No," Luca answered. "I know how to be discreet."

"Have you told anyone else?"

"I have not," Luca said, shifting the satchel on his shoulder. "But I would not advise going alone. If you intend to confront Jules, I would bring a small army."

Alistair's brow arched. "Why are you telling me this? Why not simply print it in your newssheets?"

Luca's mouth curved into a humorless smile. "Because some things are more important than a story. I have been watching, Alcott, and you deserve to know the truth." He lowered his voice. "And I assume you will not move against Jules without Warwicke at your side."

"I would be mad to," Alistair replied.

Luca nodded, seeming satisfied. "Warwicke is a competent man. I have trusted him with my life more than once."

Jane glanced between the two men. "Does this mean we no longer need to leave the sheet up?" she asked.

"No," Alistair said. "We still need to speak to Jules's man, to gain more precise information about the townhouse. But you need not worry."

"How can I not?" she asked. "You want to walk into the jaws of death, Alistair. He is surrounded by guards. And he wants you dead."

Lord Luca cleared his throat. "I believe that is my cue to take my leave." He handed Alistair a folded paper. "This is the address in Mayfair. I wish you luck because you are going to need it."

"Thank you," Alistair said, tucking it away before turning to Jane. His gaze softened, breaking through her fear. "I promise you that I will come back to you."

"You cannot promise that. It is not fair to me."

He cupped her cheek. "Jane... here I am, infinitely yours. Every day for all the days. I choose you."

Her heart soared. What did he mean by such a declaration? Emboldened, she asked, "What are you saying, Alistair?"

"I lo—"

His words were cut off by Rupert's voice. "Marie is now in the custody of the constable," he announced.

Alistair dropped his hand at once, his expression shuttering as he turned towards Rupert. "I have the address where Jules is staying."

Rupert's eyes narrowed. "How did you acquire that?"

"From Lord Luca," Alistair replied, passing him the paper.

Rupert glanced down. "I know this place. It once belonged

to the Baroness Amberleigh. Solidly built, heavily fortified." He paused, his eyes calculating. "I will return before dusk to question anyone who comes for Marie's signal."

"Where are you going?" Alistair asked.

Rupert's eyes grew guarded. "It is best you do not know." Without another word, he strode away.

Before Jane could gather her thoughts, Aunt Cosima swept into the courtyard, relief softening her features. "There you are. I have been looking everywhere."

Jane forced a small smile. "Here I am."

"Your breakfast is getting cold," her aunt scolded lightly, reaching for her hand. "I cannot have you wither away and die."

"No one wants that," Jane murmured, though her mind was far from food.

"Then let us return to the dining room."

Jane allowed herself to be led back inside, but her thoughts lingered in the courtyard, clinging to Alistair's unfinished words. He had been about to say he loved her—she felt it in her very soul. And yet the confession hung unfinished, waiting for another moment that might never come.

Alistair sat in his study, the fire at his back giving off more heat than comfort. The shadows were beginning to stretch long, dusk creeping ever nearer, but his thoughts were far from steady. He still could not believe how close he had come to telling Jane he loved her. The words had been on his tongue, rising unbidden, when Rupert's sudden interruption had stolen the moment.

He pressed his fingers to his temples, willing away the tormenting ache. Fool that he was—what if he confessed and she did not return the sentiment? It was evident that she cared for him, but did she love him? Did she even understand what she meant to him?

He had meant every word he'd told Lady Cosima earlier: when this nightmare ended, he would court Jane properly, honorably. He would make her his wife. He could not imagine a life without her. Jane was his future. He was certain of it.

But he couldn't do anything, not while Jules Leclerc still drew breath. Before he could give Jane his heart fully, he had to make certain her life would no longer be threatened by his past.

The door creaked open. Warwicke strode in, Rupert close at his heels, both men carrying the grim weight of their expressions into the room.

"We have a problem," Warwicke announced.

Alistair forced his voice to remain calm. "Which is?"

Warwicke's frown deepened. "I rounded up twenty Bow Street Runners but every last one of them wants Jules dead after what he did to three of their own. They're out for blood."

Alistair leaned forward in his chair. "And you see that as a problem?"

It was Rupert who answered, his tone clipped. "The Home Office does. They want Jules alive. They mean to interrogate him, draw out the breadth of his dealings in France—and beyond."

"Even if captured, how do you know he will talk?" Alistair asked.

Rupert's mouth curled with dark amusement. "I can be rather persuasive when I need to be."

Warwicke's expression hardened. "I'd prefer you make him suffer for killing three of my men in that explosion."

"That," Rupert said dryly, "will not be an issue."

Alistair rose, restless energy surging through him. He crossed to the window, staring into the gardens. "We may know where Jules is, but how do we get past all the guards? Charging in blindly is certain death."

Warwicke's gaze grew solemn. "Leave that to me. I'll take ten men into the gardens and silence his guards, one by one, quietly as shadows."

Rupert nodded. "That leaves you and me, Alcott. We'll lead the others inside, and deal with whoever is left."

Alistair hesitated. "And the household staff? They may be innocents in all of this."

Rupert gave him a pointed look. "Are they? No one serves a man like Jules Leclerc in ignorance."

The words struck Alistair hard, for he knew they carried truth. Still, he hated the thought of innocents caught in the crossfire.

Warwicke moved to the window, eyes narrowing at the dimming street beyond. "It is nearly time. One of Jules's men is meant to meet us."

"Let us hope it isn't a waste of our time," Alistair muttered, though unease curled low in his stomach.

They left the study together, stepping out through the servants' entrance into the courtyard. The air was damp and heavy with the scent of coal smoke drifting from the city. They waited in the shadows, every heartbeat sharpening Alistair's nerves. What if the man never came? What if Marie had betrayed them, warning Jules of their suspicions? The thought twisted like a blade in his chest. He despised uncertainty. It left him feeling exposed. Weak.

At last, a figure appeared—a man in a brown suit, cap pulled low. He strolled in with studied ease, leaning against a gate post, scanning the laundry yard as though he had every right to linger there.

Was this their man?

Rupert must have thought so, for he stepped out with his pistol raised. "Stay where you are."

The man froze, hands twitching. "What is this?"

"Are you here to see Marie?" Rupert asked. "A petite girl with brown hair?"

The man faltered. "No... I was merely—"

Alistair moved from the shadows, his voice demanding. "Merely what? Trespassing?"

Recognition flashed in the man's eyes. "My lord."

Alistair's brow arched. "So you know who I am. Yet I don't have the pleasure of knowing you."

"I am nobody," the man said quickly. Too quickly. "I just came to see if you were hiring. That is all."

"How convenient," Warwicke murmured as he closed in. "Tell me—how does a nobody recognize a viscount at a glance?"

"I know of him, that is all," the man stammered.

"Yet you recognized him," Warwicke pressed. "So you have seen him before. Where?"

The man took a step back, his hands rising in protest. "I will not be interrogated. I've done nothing wrong."

Warwicke cocked his pistol, the sound loud in the quiet courtyard. "One more step and I'll put a ball through you."

The man swallowed hard. "What do you want?"

"We want Jules Leclerc," Warwicke stated simply.

"No," the man shook his head. "If I say anything to you, he'll kill me."

Alistair's temper snapped. "And if you don't, *we* will kill you. Do you understand?"

The man looked between them, sweat beading on his brow. "I fear Jules more than I fear you."

"Then you are a fool," Alistair responded. "You should fear us more since we are the ones pointing pistols at your head!"

Rupert lowered his pistol slightly, his voice deceptively calm. "We already know where Jules is hiding. He is residing in a Mayfair townhouse, not far from here. What we want from you is answers. How many guards are protecting him?"

The man's eyes widened. "How... how did you know that?"

"It doesn't matter," Rupert said. "Now answer the question."

"You don't want to go there," the man muttered. "He means to kill you both. You'll be shot on sight."

Alistair's lips thinned. "So you recognize Lord Rupert as well."

The man dropped his gaze. "Just let me go."

"And let you run to warn Jules?" Warwicke asked. "I think not."

"I won't say a word!" the man insisted.

Warwicke's smirk was merciless. "I don't believe you. Not for one moment." He paused. "But I do like your clothing."

"My clothing?" the man repeated.

"Yes. You're about the same size as Lord Rupert. From a distance, you could very well even pass for him," Warwicke explained.

"I will not strip down to my drawers," the man snapped.

"You haven't a choice," Warwicke responded, nodding towards a constable lurking near the gate. "Constable Welker there will be happy to escort you to Newgate—in your drawers."

Welker stepped forward, pistol drawn. "You heard his lordship. Take your clothes off. Now."

The man's bravado crumbled. With trembling hands, he undressed until he stood shivering in nothing but his smallclothes.

Warwicke retrieved the garments and tossed them towards Rupert. "Change into these. From a distance, you'll be Jules's man."

"You are all fools if you think you are any kind of a match for Jules!" the man bellowed as Constable Welker dragged him away, his defiant voice echoing through the narrow courtyard.

Alistair exhaled slowly, forcing down the gnawing unease in his chest. Was it bravado, or had the man spoken truth? Jules Leclerc had always been a step ahead—ruthless, cunning, unflinching in his violence. And yet, they could not back down. Not now. Besides, if Jules truly commanded the numbers they feared, what would stop him from laying siege to Alistair's townhouse before the night was out? No. He would not wait for Jules to make the first move. They had to strike first, or there might not be a tomorrow at all.

He turned to Rupert. "Do you think you could rally any men from the Home Office?"

"They will be there," Rupert replied.

Alistair arched a brow. "Did you already ask?"

"I did," Rupert admitted. "They are more than willing to see this criminal taken off the streets."

Alistair studied him for a long moment, then gave a curt nod. Rupert's methods were often shadowed, his answers vague, but the man delivered results. That was what mattered tonight. "Then between them and the Bow Street Runners, we should have enough men to surround the townhouse," he said.

"Surrounding is not enough," Warwicke interjected. He tugged out his pocket watch, snapping the case open. "We must keep to the shadows. No warning, no noise. If Jules suspects a siege, he'll slip through our fingers again. The Bow Street Runners will be assembled in one hour's time."

"As will the team from the Home Office," Rupert added.

Alistair's gaze flicked between the two men, the weight of their words pressing on him like iron chains. An hour. In sixty short minutes, they would either end Jules's reign of terror—or walk blindly into a trap of his making. He clenched his fists at his sides as he thought of Jane.

One hour. That was all the time left to marshal his courage and prepare for the fight that would decide not only his fate, but hers.

20

Alistair followed Lord Rupert into the foul-smelling alleyway, trying not to gag as the stench of rotting refuse clung to the air. The shadows seemed alive, stretching long and jagged under the pale moonlight. A group of men loitered near the wall, grim-faced and sharp-eyed, their gazes flicking from Rupert to him with silent expectation.

Rupert strode forward as if he had commanded them for years. "Has anyone left the townhouse?"

One man shook his head. "No, my lord. The place has been quiet. Lights inside, movement through the windows, but no one has come or gone."

"Good," Rupert said briskly. "At least we know it's occupied, and let's hope it is not a trap this time."

Alistair watched, uneasy. These were not ordinary men—they obeyed Rupert as though he were a seasoned commander. How did a barrister manage that? Rupert's composure, his authority, the ease with which he spoke to hardened men—it all unsettled Alistair. There was more to Rupert than being a barrister, that much was clear.

Rupert turned to him, his expression hardened. "Are you ready?"

Alistair drew his pistol. "I am."

"Warwicke and his men should be at the rear gate by now," Rupert murmured, flicking open his pocket watch. His calm unnerved Alistair further—too calm, as though storm and bloodshed were nothing unusual.

"Follow me, and be prepared for anything," Rupert ordered.

They slipped from the alleyway, cloaked by the deep shadows of the street. The moon hung above them, casting just enough light to show the path forward.

At the door, Alistair tried the handle. Locked. His heart thudded. If they tried to break through the door, it would alert everyone inside of their arrival.

Swiftly, Rupert crouched, producing two slender lengths of metal. Alistair's brows rose. A barrister with a lockpick? He bent the tools with practiced ease until the soft *click* of surrender came from the mechanism. Rupert opened the door and gestured for Alistair to take the lead.

There would be time for questions later. Alistair slipped inside, his pistol raised. The entryway was dark, and the silence broken only by the faint creak of the hinges. A liveried footman appeared suddenly from a side corridor, eyes widening in horror. His mouth opened to no doubt scream.

Alistair acted on instinct, crossing the space in two long strides and striking the man across the temple with his pistol. The footman crumpled soundlessly. Guilt pricked him since this man was only doing his duty, but there was no time for hesitation. This was war, no matter how domestic the setting.

Men fanned into adjoining rooms, boots thudding against the floorboards. Alistair ignored them and took the staircase, Rupert at his heels. His chest tightened. Jules would be in his bedchamber at this hour—sleeping, or worse, planning.

At the landing, a guard lunged from the shadows, fumbling

at the pistol stuffed in his waistband. Rupert was faster and he slammed a fist into the man's jaw, but the guard shouted, "Intruders!"

"Well, when in Rome," Rupert muttered, drawing his pistol and firing point-blank. The man collapsed, and Rupert grimaced. "So much for stealth. I wore these blasted uncomfortable clothes for nothing."

Alistair had no time to retort. More guards poured from the darkness. Gunshots erupted and smoke filled the hall. Alistair lunged at one who was reloading, smashing his pistol against the man's skull. The guard fell, bleeding, his weapon clattering uselessly to the floor.

Ahead, a line of lamplight glowed from beneath a door. That had to be where Jules was.

"Go!" Rupert barked. "I'm right behind you."

Alistair charged forward, flinging the door wide. Inside, a dark-haired man sat upright in bed, dressed in a nightshirt, his posture calm, and his eyes cold. Jules Leclerc.

Alistair leveled his pistol. "Hands up!"

Jules obeyed lazily, an unconcerned smile tugging his lips. Alistair's gut clenched. No man facing death looked so at ease. He shifted forward, every nerve taut.

The sound of another pistol cocking froze him. He turned his head to see Rosalie standing in the corner, her weapon trained on him. Two armed guards flanked her.

Rupert entered behind Alistair, his pistol still aimed at Jules. "You've got him!"

Alistair felt his gut twist the moment Jules's smile curved. That smile meant trouble. He had seen men wear it on the battlefield, right before unleashing carnage.

"Good. Both of you are here," Jules said. "Now do something useful and close the door behind you."

Alistair stiffened, pistol steady in his grip, but Rupert spoke before he could. "And why would I do that?"

"Because if you don't," Jules drawled, "you will be killed. You are outnumbered, outgunned, and outwitted."

Rupert moved with infuriating calm, swinging the door shut with a click while keeping his aim on Jules.

"This won't end well for you, Jules," Rupert said flatly.

Jules's laugh was low and cruel, the kind that seeped under the skin. "Ah, there is that delusional sense of confidence that I know so well. You think you are clever, but you are not."

"You don't know me," Rupert countered.

"But I do." Jules's eyes gleamed as he gestured towards Rosalie. "I have made it my mission to know everything about the men who killed my father. Our father."

Alistair's temper snapped. "Your father was responsible for the deaths of thousands of British soldiers."

"Good," Jules spat. "My father was a hero, and you killed him."

Alistair's chest tightened with the memory of battlefields littered with bodies. "It was nothing personal. It was our mission."

"Well, I took it personally!" Jules exclaimed.

Alistair decided to try a different tactic. "We saved you," he said to Rosalie. "Does that not count for anything?"

"Don't you dare talk to her!" Jules exploded, rising from the bed. "This is between you and me. Not her."

"She is pointing a pistol at me," Alistair remarked, not flinching even as Rosalie leveled her weapon at his chest. "So I do believe you have included her in this mess."

Rosalie moved closer to her brother, her face a mask of hatred. "You made a mistake letting me live. You should have killed me."

Alistair's instincts warred inside him. He wanted to believe her innocence still lingered somewhere, but her eyes... her eyes were guarded. "We couldn't kill you. You were an innocent," he said, attempting to reason with her.

Her voice cracked with fury. "So was my father. Jules is merely finishing what he started."

"Murder and mayhem?" Rupert muttered.

"I am going to take great pleasure in your death," she said, steadying her pistol on Rupert.

Alistair's pulse pounded in his ears. He shifted slightly, keeping both siblings in his sights.

"What is stopping you?" Rupert pressed on recklessly. "Or do you take all your orders from your brother?"

"My brother is a visionary!" Rosalie cried.

"No," Alistair cut in. "He is a smuggler. A criminal. And a murderer. Do you truly want to align yourself with him?"

"Rosalie is family," Jules said. "My blood. And she is loyal. Now, lower your pistols."

Every instinct screamed at Alistair not to comply. He tightened his grip. "No."

"If you don't," Jules said, signaling to the two men lurking in the shadows, "I will order them to shoot you where you stand. You'll be dead before your pistols hit the floor."

Alistair's mind spun. He could almost feel the barrels trained on him and sense the tension of men waiting for a single order. "Or I could shoot you," he said. "I am as good as dead anyway."

Jules smirked. "If you put your pistol down, then I promise I won't kill your precious Lady Jane."

The sound of Jane's name was like a blade to Alistair's chest. He forced himself not to react, but the room tilted, suffocating with the weight of that threat. "You already tried once," he growled.

"Yes," Jules admitted without shame. "I underestimated her. I won't make that mistake again."

Alistair's hand trembled, though not from fear—from rage. He was cornered, and every choice ended with his death. But Jane... perhaps she could still live.

Before he could decide, Rupert tossed his pistol down with a clatter. "You won't make it out of here alive, Jules. Even as we speak, Bow Street Runners are surrounding this townhouse."

"I am so scared," Jules mocked, drawing laughter from his men.

Alistair met Jules's gaze, his voice raw. "I have your word that you won't hurt Lady Jane?"

"Yes," Jules said simply.

It was all Alistair had left. Slowly, painfully, he crouched and set his pistol on the floor.

Jules's sneer widened. "You are a fool. Why would you be stupid enough to believe a word that comes out of my mouth?"

"But you promised—"

"I lied." Jules's tone was devoid of emotion. "Now. Shoot them."

Everything happened at once. Rupert retrieved a hidden pistol from his boot and fired into the chest of one guard. The crack of the shot rang in Alistair's ears.

Alistair dropped instantly, snatching his own weapon from the ground, and fired before the second guard could react. The man fell, choking.

Smoke stung Alistair's eyes, but his reflexes were sharp. He swept up Rupert's discarded pistol from the floor and pointed it at Jules.

This wasn't over—not by a long shot. They still had Rosalie to contend with.

Alistair's breath caught in his throat. For one dizzying moment, he thought Rosalie meant to shoot him—or worse, Rupert. But then his gaze followed the barrel of her pistol. She wasn't aiming at them at all. Her weapon was leveled squarely at Jules.

Jules faltered, his eyes widening in disbelief. "What are you doing?"

Rosalie's voice shook, though her hand was steady. "I am

tired of following your orders, Brother. You are no better than Father. You kill without thought. You're merciless."

Jules's expression hardened, his eyes narrowing to slits. "You would betray me? Your own family?"

"I would," Rosalie replied. "These men saved my life."

"They killed Father!" Jules roared, his voice raw and jagged. "How can you stand to let these men live?"

"Easily," Rosalie shot back. "Considering I went from one prison to the next with you. You never gave me a choice."

Jules's eyes all but bled hatred. "Don't do this, Rosalie."

"It is too late," she responded. "It is done."

The words seemed to echo in the charged silence. Then Rupert moved swiftly to the door, yanking it open. A flood of men surged inside, pistols drawn, all trained on Jules.

"Now who is outgunned, outmanned, and outwitted?" Rupert said with a mocking edge, satisfaction blazing in his eyes. He seized Jules by the arm, twisting it forcefully behind his back. "There are many people waiting to talk to you."

"You may as well shoot me now," Jules declared. "I will never tell you anything."

Rupert grinned. "We shall see."

Alistair stood rigid, his pulse still hammering, as Rupert marched Jules out of the chamber, surrounded on all sides by armed men. The door closed behind them, leaving him alone with Rosalie.

His eyes met hers, and disbelief warred with gratitude in his chest. "Thank you for what you did," he said.

She lowered her pistol until it hung limp at her side. "Now we are even."

"No, you are wrong," Alistair countered. "You saved Jane. I owe you everything."

Rosalie's gaze softened for the briefest of moments. "It was wrong that Jules tried to kill her," she murmured. "I could not stand by and let that happen. She was an innocent."

"Jules would say you were wrong," Alistair answered. "He would call her guilty by association."

Her lips twisted faintly, sorrow bleeding through her composure. "My brother is not always right."

Alistair slid his pistol back into his waistband, studying her. "How can I show my gratitude?"

Her voice was solemn, almost weary. "All I ask is that you forget about me."

"How could I do that?"

"Because I had a job to do, and it is over," Rosalie said. Her eyes seemed older than her years, filled with secrets he could not fathom. "I can finally go home now."

Realization dawned on him. "Was your job to take down your brother?"

She said nothing. Instead, she turned, moving past him with silent grace. At the threshold, she paused, then looked back over her shoulder.

"Thank you for setting me free," she said.

And then she was gone, leaving Alistair rooted to the spot. He thought about running after her and asking questions that he had no right to ask. But he let her go instead. He had far more important things to attend to now.

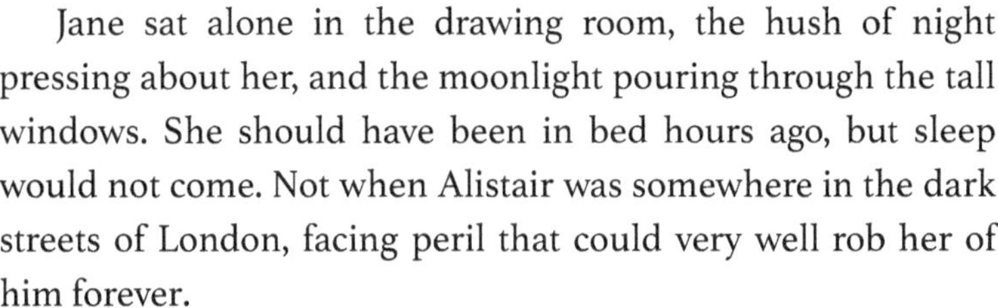

Jane sat alone in the drawing room, the hush of night pressing about her, and the moonlight pouring through the tall windows. She should have been in bed hours ago, but sleep would not come. Not when Alistair was somewhere in the dark streets of London, facing peril that could very well rob her of him forever.

A forgotten book rested beside her on the settee. She had not read a single line, her mind too restless. What use were novels when reality held her heart in such torment? The question circled endlessly—what if Alistair did not return? What would she do with the love she had not yet spoken aloud? For she did love him—deeply, desperately—and no misfortune, not even death itself, could lessen it.

The quiet broke when her aunt's gentle voice carried across the chamber. "You should be in bed, my dear."

Jane turned. Aunt Cosima stood framed in the doorway, her cap ribbons swaying slightly as she approached her niece.

"Yes, I should," Jane admitted. "But I cannot still my thoughts."

"And what thoughts keep you awake?"

Jane drew in a breath. She could no longer pretend, not even to herself. "That I love Alistair."

Her aunt settled beside her on the settee, her expression thoughtful. "You know I do not approve of him. If you wed him, you will cease to be my heir."

Jane lifted her chin, her voice steady. "I know. But if he offers, I will accept. I cannot go on living my life for others."

"Even at the risk of losing your inheritance?"

"Yes," Jane said without hesitation. Her chest ached with the truth of it. "I do not know why you disapprove of Alistair. He is the only man who has ever seen me as myself. He is kind, loving, and asks nothing of me but to be who I am. I could never unlove him—not if I tried, not even if you forced me. When we are apart, I feel half-lost."

Aunt Cosima studied her for a long moment before her lips curved into a broad smile. "I am glad to hear you speak with such conviction. You and Lord Alcott do suit."

Jane blinked. "Then... why do you not approve?"

Her aunt waved a dismissive hand. "I wished you to fight for him. To discover for yourself that he is the one you cannot live without."

"So you do approve?"

Her aunt gave her a sidelong look. "Does it truly matter if I do?"

"No," Jane whispered. "Not anymore."

Her aunt touched her sleeve gently. "That is what I wanted to hear. You remain my heir, no matter whom you choose. I love you, Jane, and I hope you know I only want your happiness."

Emotion pricked Jane's eyes. "Truly?"

"Truly. And I do believe Alistair loves you as well."

Her heart leapt. "You think so?"

"I do, assuming he survives the night."

Jane pressed her lips together against the fear rising in her throat. "He will. He must. I cannot imagine life without him."

Understanding softened her aunt's gaze. "I felt the same when my husband died. The grief threatened to consume me. I only survived by taking one day—sometimes one hour—at a time. The ache never vanishes, but one learns to breathe again."

Jane clasped her aunt's hand. "I am sorry."

A tear slipped down Cosima's cheek. "When you give everything to one person—your heart, your soul—a part of you feels missing when they die. Even now, the tears come when I think of him."

"I hope I find a love as deep as yours."

Her aunt squeezed her hand. "I believe you already have."

Just then, a knock came at the door. She turned, and there he was—Alistair—standing at the threshold. He was alive. He was here.

"May I speak to Jane privately?" he asked.

Cosima inclined her head. "You may. I shall wait in the entry hall for propriety's sake."

Jane nearly laughed at the word propriety—how little it mattered in this moment.

When the door closed behind her aunt, Alistair crossed the room and sat beside Jane. "How are you?"

She lifted her brow. “How am I? I am far more concerned about you.”

A smile touched his lips. “We got him.”

Her breath stilled. “You captured Jules?”

“Yes. He will spend the rest of his life in prison, if he even survives the interrogation,” Alistair informed her. “Which means—you are safe now.”

She reached for his gloved hand, boldly twining her fingers with his. “*We* are safe now.”

“Yes,” he agreed, his eyes dark with something she had not dared hope for. “And now… I have something important to ask you.”

Her heart pounded in her chest so hard that she thought he must hear it. “Yes?”

He faltered, uncharacteristically hesitant. “Lady Jane… would you consider allowing me to court you?”

“Court me?” she repeated, disappointment flickering. She had hoped for more.

“I know it is sudden—”

She cut him off. “Yes.”

Relief softened his features. “I feared you sounded disappointed at the notion of courtship.”

“I am disappointed,” she admitted.

“Oh.”

Her grip on his hand tightened. “Only because I hoped you would offer for me.”

“You did?”

She nodded, willing her courage to hold. “I love you, Alistair. I would marry you today, tomorrow, or any day after. I need no courtship to know you are the man I belong with.”

He grinned. “I love you, too, Jane. I have loved you for some time, but I feared the danger I carried into your life.”

“That never mattered,” she assured him. “It’s you. In a thousand lifetimes, in a hundred different ways, it would still be you. It will always be you."

His hand lingered in hers as he lowered himself to one knee. The sight stole her breath, for never had she imagined such solemn reverence directed at her. "Lady Jane, will you do me the grand honor of marrying me?"

"Yes," she said. "Yes, a million times yes."

He lifted their joined hands and pressed a fervent kiss to her fingers. "I can secure a special license tomorrow, if you wish."

She smiled through her tears. "I would wish it. Three weeks feels far too long to wait to marry the man I love."

His eyes closed briefly. "I do not think I will ever tire of hearing you say that. But now—it is time I kiss you properly."

Her lips curved. "I suppose I could allow that."

He stood and leaned close, brushing her cheeks with tender kisses before his breath warmed her lips. She closed the distance, pouring all her love into the kiss. His lips, at first gentle, soon grew more insistent as his arms wrapped around her, holding her as if he would never let her go. And in that moment, Jane knew—this was the beginning of forever.

The door swung open with a creak, and Aunt Cosima's voice sliced through the stillness of the drawing room. "Unhand my niece, my lord."

Jane startled, heat rushing to her cheeks. Yet she could not bring herself to feel guilty. Not when her heart was so full.

Alistair leaned back slightly, though he made no effort to remove his hand from hers. "Jane has agreed to marry me," he announced.

"She had better," Aunt Cosima huffed, sweeping farther into the room, "or else I would have had no choice but to challenge you to a duel myself."

Alistair chuckled. "I would have liked to see that," he

remarked, amusement glinting in his eyes. "Shall we retire to bed?"

Before Jane could answer, Aunt Cosima interjected sharply, "Separate bedchambers, I trust, is what you meant."

"Yes, separate bedchambers," Alistair replied. "For now."

Aunt Cosima sniffed. "Perhaps Jane will sleep in my chamber tonight. As a precaution."

Jane rose, still holding Alistair's hand, and together they walked towards the doorway.

"I will ride out first thing tomorrow to acquire a special license," Alistair said in a hushed voice. "If I have my way, we shall be married by noon."

Jane's heart swelled so greatly she thought it might burst. "I have no objections."

And she meant it with every fiber of her being. She wanted nothing more than to be his wife, to stand at his side in every triumph and every trial. Alistair would always be her once-in-a-lifetime.

EPILOGUE

Alistair leaned against the paneled wall just outside Lady Cosima's bedchamber, his shoulders pressed into the wood as he waited. The special license rested safely in his pocket, secured at first light after a restless night. He was bursting to tell Jane the news. For once, fortune had not eluded him, and he was on the cusp of marrying the only woman who had ever truly seen him.

He had never thought himself worthy of such devotion. His past was a tangle of mistakes and shadows, yet Jane had given him her love without demand, without hesitation. That gift alone undid him.

"Why are you loitering outside of Lady Cosima's bedchamber?" came Charlotte's voice from farther down the hall.

Alistair turned his head to find his sister approaching, her brows arched in suspicion. "I am waiting for Jane."

"Why is Jane in her aunt's chamber?" she pressed.

He almost laughed. Clearly, Charlotte had slept through the entirety of last night's chaos. He opened his mouth to explain, but the latch turned, and Jane stepped out into the corridor.

He straightened. "Good morning, Jane."

Her answering smile was enough to undo every knot of tension in him. "Good morning, Alistair."

From within, Lady Cosima's voice carried out, curt and unimpressed. "Dear heavens, can we save all this lovey-dovey nonsense until I've had a cup of coffee?"

"You drink coffee?" Alistair asked before he thought better of it.

"You sound surprised," Lady Cosima challenged, appearing just long enough to pin him with a look. "My husband drank it, and I suppose it reminds me of him."

He inclined his head. "That is reason enough."

"Glad to know I need an acceptable excuse for my choice in beverage," she muttered before disappearing again.

Jane leaned subtly towards him, her hand half-raised to shield her mouth. "My aunt can be rather cantankerous until she has had her coffee."

"I feel the same way about chocolate," Charlotte chimed in. "Not that it matters."

Jane laughed softly. "It does matter, Charlotte. How did you sleep?"

"I slept well," Charlotte answered, narrowing her eyes at Alistair, "but I find myself more curious about why Alistair was lurking outside Lady Cosima's chamber."

Alistair's lips curved. "Because I wished to be the first to tell Jane some news." He paused for effect, savoring the moment. "I acquired the special license."

Jane's eyes widened with delight. "That is wonderful!"

"And," he added, unable to contain his eagerness, "I spoke with a vicar at a nearby chapel. He has agreed to marry us after breakfast, assuming that is acceptable to you."

"It is more than acceptable." Jane's smile nearly stopped his breath.

Charlotte gaped. "You two are engaged? And you didn't tell me?"

"We are," Alistair said, never taking his eyes from Jane.

"When did this happen?"

"Last night—after we captured Jules Leclerc." He gave a small shrug. "It happened rather quickly."

"Apparently," Charlotte muttered.

He offered Jane his arm. "Shall we go down to breakfast before we depart?"

Jane's eyes danced with amusement. "Only if it is a quick breakfast. I find that I am rather eager to marry you."

He bent his head, his voice low. "The feeling is entirely mutual, my love."

Lady Cosima's voice carried after them. "I might need two cups of coffee to endure this level of mush."

"Perhaps I should take up the habit," Charlotte mused.

"You hate coffee," Alistair reminded her.

"It is an acquired taste," Cosima countered.

They had barely taken a few steps towards the stairs when a sharp pounding shook the front door. The butler hurried to open it, and the stern, disapproving figure of Lord Ketteridge strode into the entry hall.

Jane froze beside Alistair. "Father," she acknowledged, moving stiffly down to the marble floor. "What are you doing here?"

"Why else?" he sneered. "I read about your engagement in the newssheets like everyone else."

Jane's brow furrowed. "You did?"

Lord Ketteridge's eyes were hard. "Are you not engaged to Lord Alcott?" he demanded.

"I am," Jane began, "but—"

He cut her off with a dismissive wave. "I am not even going to question why you reside here before marriage. It is none of my concern, at least, not anymore."

Lady Cosima swept forward. "Not that it matters to you, but

Jane's life was in danger. I personally ensured she was properly chaperoned."

"I'm sure you did," Ketteridge scoffed. His gaze cut to Alistair. "Lord Alcott, a word."

Jane clutched his arm tighter. "Why are you here?"

"About your dowry, of course," he replied. "Why else would I be here?"

Jane's voice trembled with contained fury. "Perhaps to offer congratulations on my upcoming nuptials."

"Why would I do that? You could have been a duchess, and you settled for a viscount," her father spat out.

Her chin lifted. "I settled for nothing. I love Alistair."

Lord Ketteridge's mouth twisted. "I hope you are happy with your choice."

"I am," Jane said firmly. "Thank you for reminding me just how little I mean to you, especially after you sent Adam to abduct me to force my hand."

"You made your choice and there are consequences to your defiance," her father responded.

Alistair slid his hand over hers. "For the record, I found her act of defiance to be brilliant."

Ketteridge shook his head. "You two belong together."

"Yes, we do," Jane answered. "Goodbye, Father."

She walked away with her head high, and Alistair's heart swelled with admiration. Her father also watched her leave and muttered, "She is your problem now."

Cosima rolled her eyes. "You are a jobbernowl," she told her brother-in-law before sweeping Charlotte off towards the dining room.

Left behind, Alistair faced Ketteridge. "Well, what is it that you wish to speak about?"

"In private," the man said tightly.

Alistair gestured towards the drawing room. Once inside, he closed the door, his stance unyielding. "Speak."

Ketteridge's sigh was heavy. "As you must know, Jane left us in dire financial straits when she refused the Duke of Brackenford. He is suing us for breach of contract."

"I am well aware," Alistair replied. "Considering your son abducted Jane to force her hand."

The man shifted uncomfortably. "That was our last resort, and it failed."

Alistair couldn't quite believe what he was hearing. "That is all you have to say about it? No apology? No regret?"

"She would have been a duchess," Ketteridge said flatly. "She should have thanked me, but instead she is marrying you. A mere viscount."

His temper flared. "What do you want?"

"Jane's dowry. It would keep our estate afloat."

Alistair longed to deny him, to let him reap the ruin he had sown. But another thought sharpened in his mind. "Very well, but only on one condition. You agree to stay out of our lives, forever."

"Done."

Alistair stepped closer, lowering his voice with finality. "Jane's life will be far happier without you in it."

Ketteridge gave a bitter smile. "She has too much of her mother in her. I tried to beat it out of her, but she still shone through."

Alistair's jaw locked. "I think Jane is perfect, exactly as she is."

The man's glare faltered. "Are we done here?"

"We are."

Without saying another word, Ketteridge stormed out, slamming the main door behind him.

Moments later, Jane appeared in the doorway, her expression tight. "What did he want?"

"He asked to keep your dowry."

She drew a sharp breath. "And?"

"I agreed—if he stays out of our lives for good."

Her shoulders eased, and she stepped closer. "That is more than fair."

Reaching for her hand, he said, "I know how cruel your father has been. I will protect you from him, Jane."

"I love you," she whispered.

He pressed his forehead against hers. "I want every day with you. To laugh with you, to hold you, to carry you when you stumble. All of it, always."

Her eyes shone with tears. "I don't know what I did to deserve you."

"You don't need to deserve me," he said. "Just give me yourself—your truth, your flaws, your fears—and I will show you how perfectly our broken pieces fit."

Her lips curved into a trembling smile. "That sounds perfect."

"For me, perfection is you," he murmured. "It always has been."

Jane's answering smile grew bolder, mischievous. "Perhaps we can skip breakfast and head straight to the chapel."

He laughed, relief and joy coursing through him. "You will hear no complaint from me."

The End

NEXT BOOK IN SERIES

Unmasking the truth means risking everything—even love.

Miss Charlotte Winslow may be the diamond of the Season, but beneath her flawless exterior lies a secret—she writes for the Society pages. Years of hiding behind her carefully crafted mask have left her doubting her own worth and believing happiness to be a luxury meant for others. That is, until she crosses paths with Lord Luca Dexter—an infuriating, perceptive man who sees far too much and refuses to be ignored.

Luca may be the younger son of a duke, but unlike most men of his rank, he earns his living as the owner of *The London Gazette*. When he discovers Miss Winslow's secret talent, he's determined to recruit her to write for his newssheets. But Charlotte refuses to be reduced to mere gossip columns—if she writes for him, it will be for something that matters.

Luca and Charlotte agree to have her write something of substance. When their investigation uncovers a dangerous conspiracy, Luca finds himself torn between his growing affection for Charlotte and his desperate need to protect her. But Charlotte is not a woman who wishes to be saved. And as tragedy looms, Luca must risk everything—including his heart—to rescue the one woman who taught him that love is worth unmasking for.

ABOUT THE AUTHOR

Laura Beers is an award-winning author. She attended Brigham Young University, earning a Bachelor of Science degree in Construction Management. She can't sing, doesn't dance and loves naps.

Laura lives in Utah with her husband, three kids and her dysfunctional dog. When not writing regency romance, she loves skiing, hiking and drinking Dr Pepper.

You can connect with Laura on Facebook, Instagram or on her site at www.authorlaurabeers.com.

www.ingramcontent.com/pod-product-compliance
Lightning Source LLC
LaVergne TN
LVHW010644110826
845149LV00014B/2943

* 9 7 8 1 9 6 2 7 0 3 3 8 3 *